KT-389-891

Philip Hensher's novels include *Kitchen Venom*, which won the Somerset Maugham Award, *Other Lulus* and *The Mulberry Empire*, which was long-listed for the Man Booker Prize, shortlisted for the WH Smith 'People's Choice' Award and highlighted by no fewer than twelve reviewers as their 'book of the year'. Chosen by Granta to appear on their prestigious, once-a-decade list of the twenty best young British novelists, Philip Hensher is also a columnist for the *Independent* and chief book reviewer for the *Spectator*. He lives in south London.

Also by Philip Hensher

OTHER LULUS
POWDER HER FACE
PLEASURED
THE BEDROOM OF THE MISTER'S WIFE
THE MULBERRY EMPIRE

KITCHEN
VENOM

Philip Hensher

Flamingo
An Imprint of HarperCollinsPublishers

Flamingo
An Imprint of HarperCollins*Publishers*
77–85 Fulham Palace Road,
Hammersmith, London W6 8JB

Flamingo is a registered trade mark of
HarperCollins*Publishers* Limited

www.**fire**and**water**.com

Published by Flamingo 2003
9 8 7 6 5 4 3 2

First published in Great Britain by
Hamish Hamilton Ltd 1996

Copyright © Philip Hensher 1996

Philip Hensher asserts the moral right to
be identified as the author of this work

Photograph of Philip Hensher © Simon James 2001

This novel is entirely a work of fiction. The names,
characters and incidents portrayed in it are the work of the
author's imagination. Any resemblance to actual persons,
living or dead, events or localities is entirely coincidental.

ISBN 0 00 715242 6

Typeset in Stempel Garamond and Diotima by
Palimpsest Book Production Limited,
Polmont, Stirlingshire

Printed and bound in Great Britain by
Clays Ltd, St Ives plc

All rights reserved. No part of this publication may be
reproduced, stored in a retrieval system, or transmitted,
in any form or by any means, electronic, mechanical,
photocopying, recording or otherwise, without the prior
permission of the publishers.

This book is sold subject to the condition that it shall not,
by way of trade or otherwise, be lent, re-sold, hired out or
otherwise circulated without the publisher's prior consent
in any form of binding or cover other than that in which it
is published and without a similar condition including this
condition being imposed on the subsequent purchaser.

For Sophia Roper

— CONTENTS —

CLOSE OF PLAY

A S FOR ME, as for me . . .
Listen to me. I had a strange dream last night. I
dreamt that the house I was in was empty, and white.
I went from one room to another, as if rushing, as if
my feet would not touch the floor. And the rooms were
empty of furniture, and the walls and the ceilings and the
floors were white. Recently painted white, I had the sense;
invisible hands had gone before me, in haste. It could not
be seen, when the windows were looked out of, whether
the windows looked out on nothing, or if the nothing they
looked out on was paint on the glass, the work of those
invisible hands. Those hands I was not permitted to see. I
rushed through the rooms and through the open doors, and
there was nothing, and there was silence. I came finally to a
room in which there was a shelf, and on the shelf there were
twenty-six books. On the spine of each book, there was a
letter, a huge gilt burning A, a huge gilt burning B; and the
letters, like signs, were hot and flaming in the white empty
room, in my head. I took down a volume, and opened it, and
it was a volume of a dictionary, a volume which contained

the words beginning with one letter. The letter was O, and I worried that it would singe my fingers.

Dictionaries are things of power, and they contain every word that has ever been spoken, or ever will be. So I turned to the words of power. I turned the pages in an empty white room, and I came to the page on which the words which began with Omni were written. I knew that there were many of them. I knew that many words had been coined, in pride, to denote the ways in which men think they, or their creations, may have dominion over everything. I knew these many words, and it was as if I began to read. But there were none; no words. As my eye went down to the page, the page was blank, was erased, and my eye met with blankness where before there had been words. As my eye went down the page, each word disappeared before I could see it. They were taken away from me, the words. I was bereft. I read Omniscient, the word Omniscient, and that was there, quickly, before it began to fade. But Omnifarious was gone, and Omneity, and a word which I knew for myself, a word which said Wanting everything, the marvellous word Omnivolent. And gone was Omnipotent, and gone was Omnipotence, and instead of words, there were blank pages, and as I turned them, they were blanker and blanker and blanker.

In the morning, as I woke, omniscience was still there, and I knew everything. I knew if I went to the dictionary that omnipotence would have reappeared, in the dictionary. I walked through my house, my suddenly strangely full house. With its plush, and its lined matching books, and the guarded view from its windows, and the distant ringing, already answered telephone. But the dictionary, when I went to it, the real dictionary, omnivolent was not in it. There was no word which meant that person, who wants everything. I am the only woman who ever wanted everything, and got it. Except one thing. When I woke in the morning, I was no longer Prime Minister.

She sat at the mirror and looked at it. She knew everything she had to do to cope, and she did it. She counted to ten, very slowly. She shut her eyes and breathed deeply. She thought of the great spaces of the sky above her, and clear weather, and thoughts of emptiness and calm. She slowly opened her eyes. It was no good. Everything was still the same, exactly the same.

Her face was sharp and not beautiful, but intelligent. Those who did not know her put the shrewish pointing of her face and her gaunt stare and her wild hair down to grief, if they were charitable. At least, they would today. If they were uncharitable, they would probably put it down to drink, or worse. Those who did know Jane knew perfectly well that this was what she looked like. Neither the death of her mother nor her habits of intoxication had made much difference. Grief made so little impression on her appearance that she might not have experienced it; drink or worse had no power to touch or change her. She fell over, but she was just the same.

All she had to do was to choose her clothes and go downstairs. That was all. But for the moment she sat in her underwear in front of the mirror and looked, not at herself, but at it.

Downstairs there were her father and her sister. They were not waiting for her, though they would. It was the thought of her father which made her stand up and, without thought, pull on the dress she had worn the day before. It was not stained or crumpled; it was lucky it was black.

'One two three,' she said under her breath as she went down the stairs, 'four five six seven eight nine ten.'

It was just the same.

'Is there anything I can do?' she said to her father, who was looking out of the window. Francesca, her sister, was sitting in a chair, without a book or diversion.

'Come and have a look,' he said, 'at the food.'

They went into the kitchen. On the table there were four piles of vegetables, raw and partly chopped.

'Do you think that's about right?' John said. 'I haven't done anything apart from chop it up. Oh, and the asparagus, I thought I'd better boil it; it's over there.'

On the sink there was a colander with a great limp mop of green fingery spikes hanging over the side.

'That looks all right,' Jane said. 'We ought to finish it before we go. We don't want to have to worry about chopping up cauliflower when we get back.'

'All right,' John said. They sat down, and in their funeral clothes, each took a knife and began to pull and chop.

'What shall I do with the corn?' Jane said after a time.

'I don't know, actually,' her father said. 'I hadn't really thought about it. I suppose – well, I had supposed – that we could boil it and hand it over to people to nibble at. I should have done it with the asparagus. I just forgot about it. Perhaps we could chop it up and they could dip it with the other things.'

'Is it nice raw?' Jane said. 'It might be dangerous.'

John looked at the corn, six green logs like dildos on the table. He chopped off a small corner, and then, on the tip of his knife, he tasted it. 'I risk my life,' he said. 'No, not very nice. Let's throw it away.'

'Seems a slight waste,' Jane said. 'Oh, well, I don't care for it. Francesca might like it.'

'Boiled with butter –'

'With those strange metal spikes that you can't use for anything else –'

'Which in any case we don't have,' John said, and, demurely, amazingly, they both quickly giggled. They went back to their chopping. They had bought the food that morning, realizing, as they reached the supermarket, that neither of them had thought what they should buy. They knew nothing about food, and neither had ever thought more than vaguely about the food at successful parties, never thought about the possibilities of caterers and canapés. John thought about tiny slivers of asparagus vividly green in tiny pastry barques, and infant prawns curled up on toasted triangles. Impossible to master now, the arts of exquisiteness, and not worth the candle, he thought. Jane had never troubled to eat the food at parties, and said the word 'vol-au-vent' to herself, with amusement. So what they had ended up with was a number of bags of raw vegetables, now partly chopped. 'For dips,' Jane said, decisively, thinking of guests, leaning and dripping over bowls of wet cheese, or whatever. But they both feared now that not all the vegetables they had bought were quite suitable for dipping. Nor were the pastes and thick soups, the inadequately complicated gloopy mixes to empty into dishes altogether the right sort of thing. It was easy, however, and neither of them had much idea what else food for a party might consist of. But it was only now that they worried that they had made the wrong choices, and the simplicity of the food would not be excused on the grounds of grief.

'What time is the car coming?' John said.

'Twelve,' Jane said. 'Is there going to be enough time?'

'Oh yes,' John said. 'Terrible things, supermarkets. You just go along bunging things into the trolley while thinking about something else. Is Francesca ready?'

'I think so,' Jane said. 'She said a couple of days ago that she wasn't going to come. But she seems to have decided to come.'

'Why wouldn't she come?'

'Well, she was quite upset.'

'Is she all right now?' John said.

'Oh, yes,' Jane said. 'I'm sure. She just needs something to do, and then she'll be all right.'

She thought, with a tang of shame, that Francesca had no monopoly on sorrow, although her evident and performing grief had prevented her, without discussion, from doing anything she didn't want to do. John and Jane had done the shopping; Jane had dealt with the undertaker. Jane looked at Francesca, sitting in a chair on the other side of the glass door, and wondered why Francesca was so upset, and she not upset at all. She knew that she had no right to a sorrow she did not feel, and considered coolly why Francesca's public grief seemed to be preventing her from feeling anything at all. And she wondered what her father thought, and knew she wasn't up to asking him.

Francesca's face was plump and pink and tear-filled, as if recently slapped. She looked downwards at the floor. This was a characteristic attitude. Jane often thought that all her attitudes were characteristic. She moved through her life as if expecting to be looked at. She moved through her life as if it were a bad film, and she were waiting for the sound-track to start. She sought out streets which she could skip down, with her scarves flagging her kooky fun behind her; she travelled, Jane suspected, miles on buses to canals which she could trail along, the same scarves dangling mournfully. Those who noticed her often felt that they were being instructed in Francesca's mood by her posture. Sometimes they went along with it; they consented to share in Francesca's mood, her fun and her misery. More often, they looked at her and were enraged.

Unlike Jane's, Francesca's clothes were chosen for a funeral. Her clothes were usually massively feminine, pastel and terrifying even to those who were not terrified by feminine things. But she had produced, from somewhere, a dark suit to show her seriousness; and a pink silk scarf to finish it off.

'Well, I wish she'd do something,' John said. 'I'm quite tired of chopping.'

'That's plenty,' Jane said. 'We can always do some more afterwards. But no one will expect much.'

'No,' John said. 'It isn't exactly a party. Tell Francesca the car will be here in five minutes.'

'It's only half-past eleven.'

'Just to give her something to do, and not sit there,' John said.

'What's that?' Jane said.

'What?'

'That car outside. That is the car, isn't it?'

'It must be. But it's only half-past eleven.'

They went, leaving the vegetables under plastic film, and endured the service; and at two they returned, taking the plastic film off. Jane quickly opened the bottles of wine;

Francesca went upstairs to check her appearance. And John stood by the door, and waited. How party-like funerals are, and how little they are parties. And when few people knew the dead woman well, and when fewer people cared much for her, and when her husband is liked, although he is a hunchback, and when he is especially pitied; then a funeral could be still more like a party, and the conventions which stop it from turning into a party are still more marked. There is nothing to do except stand by the door, awkwardly, and let the party be awkward, which is what happened.

The first people to arrive were Henry and his sister Nancy. They shook John's hand in a serious way, and, for the lack of anything serious to say, Nancy remarked that they could quite easily have given somebody a lift from the crematorium. John told her it was quite unnecessary, and Henry and Nancy passed into the room.

There was nobody they could talk to except Jane. She noticed their problem. Nancy was her best friend. Henry, on the other hand, was a former boyfriend of hers, whom she no longer saw very much. He had no reason not to wish to see her. She wanted to see him all the time, very much; and yet they did not see each other at all. Jane noted Nancy's nervousness, and Henry's determination to walk forward and shake her hand. She was mildly, obscurely displeased that they had come at all, but she let them come in. They stood and waited for people to arrive.

'Thank you for coming,' Jane said, in the end.

'Not at all,' Nancy said. It was the wrong, the party-like thing to say.

'We couldn't not come,' Henry said. He was far more

tactful than his sister, and went back to talk to John until other people arrived.

'What do you think they find to talk about?' Jane said.

'Work, I think,' Nancy said. John and Henry worked together, in the House of Commons, as Clerks. 'You know how they like to talk about it.'

'Not pa,' Jane said. 'Never mentions it.'

'Jane—' Nancy said.

'Do you want something to drink?' Jane said, going off in the direction of the kitchen.

Jane's role in the funeral was marked; the elder daughter of the dead woman. Henry would have found no difficulty; he was easily shaking John's hand and looking him in the eye, and not appearing insincere or practised. But Nancy found it hard to say the correct things to Jane. She seemed only vaguely aware that this was not an ordinary party. Jane's clothes were strangely inappropriate for a funeral, but it couldn't be said why. They were not terrifyingly feminine, like Francesca's; they were black, and sober. Nor had she dressed, like Nancy, for a party exactly. Nancy had; was elegant. She looked as if she had set out for a wedding before falling in her ribboned fine pastels and purples and cheerful greys into a great pool of black ink. Nancy looked not sombre but, like a dwarf in Velazquez, blackly festive.

'What have you got on?' Jane said, coming back with two glasses of wine.

'I've only got one black dress,' Nancy said, gesturing hopelessly at her lace and ribbons.

'It looks like it,' Jane said. She had not thought of the clothes to wear, apparently, but it would not occur to those she spoke to that her approximately black dishevelment was in any way the mark of a grief. It was the mark of how Jane was, and the nearest she could come to mourning, which was not near. It did not seem like a mourning to Nancy; her wardrobe did not seem like a formal choice to mark a death; rather, it seemed like the clothes Jane always wore, because those were the clothes that suited her. She would not mourn her immaculate mother in her clothes; her mother's death, so sudden, had not discomposed or wrecked her daughter, in her customary discomposed and wrecked wardrobe. Francesca's careful suit, and Jane's father, who had taken time off from sorrow to think about his zinc-black suit and his dark tie and his polished shoes, and arranged time to have his hair cut, both seemed much more sincere. And now the party was beginning to fill up with people who had been driving round the block for ten minutes, tactfully.

'Good of the Secretary of State to come,' Nancy said, observing a middle-aged man coming through the door with something of a retinue.

'Yes, wasn't it?' Jane said. 'It's odd that he knows my father. I suppose they got to know each other years ago when neither of them was famous or important. And now he's famous and important, and my father still isn't.'

'How did they meet each other?'

'My mother was his secretary for a while, actually,' Jane said.

'Really?' Nancy said, wanting to get Jane to go on talking rather than out of interest. 'I never knew that.'

'Yes,' Jane said. 'That was years ago. And she didn't do it for long. But he probably remembers her. Anyway, she had to stop pimping for Tories when she married my father. They wouldn't stand for that for a second.'

'Who wouldn't?'

'Oh, the House of Commons, of course,' Jane said. 'You know they're not allowed to be political if you work there, for some reason, though of course they all are. Do you know that man, I can't remember his name, bald, polished head, silly beard? My father always says he's supposed to long for armed revolution or the reintroduction of slavery or something. Used to write pamphlets about it, and then he had to stop. They're just not supposed to say so or let on in any way that they're human beings. I don't know how my father stands it working there.'

'No,' Nancy said. 'I often wonder that about Henry, how he puts up with it.'

'Oh well,' Jane said. She sometimes couldn't stop herself, she couldn't stop a hurt coming out like this. 'I can believe it about Henry, it would be a great relief for someone like him not to have to be political and believe things, commit himself to anything. Someone like Henry. Not that I believe in anything much or you do, I suppose.'

'I believe in lots of things,' Nancy said.

'No you don't,' Jane said. 'You just think you ought to. Anyway, what they said was that you can't let your wife work for a Tory party activist – that was what he was, then – because all the Tories would assume that you were on their side and all the others would think you were a traitor or a quisling or something. So she stopped.'

'Good of him to come, though,' Nancy said again, looking round her.

'Yes,' Jane said. 'Lucky really. It's the party conference next week, apparently. If my mother had died a few days later, he wouldn't have been able to come.'

'Oh Jane,' Nancy said.

'It's all right,' Jane said. 'I'm just going to get another drink.'

She did not ask Nancy if she wanted anything, and left her stranded as she went to the far end of the room. She poured herself another glass of wine, drank it quickly and filled the glass again. Those who observed her thought that her behaviour was due to her being upset. This was, in fact, the way Jane always drank. She felt just the same, but she turned with her glass to the room.

The party was filling up quickly in its un-party-like way. People did not come into the room, but waited at the door until they could be welcomed by John. As he shook their hands, they took the opportunity to say how sorry they were, or something. There were few people who did this easily or gracefully or without embarrassment, although all of them had been thinking of what to say while driving to the party. The more practised among them knew that an appearance of awkwardness conveyed their sincerity. John had a face which could not but make a half-smile; he was liked because of it; and it made the job of saying I am so sorry, and If there is anything at all I can do, anything practical, much easier for the little queue of guests. He thanked all of them, and said that there was nothing to be done, and they passed into the room, where their voices lowered and, quiet, made a quiet crowd, like a surprise party waiting for the surprise guest, or, in their black, like a black cloud after thunder or before.

Nancy was stranded. Her brother, Henry, observing this, came to talk to her. Normally it would be thought wrong for a brother and sister at a party to talk to each other if they came together. But this was all right, by the unestablished rules they acted by. At a funeral it does not do to mix.

'How is she?' Nancy said.

'I don't know,' Henry said. 'I haven't spoken to her. You were talking to her.'

'She seemed pretty bad,' Nancy said. 'You know when people can't stop talking about something that's really hurt them. You know, she's still knocked sideways by the whole business.'

'Well, it was only a week ago,' Henry said. Nancy looked at him, since she had not been thinking of Jane's mother's death the week before, but of Henry's leaving her, some years before.

'You could be nicer to her,' Nancy said. 'You ought to go and talk to her properly.'

'No point,' Henry said. 'She doesn't want to talk to me.'

'Yes she does,' Nancy said. 'She talks about you all the time. Quite casually, but you can see she's always thinking about the same things.'

'Well, she oughtn't to want to talk to me, and it would only make it worse,' Henry said. 'Anyway, she could be pining over a boy in Boots the Chemist.'

'You know she's not.'

'I suppose so.'

'You know, what with her father always talking about you and what you've been up to at work, and me, it can't be that easy. You don't get over something like that as quickly as all that.'

'I did.'

'That's different. She wouldn't, and she thinks of it as unfinished business.'

'All business is unfinished,' Henry said. 'And all of us cope with it somehow. Look at John, he's coping. Good of the Secretary of State to come.'

'I was just saying that to Jane,' Nancy said. 'She didn't take it that well.'

'Still, it is,' Henry said. 'You can imagine how busy he must be, even in the summer, and I doubt he knew Helena much at all.'

'Actually, years ago, before they married, she used to be his secretary, Jane said.'

'What, before he was a Member? John never mentioned that.'

'Funny little man,' Nancy said. 'Not at all as he looks normally. I dare say these people are always glad of a chance to show how human they are, in their private lives.'

'He is human, of course,' Henry said. 'He might well feel sorry for John, or have been fond of Helena, if she was his secretary. I don't know how much they see of each other, him and John.'

'I can't imagine they can see each other often,' she said. 'A House of Commons Clerk and a Secretary of State. Such public things. They have such public lives, as if they only have a job to do, like a role to step into, and no real life at all. There is something inhuman about you all, what you all do.'

'Thank you,' Henry said. 'Just what one wants to be told.'

'I'm joking.'

'No you weren't. They're just jobs,' he said. 'Even you have a job.'

'Not a job like a mask or a coffin, not a job that's been going on for six hundred years without any gaps at all,' she said. 'Look at him now. Look at John. You can see he's sad, but it's all terribly public. He's not going to cry, or if he is, he'll wait until he's on his own and, probably, there's no one else in the house. All that self-control. The way he's taking it, it's so correct and public. He never stops. None of you do.'

They observed John, shaking hands for precisely five seconds, giving the appearance of gratitude, sorrow, and feeling, precisely gauged, smiling wanly.

'It is a funeral,' he said. 'You can't just indulge your feelings here. You have to put up a bit of a brave face.'

'I'd rather people wept and wailed and tore their hair at mine,' Nancy said extravagantly. 'In a way.'

'No you wouldn't,' Henry said. 'And you wouldn't be there to know anything about it.'

'I just wonder whether there's anything to John, anything private behind the brave face and handshaking,' Nancy said. 'To tell the truth, I've always been a bit scared of him.'

'He's terribly nice,' Henry said, looking round.

John. It was not his fists that took the attention, but the hump on his back. His twisting spine which made him stand awkwardly and made him shift from foot to foot, like a slow courtly dance, and gave him an evident perpetual ache and restlessness. And, after a while there was his kind smooth face, with its half-smiling patience which was only the way his face was formed, and perhaps, in the eyes, a little suggestion of the pain he must always feel, must always be just behind him. But it was the fists that mattered. As people came up to him with their practised expressions of sorrow and offers of help, they did not see his fists, clenched. If they had seen them, what they would have seen was fists clenched as if in nervousness and terror and grief, and not fists clenched to strike. But violence is what they were gripped for. Look at his fists, their rictus, and the unvarying expression of his face; worry about the private violence to come, and the public mask. It was as if he were not a victim of death, not the bereaved, but the perpetrator of it. As if, from the way he held down his hands before the many guests he barely knew, he wanted to kill.

'Thank you for coming,' Francesca said to Nancy and Henry. She had come up without them noticing. She was pulling a face which was evidently meant as an expression of sorrow, but which gave a practised and an actressy impression. She seemed to speak to both of them, but Nancy understood that she meant to speak to Henry, whom she did not know well. Taking the opportunity which in five minutes might no longer exist, she said, 'It was the least we could do,' and moved off.

'I'm glad so many people have felt able to come,' Francesca said.

'It isn't surprising, though,' Henry said.

'I'm particularly glad,' Francesca said, taking Henry by the elbow and looking into his eyes, 'that you felt able to come. I think we would all – all of us – have understood if you hadn't, and yet I'm more pleased that you're here than anyone else.'

'It would have been unforgivable not to come,' Henry said.

'It feels so strange,' Francesca said straight away, guiding Henry firmly to a sofa with a shadow of her mother's perfect party polish. 'It's difficult to believe that she's dead. She was always so full of life and fun. I think now I'll always remember her laughing, or chatting, or making something delicious in the kitchen.'

'Oh yes,' Henry said. These were not his memories of her mother, nor were they very likely to be anyone else's. Henry remembered her, at a party like this, or in a bar at the opera house – a modern German opera, in July, a terrible mistake which no one quite owned up to – talking to him. The cost of wallpaper, the decline of men's tennis, last year's holiday to the Languedoc and this year's holiday to Umbria and next year's or the year after's to Brazil, maybe – and all the time her looking over his shoulder for the next person to talk to. She was not fun; she was not full of life; he shrank from the word that came to mind.

'Didn't she?' Francesca said.

'Yes,' Henry said, paying attention again. 'I think that's my memory of her.'

'I know it's a terrible cliché,' Francesca said, 'but when someone dies, it takes such a long time for the fact of it to sink in. I know that I've hardly understood that she won't just now walk through the door, laughing as she always did. That's the first step to the acceptance of death, isn't it? Once one truly understands that someone is gone, then one can truly come to terms with one's own grief.'

'I think that's terribly true,' said Henry, thinking that he had never heard anyone use the word truly in conversation before.

'I've been reading a book about bereavement,' Francesca said. 'It's helping me a good deal.'

'Did you buy it?'

'Yes,' Francesca said. 'Of course. What funny things you say, Henry.'

Henry tried to imagine Francesca going into a bookshop and asking for the bereavement section. Perhaps it would be called personal growth. He imagined her taking down a number of books from the shelf, and examining them carefully; weighing the claims of an intimate, comforting style of writing against a psychological acuity. Thinking

whether it was better to have something consoling or something which genuinely understood all the issues involved.
Perhaps she would prefer not to buy a book on such a
serious subject in paperback; or, then again, perhaps she
would prefer something which she could read quickly and
then throw away. He imagined her, having made her choice,
going with it to the till, and giving a ten pound note, and
waiting for her change. When had she done all this? Had
she waited until the day after her mother's death, or the
day after that? What was a decent interval? Had she begun
to read it on the way home in the underground train, or
would there be more comfort in shutting one's bedroom
door and concentrating on it? Would it have been more or
less extraordinary to have borrowed a book from the public
library, if there was still one open around here? Perhaps the
thing to do would have been for some sympathetic person,
themselves unaffected, to have gone through the transaction
on her behalf, uncommissioned, and then, finally, to have
handed over the book. Would he have thought of doing
such a thing? Would anyone?

'Who wrote the book?' he said.

'An American,' she said. 'But it's really very helpful.'

'It sounds it,' he said, looking over her shoulder.

The Clerk of the House now stood at the door. He had
come very promptly to the funeral, and had sat tactfully at
the back, and not intruded on the family. He was the head of
the department in the House of Commons in which Henry
and John both worked – daringly, they sometimes said 'my
boss', which seemed an incongruous sort of word for the
post he held. It was good of him to come. As they all said.
He moved in his self-effacing way through the now full
room, appearing awkward and out of ease in his clothes.

His tweed suit, unfamiliar, and his bald head, wigless, were not what anyone expected; they might have thought of his usual wig and gown.

'Gavin,' John said to the Clerk of the House.

'John,' the Clerk of the House said in return, in his heavy manner, not comforting, not offering much beyond the name he produced. He radiated consciousness of his goodness in coming. They had nothing else to say to each other.

'Have you met our new recruit?' the Clerk of the House finally said.

'No,' John said. 'Has he started yet?'

'We had to take him on at the beginning of the recess,' the Clerk of the House said.

'What is he like?' John said.

'Extraordinarily fat,' the Clerk of the House said. John looked at the Clerk in a little surprise, and contemplated the fat sweating pinkfaced blond boy the Clerk had been when they had first known each other; he thought what a humourless bore he had always thought him and remembered the sickening feeling he had had when he realized that no sense of humour and an ability to bore on endlessly were vital qualities for anyone wanting to be Clerk of the House.

'I don't want to talk shop,' the Clerk said.

'No, fire away,' John said.

'I didn't mention this, for obvious reasons, or want to trouble you.'

'No, please, carry on.'

'Well,' the Clerk said. 'It looks as if there might be a Petition for leave to produce evidence in the offing. I thought you'd like to know.'

'What's the story?'

'Oh, no need to go into it now. But we ought to talk about it pretty soon.'

'I could come in next week,' John said.

'No, the first day back would do. Or better Friday,' the Clerk said. 'Shall we say close of play on the first Friday? You don't have to dash off? It might take all afternoon.'

'No. Close of play. If you could send me the papers.'

Jane observed all this. She had known this was how it was to be. She had known she would want to speak to no one except Henry; she had known that the event of her mother's death, like every other event in her life since Henry had left her, would change nothing for her, would leave her life suspended as it had been. From time to time men and women spoke to her, seemingly concerned about the state she might be in, but knowing nothing about it. The Secretary of State, even, had tried to speak to her, once she had been identified by one of his retinue as the daughter of the dead woman. She suspected him of lechery, of using her name as if to remind himself who he was talking to, and of neglecting to wash himself enough. She ignored him.

She went into the kitchen and saw two big plates of vegetables and the four bowls of improvised dip. She realized immediately the terrible inadequacy and pathos of the dips; she saw no one would eat them. But there was no obvious way to ask people to eat them, anyway. She could not carry these plates through the party, being bereaved and more than half drunk. Nor could she decently summon people to come and fetch the food themselves. While she thought about it, she picked up a plate, and put things on to it, beginning with the asparagus, and two puddles of sauce, one red and one white. Then she forgot about it, and went into the drawing room with her plate. This proved a successful way of announcing that the food was there to be taken, and when, after a while, the room was fairly full of people balancing plates, and eating, with difficulty and not much dignity, the asparagus they had all taken care to take first, Jane could put the plate she had filled with food down on a table, with its untouched load, and went to her grand-mother.

When the room cleared slightly; when people moved; when people fetched food; at the far end, upright and alone, Jane's grandmother could be seen. She stood firmly at the funeral of her daughter. She took no prisoners; was uncompromisingly dressed in formally funereal black. She seemed to see nobody and to wish to speak to nobody. It was as if it was apparent, from the way she stood, that she knew that it was always going to happen, your children dying pointlessly. And whatever politenesses she voiced to those she hardly knew, the guests seemed to understand that, in her mind, it was all she deserved, all her daughter deserved, all any of them deserved, in the end, really, and they moved away, quite quickly. Only Jane stayed to talk to her.

'You are clever,' she said in the end, 'to find asparagus. I thought the season would have finished by now.'

'I don't know,' Jane said. 'It was in the supermarket. I think it's Chilean or something.'

'Still, very nice,' she said. 'It is extraordinary now, what you can find. I remember when you used to wait for the first asparagus, and then after a month or two it would just disappear for another year. I do love it.'

'So do I,' Jane said. 'Makes your pee smell, though.'

'Yes, it does,' she said. 'I remember your mother would never eat it.'

'Really?' Jane said. 'I never knew that.'

'Well, your grandfather and I were mad keen on it – friends always used to tell us if they'd happened to see some especially early asparagus, and I remember once inventing an excuse to go to Suffolk because someone said they'd seen some there in February. It was all the most shocking prank, of course, in the end.' She laughed, abruptly. 'But we used to gorge ourselves on it whenever we could, and, whether it was that that disgusted your mother or the taste I don't know. But certainly she would never touch it. Who are all these people?'

'Oh, friends of father's, and mother's, mostly,' Jane said. They sat down on the sofa.

'I've never seen one of them in my life,' her grandmother said. 'Are you sure?'

'Well, I don't know most of them either,' Jane said. 'But I assume father wouldn't let them in if they weren't genuine. I can't see why anyone would want to come if they didn't have to.'

'There is that,' she said. 'That man looks familiar.'

'That's a member of the Cabinet.'

'Really? I thought I knew him, and it turns out to be off the telly. Why is he here?'

'Years ago, mother used to work for him. Before I was born, didn't she work for politicians?'

'Oh, yes, for a while, I remember. So that's what they turn into. Not very remarkable, apart from his job.'

'None of them are,' Jane said. 'It's only her who's at all remarkable.'

'Yes, her,' her grandmother said. Always, in political circles, there was no need to name her; no need for anything but a title and a pronoun; and the pronoun could mean no one else. 'Don't drink too much, will you.'

'Why not?' Jane said.

'Save it for later,' she said, and quickly, suddenly grinned. They had talked about nothing, but Jane still took her hand and held it tight.

'Papa,' Jane said as John came up.

'Girls,' John said in his heavy manner.

'Go on,' Jane's grandmother said. 'I'm sure your father needs some help.'

'Are you all right?' Jane said.

'I'll be quite all right,' she said.

'Not too bad, after all,' John said, as they went into the kitchen.

'No, not at all,' she said. 'No one's mentioned the food, though. Only granny, who liked the asparagus.'

'Once they've got through the food, they'll think about going.'

'Shall I hurry them along a bit?'

'No, no. It's quite all right. Shall we get another drink?'

'Why not?' Jane said.

'You know, we ought to have got some caterers in, or something.'

'Oh, I couldn't have felt much like discussing canapés. You have to start thinking about the six pounds menu and the five pounds menu, and how much more the five pounds menu would be if you took out the sardine tartlets and put in the smoked salmon roulades. It's all such hard work.'

'Frances might have enjoyed it.'

'Yes, she would. Francesca.'

'Sorry. I do keep forgetting.' Francesca had changed her name from Frances some months before, for no apparent reason. 'Someone ought to go and rescue poor Henry.'

'Not me,' Jane said. 'I've done enough of that in my time.'

Francesca and Henry were still on the sofa. Francesca was still talking about her recent bereavement. Henry was still giving a poor impersonation of someone listening to what she was saying when the Clerk of the House came within hailing distance. Henry got up.

'Gavin,' he said.

'Henry,' the Clerk of the House said. 'And it's Frances, isn't it?'

'Francesca, actually.' Francesca said. The Clerk sat down. Henry moved past him, as if to get a drink.

The Secretary of State was preparing to go.

'Appointment at four, Secretary of State,' his private secretary had said.

'They would have been able to reach me, wouldn't they?' he said to his wife.

'Of course they would,' she said. 'They knew where you were going. But why would they have wanted to reach you?'

'Things come up all the time. What would happen if the Prime Minister wanted to talk to me?'

'I've no idea,' she said. 'What would happen?'

He looked at her sharply. He suspected her of not being especially keen on his career.

'Always sad,' he went on, 'a funeral of someone younger than oneself.'

'I never knew her,' his wife said. 'When did you last see her?'

'Quite recently, actually,' he said. 'Just by chance. I always liked her.'

'I don't remember you ever mentioning her,' she said. They stood side by side and looked at the room, and not each other, as they spoke.

'I think I'd better find the husband and say goodbye,' the Secretary of State said.

John was already standing near the door.

'Not at all, Secretary of State; kind of you to think of coming. Thank you. Yes, goodbye. Henry.'

'John,' Henry said, feeling lightheadedly that he had done nothing but hail people by their names since he had arrived. It was not his fault; there was nothing else to say.

'Would you come for dinner this week?' John said. 'It would be nice to have a chat, you and the girls as well. This is hopeless, I'm afraid.'

'Yes,' Henry said. He tried to look John in the eye in a sincere way, and knew he failed. 'I should like that.'

He did not think of Jane. He felt that he would do John a necessary favour by going to dinner there; he felt that John's appearance of vagueness, his looking past Henry and through the party, were a means of not looking at anyone. And, just as he spoke, he saw John's clenched fists, clenched as if to strike, and he had never seen them before. He did not know what to make of his gaze, suddenly, into the middle distance, and his constrained violence.

The party had begun to thin almost as soon as it had begun. People arrived promptly and politely, had taken one plate of food – taking the asparagus first – and a single glass of wine, as if eating and drinking were only gestures. They had spoken to the people they had come with, and to the family. They talked about few things. They talked about the Government and the Prime Minister. They talked about the weather, which had persisted with heat long after it could have been expected to. And, perhaps a little self-consciously, perhaps with a slight sense that this was expected of them at the funeral, they talked about the dead woman. And when they had done these things, they went. As Francesca went over to talk to her grandmother – the Clerk of the House had defeated her – there were only fourteen or fifteen people left in the room.

'It's difficult to believe that she's dead, isn't it?' Henry heard her beginning as he moved away.

'You did well with her,' Nancy said to Henry as he came through.

'Oh, she's not so difficult.'

'I have trouble with her, I must say.'

'I know. I don't see any reason to dislike her, though.'

'Oh no, I don't dislike her. I see why some people might, though.'

'After all, Jane's just as difficult in the end.'

'Yes, but Jane is fun,' Nancy said. 'That's the difference. I don't think I'd ever let myself go on holiday with Francesca, for instance. I don't dislike her. I just don't care for her much.'

'Would you phone her up?'

'No, but if she phoned me up I wouldn't invent excuses. But I know she wouldn't.'

'Why not?'

'She's got no use for women,' Nancy said. 'We ought to go.'

'The difference between them is,' Henry said, 'that Jane drinks more than Francesca.'

'I'm not so sure,' Nancy said. 'She certainly holds it better. Look at her now.'

Francesca and her grandmother were sitting down, but upright and shell-shocked, her grandmother seemed quite as stiff. With a glass in her hand at a dangerous angle, Francesca appeared to be crying. It was the first time anyone had seen anyone crying all day. They all started preparing to leave.

'I had no idea,' somebody said, 'that the daughter was as close to her mother as all that.'

'She wasn't,' a woman said. They prepared to go, noticing that they were standing next to John, and, not shamed, but disliking their own embarrassment, they moved off.

They would all leave, and in one hour, or two, or three, or four, or more, each of them would piss; even the Secretary of State and the Clerk of the House would piss; even the old ladies; even the bereaved. And when they pissed, the stink of asparagus would remind them of what they had eaten, and where they had been. For a time the chemical, the physical traces would remind them, but not forever; and soon they would forget. And in a year, or two, or three, or four, or more, some of them would come across a photograph of the dead woman, or a letter, and they would look at it, and think that she was dead. But soon the photograph, or the ink, would begin to fade, and soon those who remembered her would be dead in their turn; and in the end, at the close of play, they would all be forgotten, and gone.

There was plenty of food left, John noted. And almost everyone had gone. He had no idea which people had come, and which people, who had been expected, had failed to come. He shook the hand of the departing Clerk of the House, and did not listen to the rubbish he was mumbling. He didn't listen to what people said to him, and he didn't hear remarks that were passed in his earshot. What he heard was a voice in his head, which was sometimes his wife's voice, and sometimes his voice, and sometimes neither. By the window, he stood and looked out at the dried-up garden. Next door, or further away, someone was mowing the lawn. There was a smell of petrol and cut grass which for John had always been the smell of happiness; the smell of his childhood. In an uncomplicated way he enjoyed it. There was a thought going around his head; something about the cutting down of grass and the cutting down of lives in their prime. It would not form properly; it was the end of summer. And the pleasure the smell and the blue roar of the motor gave him; it was not anything which meant anything. It was just memory, too vague to specify, and too vague to give anything but happiness.

He let his thoughts run on emptily for a while. Soon they passed into blankness, and they stayed blank while he said goodbye in his natural way to the last people going. 'Poor John,' they said in their cars, going home. They thought as much of his hunchback as of the death of his wife. But he stood at the closed window, and, at the hot day's end, at the hot summer's end, he let his thoughts go blank. Something had gone wrong; many things had gone wrong; and many more things were to go wrong. What were they? For the moment he could not remember them. They were somewhere in his blank mind, on the other side of the glass from the garden. Then his mind was not blank at all, but full of an idea, an idea of Giacomo; and, with his perfect public face, he turned to say goodbye to the room he was in; which had once been empty of people, and soon would be again.

HAVE YOU EVER BEEN FUCKED

OFTEN, WHEN HIS mind blanked over, he would find himself thinking, 'How many men have I fucked in my life?' His mind blanked over in this way more and more often these days. His age, he supposed. He sat in his office, and looked out of the window like a schoolboy at a quarter to three (but when did schoolboys come out of school now?); or he sat in his study with a glass of gin and tonic an hour before dinner (and it was not a drink he would have drunk even ten years ago); and a book he used to know that sooner or later he would definitely read; but now it was a book he only meant to read and never would. He would let his mind blank over, just blank, and he would begin to count the men he had fucked. And, beginning to count, he would come, after seven or eight more or less shadowy figures, whose names he couldn't recall, to a boy he met, in the end, ten times, an Italian boy he fucked, in the end, ten times; whom he gave five hundred pounds to; and afterwards – afterwards – he never knew what happened to him; or where, afterwards, he went.

'Let's go,' said Giacomo.

'Mm,' said John.

'Do you like that?' said John.

'Again,' said Giacomo, later.

'Yes,' said John.

'Have you ever been fucked?' said John.

'No,' said Giacomo, after a suitable pause.

'Would you like to be?' said John.

'We don't have to make a whole discussion out of it,' said Giacomo.

Often, when John's mind blanked over, and he looked out of a window, and out of the small closed space of his mind, he thought of this room, a room he was in ten times. There was a mattress, on the floor, and a clean towel, and a painted chest of drawers. He could never imagine what was in the chest of drawers, and he wondered if he wanted to know. Were there props? Were there devices? Were there towels, more clean ones, for those who came before him and those who came afterwards? He wondered if he wanted to know. He had never seen the room when the curtains were not drawn, and did not know what the view from the windows was; what the room would be like. He thought about the room, in a nowhere sort of place; the thought made him happy, and then he thought about Giacomo. When he thought of Giacomo, just as when he thought of the room, he did not think of appearances; he did not think of what he was like, nor what he looked like. It was what he felt like to John. It was the skin, like rough silk falling through the hands, unstoppably, and the hard wriggling inside pleasures of fucking him, and seeing him absolutely still in every respect but his mouth, moving, silently, in the silent motions of pleasure.

'Where do you come from?' John asked him once.

'I come from Italy,' said Giacomo, like a boy told to answer in sentences by a good teacher.

'Where in Italy?' said John.

'The south,' said Giacomo, politely, and John let his mind, just for now, fill with the baroque, unproffered erotic truths of Palermo, of Naples, of Lecce, Basilicata and Noto. He left it.

'Have you got any brothers?' said John.

'Yes,' said Giacomo, with an abrupt grin which reminded John why he liked coming here.

'Older?' said John. It was all he could get out.

'Wait one moment,' Giacomo said. 'Yes. All right?'

'Yes,' John said.

'One older, one younger. Luigi did well at school, and he's a dentist, and Giuseppe didn't do so well, and he's a boxer. But he's quite good. I trained to be a dentist as well. I failed all my exams, though.'

'A boxer,' John said. 'I thought your name was Luigi.'

'No,' Giacomo said. 'My name is Giacomo really. I don't like it though. I just say that my name is Luigi.'

'Why don't you like it?'

'It's my grandfather's name. So I say in adverts that my name is Luigi.'

'Not to me, though,' John said.

'No,' Giacomo said. 'Not to you, anyway. Not now you ask me.'

'Do that again,' John said.

'Yes,' Giacomo said, later. 'Giuseppe used to be very beautiful, but now his nose is broken.'

'Do they know what you do?' said John.

'Of course,' said Giacomo. 'Why not?'

'You surprise me,' said John, with the irony he sometimes

found himself using here, which he always used everywhere else. 'Do you like what you do?'

Sometimes, before they began to have sex, or after, John would lie and imagine the touch of hands. In their momentary absence, he would think of them; the pleasure of their not being there, the pleasure when they were there. The room they were in, and the flat, seemed to be Giacomo's alone. There was no question of any other presence. It seemed, too, to be not a professional flat; not one hired for the afternoon and evening, but one in which Giacomo lived. There was food in the kitchen, and colognes and shampoo in the bathroom. Giacomo's life was unimaginable, a matter perhaps of gyms and clothes-buying and perhaps clubs; did he have friends? Who did he see? Did he spend time, freely, with men who had started by paying him? Did he? And would he?

'Fuck me,' said John.

'Fuck me,' said Giacomo, on a different occasion.

'Do you like it?' said John.

'Yes,' said Giacomo. 'I like it. What did we agree on?'

'We didn't agree on anything before,' said John.

'No,' Giacomo said. 'I meant, how much did we agree on?'

'Oh,' John said. 'I see what you mean. Fifty pounds, I think.'

'Not exactly,' said Giacomo, whose English, it seemed, improved every time John came to see him.

John's hand moved over the perfect smoothness of Giacomo's shoulder, and there, like a solitary imperfection, under his thumb, was a little pin-head, embedded in the skin. His hand slowed.

'What is it?' Giacomo said.

'Nothing,' John said. 'A blackhead.'

'There are many?' Giacomo said.

'No,' John said. 'Only one.'

'Squeeze it,' Giacomo said.

He turned and momentarily grinned. John ran his fingers up and down the spine once more, and then, with the thumbs, he took a half-inch of skin, and quickly pressed. A muffled noise came from the boy; a little shout of pain, and he was purified, his flesh was clean. A small yellow worm, the last tenth of an inch of black, lay on the perfect back. John wiped his hand over it; it was gone.

'Has it gone?' Giacomo said.

'Yes,' John said. 'Did it hurt?'

'No,' Giacomo said. 'I'm sorry.'

'That's all right,' John said, and he was surprised, in his voice, to hear the gruff edge of lust, the vulnerability of desire, and he wondered what the tiny act of violence had done to excite him.

'Do you want to fuck me?' Giacomo said.

'All right,' said John. 'We'll talk about it later.'

'Fifty pounds is fine,' said Giacomo. He smiled; it was a small personal fondness, or like one.

'How old are you?' John said, later.

'Twenty-one,' Giacomo said.

'I'm forty-five,' said John. They both lied, and each knew that the other was older than he said.

'Do you like me?' said Giacomo.

'Yes, of course,' said John. He meant that he liked coming to this place, and he assumed that was what Giacomo had meant to ask him. 'I mean, I like coming here.'

'Why?' said Giacomo.

'Because it's so peaceful and separate,' said John, lying with his face down in a pile of pillows.

'Separate,' Giacomo murmured, moving his hands over the hump on John's left shoulder. 'Separate from what?'

'From everything,' John said. 'From everything else. Don't touch that.'

'Why not?' said Giacomo.

'Because –'

'It's all right,' Giacomo said. 'Relax yourself.' His hand moved down the back, ran softly down and underneath; took hold; began to move and caress and knead. John's eyes were shut. He felt at these moments that, in the unhesitating strength of this paid boy's grip, there was no revulsion to be felt, nothing but patience and a fondness which, in the end, could not be bought. 'Separate?' Giacomo said.

'It's like,' John said. 'It's like anger.' He knew Giacomo could hardly understand. He knew Giacomo could not understand what John himself hardly understood. That it wasn't his job to understand but just to be there, and to listen. 'You can be angry about something, and then shut it off from everything else. It doesn't have to infect anything else. This is just pleasure. Just pleasure. It doesn't matter to anything else, and nothing else matters. Matters to it. I'm just forgetting. Forgetting everything else, everything else in my life, just lying here. With you. With you. You.'

'Was that good?' said Giacomo, after a pause.

'It's always good,' said John, politely. 'How do you do that thing – you know –'

'I don't know,' Giacomo said. 'I can't say it.'

'Can you tell me in Italian?' said John.

'I can, but I can't,' said Giacomo.

'What do you mean?' John said.

'I mean I don't want to,' said Giacomo.

'All right,' said John. He was just the same as ever, in the end, afterwards.

'You speak Italian?'

'*Si,*' John said, hopelessly.

'Would you like a shower and a cup of tea?' Giacomo said.

John was silent. He was dead; he felt it; already. Often, when his mind blanked over in the middle of the afternoon, or just before he fell asleep, he would find himself thinking. 'How many men have I fucked in my life?' And, beginning to count, he came, after seven or eight shadowy figures, to a boy he met ten times, and fucked ten times, and gave five hundred pounds to, and never saw what happened to him. In the end. He thought of the boy's rumpy wiggle across the room on his way to get a towel. And then he thought of the boxer, the prostitute's brother, the boy who used to be beautiful, but whose nose, the prostitute said, was broken.

That day, all manner and rank and order of men thought about something they had never thought of before; or of something they had often thought about. They all said that they had never thought of it. They thought about the air. Something had happened to make it visible. A fog of water, suspended in itself above the pavements and which the pigeons, clattering with their wings, panicked through. An ordinary thing, but the fog was an unusual one; it seemed dirty; yellow; old. The Prime Minister in her room looked out of the window. It seemed to her a fog like the fogs she remembered from the time she first came to London. Then, they had seemed like an emblem of everything that had gone wrong with London, and with the nation; they seemed like something which could be put right, given enough will and energy. Something had again, inexplicably, gone wrong. What could be done about it? Her hands, she noticed, had begun to finger the lapel of her silk jacket; they had a pleasure of their own. A momentary lapse, and she turned her attention back to her patient paid interlocutioner, who had not stopped talking. Clerks in the offices of the House of Commons and the House of Lords commented on its thickness; they said they would remember this fog, just as they remembered the fogs which this fog reminded them of. Civil servants apologized to each other for their late arrival in their offices. They blamed the visible yellow air. The municipal modes of transport, and the national modes of transport, went on explaining quietly over their loudspeakers that travel would be delayed. A man – perhaps several men, but who cared? – sat on a bench and coughed, and prepared for death.

This is the way the city worked. A river ran through it, and divided the city into north and south; those who lived in the north said they never went south of the river. Those who lived in the south said that they would be glad never to have to go north of the river. But, in the west of the city, a great court had once lived, and spawned houses for the grand, and then the rich, and then those who merely hoped to be rich, and then nobody in particular. In the east, a great district which dealt with money was trapped in its mile-sized boundaries, and grew upwards, into the sky, into space which would never be needed. And east of that, nobody at all lived, despite the acres and miles of houses, stretching on and on to the edge of the country and into the sea, and despite the sums of money poured daily into this part of the great city, it was a part nobody lived in and nobody went to.

That day, those who worked or walked or lived next to the river which carved up the miles of city, a river which was there before the city, and would be there after, were struck by its silence. When a boat hooted to make itself known, the noise echoed from building to building from the City to Chelsea, and when the noise died away, there was nothing left behind it except the clatter of a pigeon, blundering through the fog in panic. They continued working, or sleeping, or walking. Some coughed, as I said.

Afterwards, that luxurious, sexy word. Afterwards, he left the flat, and stretched as he stood inside the hallway. The fogged street looked new, as if it didn't want to unwrap itself just yet. He had to make two telephone calls. He paused to button his coat before he shut the door behind him. It was only when leaving Giacomo's flat that he ever wondered if it was more natural to wait for a second, or to leave quickly. But he wondered every time he left Giacomo. A distinguished, fifty-five-year-old (hunchback) newly widowed public man. The Clerk of the Journals in the House of Commons. What could be more anonymous, more distinguished? Perhaps he was visiting a friend's son for lunch, in this street in Earl's Court. The parking here was, naturally, fiendishly difficult, and he had, naturally, been obliged to leave his car some streets away. Not wanting, either, to drive too far in the weather. He walked for a while before hunger nudged him. He thought all the time about the two telephone calls he ought to make: No telephone box was in sight. He went into a pub, thinking to have something to eat, and to telephone.

The pub was nearly empty. It was a pub which might be unchanged from forty years ago, or, far more likely, had been done up by the brewery in a nostalgic way in the last year or two. He stood at the bar in his distinguished, portly (hunchback) way, while the barman finished a conversation with another customer. John looked at his watch. It was just twelve. It was the hour his secretary had lunch, but none of the other Clerks would be having lunch for an hour or an hour and a half. Good. He needed to catch them to tell them – he hadn't mentioned he was going out – that he was on his way back. The barman glanced over, and carried on talking for a moment. John rapped the bar with his fingernails, not summoning, just tapping. The barman performed an elaborate camp pantomime of noticing the unserved customer for the first time in the empty pub.

John ordered a pint of beer and a beef sandwich. As the barman leant forward to write down Beef sandwich, on the doubled raffle tickets of his pad, he caught his own eye in the mirror behind the bar. Pale, pudgy, slack-mouth cripple, he thought; a look of fear in the eyes. He shut his mouth. He thought about his mouth, exploring the furred warm cavities and sudden odd softnesses of Giacomo, whose name he had just learnt. It did not occur to him that Giacomo might have told him another false name, and he was right not to doubt him. His bristled jaw, the odd hard skin at the edges of his hands and feet, his secret pinks and blushes. Unasked for, the word *sated* came to mind. He dismissed it.

(In other parts of the same city, north or south or east,

his two daughters, his colleagues; lines of electricity and thought connected them.)

He left his pint of beer on the bar and went to the payphone at the back of the pub. He was unable to remember any telephone numbers in his office, and rang his own. It rang five times before anyone answered it.

'John here,' John said. 'Who's that?'

'Louis,' the voice said.

'Oh yes,' John said. 'Hello there. Getting on all right, are you?'

'Oh, yes,' Louis said.

'Look,' John said. 'I've been a bit held up here. In this meeting. I should be back quite soon. Has anything come up?'

'No,' Louis said. 'I don't think so. Hang on.'

'I only wanted to know if the Clerk had telephoned. I was supposed –' John said, but found himself talking to an abandoned telephone. He put some more money in. 'Hello. Hello.'

'Hello,' Louis said. Just as he did so, the barman dropped a glass on the wooden floor, breaking it. The barman's friend let out a brief violent shout of laughter. 'What was that?'

'Oh, nothing,' John said. 'I'll be back soon. Before one, anyway.' He went back to his pint of beer and sat drinking it, thinking, as he always did on leaving Giacomo, of decay and death, of ageing and corruption and beauty. He thought about Louis, who had just become a Clerk, and how he was young and fine and fat, and would grow old in the service of the House of Commons, and nothing would change for him, just as nothing had changed for John, except that ruination would come upon him. John sat with his thoughts of decay, and waited for the meat, and the bread, and the other customers to arrive.

If you had said to John, What do you want, what would he have said? He would have said Luigi, 23, muscular, Italian, tanned beach-boy, good-looking, well hung, full service, 437271. No he would not. He would have said he wanted a drink or a cheese sandwich, or a bit of peace. In more serious moments he would have said he wanted security for himself and his children, and he wanted to go on just as he was. These were things he thought he could have; he was wrong.

But there were two things John wanted. He said to himself that he wanted a boy. And that he wanted sex with a man. He would have said these things, but he would have said them only to himself. He prided himself on his honesty, but in truth, his honesty only resided in his not lying to himself. Which is no honesty at all. His real desire – what he said he wanted to nobody at all, not even himself – stopped him from saying this to anyone else.

It was true that John wanted a man. He did want it; wanted one all the time, and thought about it constantly. Sometimes he shocked himself with the honesty of his desire, his honesty to himself. It was only unclear to John whether he wanted a man for the afternoon, or whether he wanted a man for good; it was unclear, because he had not addressed the question, what he would do if a man wanted him in return. He did not know.

This is what he said to himself he most wanted. But this was not true. There was something he wanted more. Because what he wanted was something he felt he could do without; something he considered an incidental, a tiresome bore, something which – he said to himself – got in the way of his wishes. His secret life was not entered upon for the reason that it was what he most wanted.

It was entered upon because it gave him a secret to keep. What he most wanted was a secret to keep. This was something he did not know, or had not formulated. It was something only I knew.

He would do anything, if it involved a secret. He would go to any lengths, and, in the end, he did.

He relished secrecy, and he created it around him. Perhaps it was why he decided to do the job that he did. He was secretive about it even when there was no need. He never told his daughters, and, before, he would never have told his wife about what he had done during the day. Not that they asked, and he was happy that they did not ask. When he met people, however, who were interested in what he did, an alarm came over him. He would never tell them the piquant anecdotes they expected. If they wrote him off as a bore, it hardly mattered.

I do not know, and John did not know, what the causes of homosexuality are. I do not know whether John's mother was strong, and his father was weak; I do not know whether he was exposed to the films of Douglas Sirk at too young an age; I do not know what he thought of my beauty, and the beauty of women like, and unlike, me; I do not know whether he was bitten and traumatized. But I know that he loved secrecy. He was homosexual and secretive; and it might be that he was not secretive because, being homosexual, he had to be. It might be that he was homosexual because he wanted to be secretive. He was homosexual because that was what best suited his secrecy.

One of the maxims he had often heard was that a man with a secret was not to be trusted. He, too, did not trust

men with secrets, and he, too, repeated the maxim. He
was a man with a secret, and held the secret because he
wanted not to be trusted. He wanted, perhaps, not to be
able to trust himself; and he sometimes wondered what
ends his homosexuality would lead him to. What ends
would preserve the need for secrecy. He wanted to get
rid of the trust in which he was swaddled, and to do
it, he would have done anything. He would have acted
in any way, to create a secret for himself. And he knew
that homosexuality was no longer enough. In a London
where the men increasingly walked the streets with their
men, hand in hand; where in nightclubs where thousands
went, men fucked each other on the dance floor, sodomy
was no longer enough. He would have done anything to
create, to sustain his laboriously maintained secret. He did,
in the end. He would have killed, with his habitually and
strangely clenched fists.

'And then,' Henry said, his arms upstretched like Liberty in
the photographs, 'she enters in a fit of rage, but completely
controlled, a sort of silent intense rage, wearing this absolutely immense gold ballgown. It's slightly absurd because,
of course, it's really lunchtime, but you just don't ask.
Anyway, she comes into this not very salubrious bar in
the middle of the morning, and they all fall away from her
in a slightly exaggerated but really very exciting way, and
then of course you realize what you've spent the whole film
trying to work out, who she really is.'

'Who is she?' said Louis, when he realized he was
supposed to.

'She's the Angel of Death, of course,' Henry said,

'descended from the heavens to gather them all up. Marvellous moment.'

Around him, he wrapped the immense black slightly mouldy gown the Clerk of Public Bills had left in the office with his lawyer's mouldy wig the night before, and strode the full length of the office in impersonation of an angel as impersonated by a great *diva* of the nineteen-forties, which for Louis he momentarily became.

'My goodness,' Louis said.

There was a man called Louis. He had started work for the House of Commons six months before, and still did not know how to get around the Palace. He knew how to reach his office from the gate, and how to get to a bar and to a canteen from his office, and how to get to the division lobby. More than that he did not know, and often he turned the wrong way, and was quickly lost. The corridors; the hundreds of stairs; the thousands of windowed rooms looking out on windowed curtained courts and spires and a scrap of sky. Whenever Louis walked, lost, through the corridors of the Palace, they were so dimly lit; so silent, private and, in their green warm light, so underwater, that into his mind often came the thought 'The secret Ministry'. In this public place, into which the public never came, upon which so many thoughts were daily bent, he walked, removed from the world of men, unsuspected by any, unheard, unwatched in this secret place, performing his secret ministry. He had no hidden purpose, but he felt like an anarchist when he walked the streets, hiding the round black bomb of his job.

At this time, Louis was sitting at his desk, and watching the Clerk he shared an office with impersonate a great *diva* of the nineteen-forties, not unimpressively.

'Anyway,' Henry said, just as John came back into the office in his blue raincoat, a little out of breath, a little head down. 'Whatever were we doing? Oh yes. Five minutes to write them down. The target is forty-seven. Appalling weather, John.'

'Appalling,' John said.

'Do we know there are forty-seven?' Louis said.

'Oh yes,' Henry said. 'I'm sure there are.'

'Have you got a pen?' Louis said.

'Haven't you got one?' John said. 'Didn't anyone tell you you ought to carry one at all times?'

'No,' Louis said. 'Why?'

'Well, there might be a division or something,' Henry said. 'And you might have to dash down to take it, and if you've got to tick off Members you can't rely on there being a pencil left in the desk by the Clerk before you.'

'Though I admit,' John said, 'that since the House isn't sitting at the moment, there isn't likely to be a division. What are you doing?'

'There was nothing to do,' Louis said. 'Actually. We were trying to remember the titles of all Trollope's novels. Oh look, I do have a pen.'

John wandered over to the long table running the length of the office and moved a book before moving it back again.

'Nothing came up?'

'No,' Henry said, writing.

'Have you really nothing better to do?'

'Patently not,' Henry said. 'I presume we'll read yesterday's Vote tomorrow.'

'Yes,' John said. 'Might as well. I'm sorry about that. I meant to be back by noon, but the – the fog.'

'Why can't we do it now?' Louis said.

'It isn't noon,' Henry said. 'It's too late now.'

There is a class of human beings, called the Clerks of the House of Commons. They do not sound grand; they sound as if they spend their days copying things from one ledger to another. But they are grand. It is not a large class of human beings, when compared to other classes, such as women, or the inhabitants of Peking. There are sixty of them. This is few, yet there are more of them than the Clerks of the House of Lords, whom they regard as drunken wastrels, and who regard them with something not short of amusement. The Clerks are grand, and the grander they become, the less grand they sound; the lowest sort of person to work in the House is called an Executive Officer, which to those outside sounds rather smart; the highest sort of person who works in the House – so high that one can hardly think of him as working in the House, more as nobly devoting a part of his distinguished hours and minutes to sit in the chamber of the House – is merely termed the Clerk.

The Clerks of the House of Commons work in the House of Commons, and they advise elected members of Parliament, whom they call Members. Follow these capital letters. They have no respect for them; they laugh at them; they compile lists of the twenty most idiotic Members, and the twenty most debauched; they do not work for them. Members treat them as superior waiters – wine waiters, perhaps, in a *Punch* cartoon, a little nervous-making – and they treat Members to their faces with civility, and behind their backs as inferior undergraduates who have mistaken their ambitions. Some Clerks are cheerful, sometimes; and some are bibulous; and some, like Louis, are immensely fat; and some are novelists. But most of them are, in the end, manic depressives, and all of them are, in one way or another, experts.

Three of them were sitting in the Journal Office of the House of Commons. Their names were John, and Louis, and Henry. One of them was reading the newspaper, and the other two were writing the names of all the novels of Trollope they could remember when a Member came in, whose name was of no account.

'Good morning, sir,' John said.

'Hello,' the Member said. 'I was wondering what the length of a Parliament was.'

'Five years,' John said, leaving the office.

'Quite,' the Member said nervously. 'But is it five years from election to election, or five years from election to dissolution. In short, I mean, what is the latest conceivable moment for the Prime Minister to dissolve Parliament?'

When the Member's inquiry had been answered and he had gone, Henry said, 'You know, I used to step out with one of John's daughters. The elder, of course.'

'Really?' Louis said. Henry was too camp to envisage being romantically involved with anyone except himself.

'You know, some people really have nothing better to do than to badger us with pointless queries. Now. *Pallisers, Barset, Way We Live Now, Claverings, Orley Farm, Ayala's Angel, Knew He Was Right, Miss Mackenzie, Dr Wortle, Popenjoy, Kellys and O'Kelly's, Castle Richmond, Mr Scarborough's Family.* They are naughty, they slip one's mind.'

'I assume you can name the constituent novels of both series,' Louis said.

'No gentleman would doubt it,' Henry said. 'Twenty-six, I'm losing my touch. Actually, I'm going to John's for dinner tonight. To tell you a tiny secret, I'm rather dreading it.'

Louis gave his list. 'And *Why Frau Frohmann Raised Her Prices, and other stories.*'

'*Why Frau Frohman Raised Her Prices, and other stories?*' Henry said. 'I don't believe it.'

'I've just read it,' Louis said. 'It's rather fine. Nine short, if we're not counting the autobiography.'

'Did you get *The Three Clerks?*' John said, coming back. 'Has he gone?'

'Drove him away,' Henry said. 'How many states in the USA can you name?'

'Oh, don't be absurd,' John said. 'If you really have nothing to do, or any prospect of it, go for lunch, why don't you. I dare say you'll come up with the missing novels in the meantime.'

'Oh, all right,' Henry said. 'How was the meeting?'

'Fine,' John said briefly. 'They actually asked some reasonable questions.'

'Who were they?' said Louis.

'Some protégés of the Clerk's,' John said. 'Nothing interesting.'

They were sitting in a long corridor-like office high in the building. It was called the Journal Office. What their job was, no Member knew; what their purpose was, not even they quite understood. From day to day, they performed small rituals, and they recorded, and they checked what they had recorded, and at the end of the day, they went home and forgot about it. For centuries Clerks had been doing the same things, and for centuries they had sat and played idle games in the morning, and carried out their rituals and their routines. And at the end of the twentieth century they sat in a room like a corridor directly above the Chamber of the House, and performed their duties at noon, and waited for half past two to arrive, when they would listen to the speeches and the Questions on a loudspeaker wired to the chamber. Burbling on, the words, disappearing into air, set down briefly on paper and forgotten forever.

Out of the window, there was a view only of roofs, and of sky, which gave no hint of the famous gargoyled building.

This is what they did. Listen carefully. They kept the minutes of the House, which was called the Journal of the House. Everything needs its minutes to be kept. Everything needs to be reduced from what occurs to what it means. We are human, and we cannot write down what happened, not everything that happened. We can only write down the significance of the events, in the end; we can only write down, and record, the decisions that are come to. We cannot record the speech of men, and their hot blushes, and the flush of breath on skin. We can only record the roles of men, and how they act, and what happens in the end. In the end. There is always the same thing, in the end.

The House of Commons was no different, although measures had been taken to make it seem different. Here the speech of men was recorded. At this time, there was an attempt to write down the words of men, and it was called Hansard. The women of Hansard sat in the galleries, and wrote what was said. They did not think about the rubbish they set down; they had no time. But Hansard did not matter. Hansard was ephemeral. Hansard had the names of men who were quickly forgotten, and the words of men which would never be read, and, frankly, the words of men which had never been spoken.

What mattered was the Journal of the House; and this is what John, who was the Clerk of the Journals, and the Senior Vote Writer, and Henry, and Louis all attempted to write. They wrote down the decisions the House had come to; and what had occurred in the House. They were not Hansard. They were not concerned with ephemera. They did not write down what people said. They wrote down truth.

They were not concerned with individual men, or individual voices. They were not concerned with speech, or breath, or pain, or snot. What they were concerned with was truth. The Journal was the minutes of the House, and sometimes, if the House talked for many hours on a matter which for the moment was significant, all they could find was that the House discussed whether it should go home or not, and, in the end, it decided that, for the moment, it should not. It was a complex matter, understanding what the Journal had said, and a full-time job. And because of it, those who had learned to decipher its eighteenth-century code relished it, and prized it, and took pleasure in it. These were few; because there are few men who have understood that truth is secret; that truth resides in secrecy; and the fewer these men were, the truer this was.

Henry and Louis got up and left the office. John picked up the telephone and began to dial. Louis could see that he was dialling slowly enough for them to have left the office before he finished. They walked in a leisurely way to the faster of two adjacent lifts, and were in the Members' lobby before they spoke. No one was in the lobby except sixteen schoolchildren and three ex-sergeant majors in tailcoats and white bow ties.

'What do you think of it so far?' Henry said.

'What do I think?' Louis said. 'It's only been six months.'

'Three of which the House wasn't sitting anyway,' Henry said. 'I can see that three months' holiday before you'd started work would make a job seem all right.'

'Why?' said Louis. 'Isn't it?'

'Oh yes,' Henry said. 'We all love our job.'

'No,' Louis said. 'I don't really understand anything, though.'

'Oh, no one does. What don't you understand?'

'Well, anything, really. Like what statutory instruments are. That sort of thing.'

'Well, you did very well with the Member this morning. If you don't understand anything, you can always ask. We understand everything, of course, as you know, and if we don't, we make it up. I can explain from the resources of my own invention, and John's quite well informed for such an idle man.'

They walked on a bit. Members were stating their forceful convictions into telephones along the hot carpeted corridors.

'I don't know what he was doing this morning,' Henry said. 'He'd been in and gone by the time I arrived, and I know for a fact he didn't talk to anyone, protégés of the Clerk or otherwise.'

'When he telephoned,' Louis said, 'it sounded rather as if he were in a pub.'

'Well, I dare say he was,' Henry said. 'The Clerk of the Journals never has much to do, of course. Look. There's going to be trouble.'

'About John going to the pub?'

'No, of course not.'

'What sort of trouble?'

'Over Europe.'

'Over Europe?'

'Yes. The Government.'

'What do you mean, trouble? I thought there was already a kind of scrap going on.'

'Yes, exactly. Quite. Quite,' said Henry, as he pushed open the double doors into the Members' Tea Room. A Member was standing just inside the room, talking quietly to a journalist.

'Should he be here?' Louis said.

'What, Harvey? No, of course not. But it's not exactly for us to apprehend a gentleman, even if he is a Stranger, you know.'

'Well, yes,' said Louis. 'What sort of trouble, anyway?'

'Let's eat,' said Henry. 'If the Clerk's there, for Christ's sake don't mention the protégés.'

'He can't have been in a pub since half past ten.'

'It's no business of mine,' said Henry. 'And in any case, I didn't get in until eleven so I'm not going to criticize. There's no fucking meat pie left. Is there any pie?'

A middle-aged woman of eccentric appearance came round the counter to hug Henry.

'Hello gorgeous boy,' she said. 'Are you my boyfriend, then, gorgeous?'

'I just wanted some meat pie, Jean,' said Henry plaintively.

'You're lovely, you are,' the woman said, irrelevantly. 'You wouldn't have wanted it, anyway.'

*   *   *

'Father rang,' Jane said. 'He's bringing someone home for dinner.'

Francesca nodded. They were sitting in their father's drawing room. It was two o'clock. They were in different parts of the long room. At some point, a central wall had been demolished, turning a sitting room and a dining room into one ballroom-like space. It was possible to stand outside the front window and wave at someone forty feet away on the other side of the house, through the two windows. The room was dark with the outside fog.

In a contrived space, let into the wall, a light had been turned on for Francesca to see what she was writing. She wrote quickly, on a computer screen which had been turned down to black, so that, in fact, it was impossible to see what she was writing. She could not correct her mistakes, or see that she was making mistakes. She wrote poetry about death; the death of her mother, and suicides, and misery, and black lakes like mirrors beneath the mourning sky; and sometimes, when everything else failed her, she wrote readily about the black face of her computer screen. Jane was lying on a sofa, at the far end of the room, smoking.

These were characteristic attitudes with them. Francesca, attempting to type, could see Jane in the reflection of the computer screen where she was writing. She was sitting stiffly upright, and now and then she looked around and yawned in a quick, wide way, like an unfanged animal. Francesca was satisfied, and yet not; from time to time, Jane stretched up and looked at the clock. It was still only two.

'How can you see to write?' Jane said, when Francesca failed to respond to her comment about the dinner.

'I just can,' said Francesca. 'I like to write like this, anyway,' she went on, as if answering Jane's question.

'Oh yes?' Jane said.

'I like to write,' she said, going on, 'when the electric green of the computer has been turned down to black, and nothing can be seen of the traces of writing. I don't need to see; I can remember.'

'Don't you speak to me like that,' said Jane. 'I'm not in your fucking poem.'

Francesca went on typing for a moment with the appearance of calmness. 'I'm reading a very interesting book,' she said. '*Lolita*.'

'Are you writing about mother?' Jane said.

'No,' Francesca said after a time. 'The odd thing is, I think it's a very moral book.'

'You often say that,' Jane said. 'I haven't read it.'

'If you read a bit more and smoked a bit less, you might be more interesting as a person.'

'I doubt I would,' Jane said.

'Well, there are some people past redemption,' Francesca said. Jane did not respond. Outside, in the fog, it could be seen that the garden was past its best. Its best had never been up to the plum-perfection of the gardens which surrounded, but now the lawn looked as if tennis had been played on it to an international standard for some months. The earth showed brown through the brown and yellow grass. John had obeyed an order, all summer, not to water the grass, and, unlike his neighbours, had not illicitly watered the grass at midnight when the fuzz, as Jane put it, were a-bed. It was October and they waited for rain. The summer's dust for earth should be replaced by something fruitful and wet; but this had not happened. Instead, there was an inadequate unlovely sliminess covering everything. There was fog, but there was no rain. This was unnatural.

'Have you really not read *Lolita*?' Francesca said.

'Yes,' Jane said. 'Of course I have. You know, if mother was here, we wouldn't be allowed to lie here like this.'

'No,' Francesca said. 'Of course, I'm not lying, I'm working.'

'No you're not,' Jane said. 'You know perfectly well, mother would have sent you out for a walk by now, or to buy something from the butcher.'

'Well, I will go for a walk soon.'

'Frances,' Jane said.

'Yes?'

'Do you think granny's all right?'

'That's an awful cold she's got.'

'No, that's not what I meant; I meant about mother.'

Francesca carried on writing, for a moment.

'It must be very hard for her,' she said.

'I suppose so. Do you think it's just going to be like this from now on?'

'No,' Francesca said. 'I don't, actually.' She turned round from her screen and looked at Jane.

'I can't think anything's going to change,' Jane said. 'I can't think what.'

'All sorts of things,' Francesca said, faltering. 'Everything could change. Are you cooking?'

'No, I'm not. It's his turn.'

'No it's not. It's your turn.'

'Well, I'm going out anyway,' Jane said. 'For dinner.'

'You're so selfish,' Francesca said, and turned back to her screen. Jane lit another cigarette.

'I know you are,' she said idly. 'But what am I?'

'Who's coming, anyway?' Francesca said.

'I don't know.'

Jane got up and went into the kitchen. She could be heard rifling through the freezer for bread, and then putting some in the toaster. She made a cup of tea, and came back into the sitting room with it, and two pieces of toast with yeast extract on them. This was mostly what Jane ate. She turned on the television, and then turned it off again.

'It could be Henry,' Jane said, in the end.

'Hen-ry?' Francesca yodelled, in quite the same way she always had when she was seventeen and Jane was twenty. Jane finished her toast, and got up and went upstairs to have a bath. When she came back, scrubbed and clean, she was wearing a different, but a similar black dress, and lipstick; her hair was combed.

'Are you all right?' Francesca said.

'Yes,' Jane said. 'Of course. I sometimes ask myself whether you are.'

'No, seriously,' Francesca said. 'How are you really?'

'Perfectly all right,' Jane said.

'Do you phone him?'

'You know I don't.'

'I know you do,' Francesca said. 'Every six weeks.'

Approximately right, Jane thought. When she was eighteen she had gone away to university. Francesca did not manage to, subsequently. Most people predicted that Jane would entirely change under the influence of the ancient stones and grassy swards and powerful intellects which would now surround her. The stones weren't that ancient.

She went away with a suitcase of translations of Dostoevsky's novels; she never quite got round to reading them in the original, which was what she was supposed to be doing. She went away as the baddest girl in the school, and that was how she came back. She used to wear school uniform, when she was young; but so approximately that it looked like a pornographer's prop rather than a serious way of dressing. She shuffled from room to room wearing an old fur coat and a miniskirt and black stockings. Her mother was still alive, and appalled. And when she came back from the university at Christmas, she was quite the same; except that before she arrived she announced she would have a boyfriend with her.

They all expected the worst; drunkenness, earrings, filth. They expected to have to ask him to leave after two days. But, bitchy, likeable and clean, the boyfriend stayed for three weeks, to her father's surprise; and, admittedly, to her mother's irritation. Henry being there gave Jane something to be interested in, and they closeted themselves away with each other and giggled. He absented himself tactfully from time to time, spending days away, and never required entertaining. He cooked, once, a dinner, and made no fuss about it and cleared up afterwards. He talked from time to time even to Francesca, and even once offered to read her poetry and even showed interest in the mother's doings, and once helped her stick photographs of the family holiday in books. Before the end of the three weeks, John was calling him Henry without a momentary collection of memory first, and Henry was calling him John. All in all, they felt, Jane had done pretty well.

This went on for almost four years. Every vacation Henry would come and stay with them. Jane went twice to his family; it was less of a success, and the second visit was in the nature of a second chance. He could be taken into her family; for her, she found she could get as far as his nice daft sister Nancy, who quickly became an old mate, but no further. It made no difference, since they laughed about it. He returned to them. His limp, friendly, amusing presence stopped being something they changed to accommodate, and when he arrived, they no longer gave the impression of lining up at the front door to shake his hand.

'Busy?' Henry said once to John.

'Yes,' John said. 'This enormous bill.'

'Why are you busy with it?'

'Oh,' John said. 'There's a rather complicated procedural wrangle going on about it.'

'Can you explain to me?'

'Well, it's all to do with this thing called hybridity.'

Jane, sitting in the kitchen, overheard some of this. Henry had gone, quite quickly, from being politely interested in the House of Commons and what went on there to being really interested in what John had to say. Increasingly, when she went into the drawing room, she would find a conversation about moving the previous Question in progress; or John speculating in an amused way about filibustering, and the doings of the Secretary of State, and the Honourable Member, and more. Helena and Jane and Francesca had always been rather bored by such conversations; Jane now liked Henry's enjoyment of them, even if it were only seeming enjoyment. As long as she knew where he was, she had no objection to not talking to him. They were relaxed and they did not need reassurance. Often, while these conversations were going on at the far end of the drawing room, she would pull two sofas together into a safe walled bed, lie down and let her cigarette burn itself out, dropping ash on her supine sleeping body. She was so safe. She would wake to find a neat grey caterpillar on her

chest and faint affectionate shrieks about private Members'
bills at the other end of the room.

'Jane,' John said once.

'Um hum.'

'What are you planning to do?'

'Go out this evening I think.'

'No, I meant next year, or the year after. Are you going
to get a job?'

'I don't think so,' she said. She hadn't thought. 'I suppose
I ought to think about it.'

'I would.'

'But no one I know's thought about it,' she said. 'I know
Henry hasn't.'

'Um hum,' John said, and moved on. A little shadow
passed over her; the shadow of a life where Henry was
taken away from her for twelve hours a day; the shadow of
busyness. She wondered what Henry had been doing, and
what planning, and what she knew about his life to come.

They finished university at the same time, and he went
straight to work for the House of Commons. John was
pleased, he said, but denied any kind of responsibility for
it; he hadn't any idea Henry was applying, and would have
been quite unable to help if he had known it. His daughters
didn't believe him, but they, too, were pleased, or gave the
appearance of pleasure.

'Are you pleased?' Nancy said.

'Yes,' Jane said.

They were sitting on the sofa. Nancy was to start university the next month; the same college as Jane.

'Are you going to get a job?' Nancy said, eventually.

'I don't think so,' Jane said. 'Haven't really the time.'

'How will you live?'

'Oh, I'll live all right,' Jane said. 'Writing something now.'

Nancy lit Jane's cigarette for her.

'A letter,' Jane said. 'No, I'm joking. I'm thinking about maybe trying to write a screenplay or something, maybe going to film school.'

The possibilities before Jane seemed endlessly open, but they filled Nancy with sadness, when she looked at her, smoking, and writing, if she was writing at all, in her head, and not setting it down.

Things got bad.

Henry stopped coming round. Once Francesca went to have lunch with her father at the House of Commons, and she met him in the corridor. In her way, she asked him why. He fluttered a little; he hadn't stopped coming round; then he had, but only because things had changed between her father and him. He saw him all the time now. He used to be a friend, but now there was rank, and a job, between them. He didn't want to be a nuisance, he didn't want to create bad feeling, he didn't want to pester John at home. He saw Jane whenever he wanted, really, whenever she wanted. Anger in him was like petulance in others.

It was untrue, what he said. They found out only slowly, and not through Jane. Even Nancy didn't know immediately. By July, Jane and Henry had seen each other only twice in the year. Henry did well, and after a year or two, he did start coming round a little, again; but as a friend of John's, and sometimes Jane didn't even trouble to be there when he arrived. They stood apart at parties, and it was good of him to come to Helena's funeral, for reasons that did not touch on Jane, and he was polite only, and it looked natural. That was that.

'Do you know,' Francesca said. 'I think we're rather like the Bennet sisters. In a way.'

'What Bennet sisters?' Jane said.

'In *Pride and Prejudice*,' Francesca said.

'Oh, them,' Jane said. 'I didn't know what you were talking about. I'm going to have a bath.'

'You've just had one.'

'So I have,' said Jane. She lay back on the sofa.

'No serious rebellions so far, though,' said Louis. 'Isn't that right?'

'You wait,' Henry said. 'So far it's only loonies, but in six months the whole thing will have gone thermo-nuclear. The loonies can't do anything on their own with a majority like this one, of course.'

'Oh yes they can,' said another Clerk. 'If there are enough, they can do anything.'

'Like introducing insane unworkable taxes and calling themselves a government, I suppose,' Henry said.

'Yes, quite,' the other Clerk said. 'I don't think we've met, have we?'

They told each other their names. They were sitting at the far end of the Members' Tea Room. It was a long thin room, divided into three; running parallel, on the other side of a court, to a division lobby. Two Members could be seen through the glass having the semblance of an animated conversation.

In the part of the Tea Room nearest the door, members of the Opposition sat and watched everyone come in. In the middle section, members of the Government party sat and ignored everyone else, talking indiscreetly about their superiors and ministers, knowing that they were not overheard. In the farthest point, under the worst and biggest pictures, the Clerks sat, and they listened.

It was here that they were sitting, half-listening to a conversation between two Members no one outside the House and the Conservative party had ever heard of.

Louis often caught himself smiling at surprising moments. Walking down the street, he would see people looking at him with more than the usual interest at his size or appearance. He would curb his grin, and walk on, another man, a fat man, in a street of men. A man had asked him once, in a bar, late at night, what he had to fucking smile about. Louis hadn't answered at the time. He had been too concerned with the idea that he was about to be hit very hard. But since then, he had from time to time felt like saying to strangers, 'Ask me why I'm smiling.' He had an answer now, and the answer was, 'Because I'm getting away with it.'

Louis had a secret, and though in general he was bad at keeping secrets, he was very good at keeping this one. The secret was, 'I don't deserve it.' There was a second secret, which was part of the first. This was, 'They've made a mistake.' All his life, Louis had succeeded; he had never once failed. But when the stiff scholarship letter, or the piano exam mark, or the proof of an article arrived in the post, Louis always thought the same thing. He thought precisely the same thing, before he suppressed it, when, after his old father died and the valuation of his father's estate came through the post, and he held the stiff headed paper and read the noughts (and how could he be so rich? Nothing but a big black house, looking at nothing in Lincolnshire, and twenty paintings, and, made liquid, sent to the broker and the bank) and re-read them, and counted. He thought the same thing. He thought, 'There's been a mistake; this is meant for someone else of the same name.'

But following this always came the pleasurable thought, the nice, the third secret. It was the only secret that in the end, really mattered. 'I'm going to get away with it. I am.' This was the secret he wanted to tell to strangers. He had never had a secret without wanting to share it; in later years, when asked if he could keep a secret, he would always, and somewhat brutally, say no. It saved time, and friendships.

Sometimes he would, in an unguarded moment, look up and find someone looking strangely at him. He knew that it was a person who had, for some reason, seen through him immediately. He always wanted to stop, and say to the Member, or to the girl on the tube, or to a guard in a museum, 'Yes. You're right.' Once it was a boy Louis had picked up in a gay bar. He had woken to find the boy propped up on one elbow, regarding him with a steady gaze, all lust and fondness drained. These shared perceptions, these silent moments with perfect strangers gave Louis the feeling of a quiet fraternity, a body of people who all saw through Louis. And the chief of the quiet fraternity, the only member who knew all the others and gave illusions no house-room was Louis himself. They never spoke about it, Louis and these strangers, these perfect strangers. Even the boy in his bed seemed to find sex an easier intimacy than talking about his perception of Louis's failure. But, like a beggar sniffing out a momentary gap of compassion in the sideways glance of a passer-by, they had seen Louis's failure, and he rather liked them for it.

They sat in the Members' Tea Room and listened to a conversation between two supporters of the Government.

One, who was hoping soon to be made a Minister for reasons not clear to his wife, his children, his friends, or his enemies, was saying over and over again, 'I don't give a damn. I don't give a damn,' impressing those around him with his incisive and accurate judgement.

'The honourable Member for Broom Hill,' said Henry with an air of irony.

'Really,' said Louis. 'Who is he?'

'Health Secretary's PPS,' the third Clerk said. 'Used to be on a committee of mine, made a perfect nuisance of himself trying to get involved with drafting committee reports.'

'Well, he's got a majority of twenty-seven, if that's any consolation,' Henry said.

'Henry,' the third Clerk said, 'how do you get your shirts so very well ironed?'

'Oh, I send them to the dry cleaners, of course,' said Henry, who was indeed very nattily turned out.

'I could never do that,' said the third Clerk, a man pale as paper, with glasses thick as a brick and shoulders too narrow, really, for use. His clothes were unironed, stained and holed. It wasn't clear whether he was debarred by nature or practice from sending his clothes to the dry cleaners.

'I could never do anything else,' Henry said. 'It saves an awful lot of time and effort, and it's important to dress well.'

'Do you think so?' Louis said. 'Here, you mean?'

'No, not here,' Henry said. 'It makes no difference how one dresses here, as far as one can judge from the Committee Office. No, I meant in life, clothes matter so much.'

'But they wear out, so quickly,' the third Clerk said for something to say.

'So does everything, really,' Henry said. 'Here comes the Clerk.'

The Clerk of the House approached wearily with a plastic tray and a Kit-Kat.

'Gavin,' Henry said to the Clerk with a slight air of bravado.

'Henry,' the Clerk of the House said, nodding to the other two. His name was Gavin; it was odd to use it.

He put his tray down and went to fetch *The Sun* from the magazine rack, and began to turn the pages. He paid no attention to the nude girl, but paused at the picture of a smiling blonde girl, an actress in a soap opera, wearing a bikini. Upside down, her grin seemed to Louis like rictus.

'I understand there's going to be a fight this afternoon.'

'Yes,' said the Clerk. 'A small one, I think.'

'You think there's going to be a big one?' said Henry.

'At some point,' the Clerk said.

'Have you come across the Member for Clapham?' Henry said to Louis.

'No,' Louis said. 'I don't think so.'

'Is it him?' the Clerk said. 'One of our more unhinged Members, shall we say.'

'Well,' Henry said. 'If you've nothing better to do this afternoon, I recommend wandering down to the Chamber around five o'clock. There might be an amusing row. Quite harmless, I think.'

The Clerk looked amused, but whether it was at the idea of the scrap or the facsimile of the plain girl on wet cheap paper in front of him, nobody could tell.

*　　*　　*

When John's wife died, then, he went through a period of decently resigned public grief, shaking his head at everyone around him who expressed sympathy or even treated him with more than usual care. His memory of the funeral was not of the vegetables, of the Secretary of State, so good to come, or of anything anyone said. He remembered his daughters and his wife's mother. Her bewildered mother, sitting on the edge of the seat in the too-big car in her uncompromising black and saying nothing. Just sniffling a little, whether through grief or – John wondered, retro-spectively – the onset of the grim cold she was now suffering from. It was as if she were waiting in a shop for someone sufficiently senior – and *sufficiently* was, a little too superbly, one of her favourite words – to deal with her complaint. John held her hand from time to time, but thought it could hardly seem a sincere enough gesture. Insincerity, too, however, could be appropriate.

No one had thought much about the service; nobody had thought that Helena would die, least of all Helena herself.

'I'm really quite sick and tired of lying here with nothing to do, and no one to talk to except the nurses,' she had said.

'They seem all right,' Jane said vaguely.

'Oh, terribly kind,' Helena said. 'Just nothing to talk about. Pass my reading glasses, would you, dear?'

John passed them over.

'Do you want some more fruit or anything?' he said, hopelessly.

'Oh, no,' she said. 'I never get to eat it anyway, people are always wandering in and taking grapes.' She smoothed the folded-back crisp white sheet with an air of dissatisfaction; what with was hard to say, and hard to ask. 'I can't wait to get home; I don't feel ill at all, just tired and bored.'

'Look, Helena,' John said. 'I'd better go. I ought to get some food before the supermarket shuts. And the House is coming back tomorrow for two days.'

'All right,' Helena said. 'Something beastly boring, I dare say. I'll see you tomorrow, I expect. You know what you could get me, another book. This one's too dull to get through.'

'Of course,' John said. 'Francesca said she'll come tomorrow.'

'Oh, good,' Helena said. And they went.

The dying finish their books; they have no time for luxury. The next day the House was recalled; there was a war, or something. It was John's day at the Table. He was sitting at the Table of the House, making notes when, quite abruptly, the Clerk of the House appeared at his side. He was sitting in the middle chair of three and the Clerk sat down.

'I'm going to take over,' the Clerk said. 'There's been a message for you to call your daughter immediately. I think you should.'

John got up and left, taking the book with him and bowing to the Speaker who, bored, nodded agreeably back.

It was only when he got to the hospital and was sitting with the professional counsellor and his two daughters in the tasteful, neutral surroundings of the private room on the ward, that he realized he had not changed out of his tailcoat and white bow tie; nor could anyone comment on the clothes the bereaved and unstable might choose to wear.

The planning of the service fell largely to people paid to do it. They asked for Helena's favourite hymn; no one could think of one. A favourite poem, perhaps? But all anyone could think of was Helena's querulous complaining and her failed cooking. The novels she read were by authors no one had heard of, and she never read the same book twice. It was impossible to discern anything resembling a favourite author, or someone who could be read out loud at a funeral service in the sad crumpled piles of fat mattressy books.

When he thought of her books, he noted with almost no shock that he would no longer be embarrassed by her.

They ended with the professional choices of the professional undertaker, the grand official sorrow of the priest from a church no one ever went to. He accepted solicitude and regret gracefully. When the Secretary of State came, John, too, was flattered, and he could not suppress the thought that Helena would have been delighted at this man turning up at her funeral, who for seven years had never managed to get to one of her parties. In a way it was enjoyable, and it wasn't difficult. He knew what to do, and he coped with the little difficulties in his mind well. He coped with his not saying goodbye to her; he coped with his visiting a rent-boy three days before she died. He was rational, and he saw what did not matter. He knew there were men outside the house he knew and liked, who liked him, who never knew he had a wife and would not have cared if she was alive or dead. That amused him, and again he waited for a shock that wouldn't come.

When the officials and the colleagues and the female relations had gone, he sat and watched his daughters, one drunk, one flushed with social success, begin the task of clearing up. No one expected him to help. He had been marvellous. The whole thing had been a great success; neither the insincerely overflowing church nor the pathetically empty chapel with a tape recording of

'The Lord Is My Shepherd'. Nobody had cried, and in the end the people who were there were the people she would have wanted to be there. Then, in his head, he heard like an explosion her voice. 'All London was there,' she was saying. It was her silly silly expression. It was an expression he would never have used himself, or used in his head. Hadn't he once or twice told her how silly the expression was, how silly and meaningless? But here it was, in his head, and there she was, saying it.

What was this feeling, not in his head, but in his stomach, this strange empty misery like physical suffering? Where were the pills to cure it in minutes? Was this grief? Like the handmaidens of the dead, the people around him who had treated him with their best solicitude had not been assuaging his grief, but preparing him for it. He had played along, and faked his grief for the purposes of decency, and now here it was; now, with no warning, she was saying, 'All London was there,' to him, and in him, and the grief of all London was in him, like a shot.

The next day he spent a morning in his study studying the adverts at the back of a magazine until he found an advert for a muscular Mediterranean man in his early twenties. He telephoned, and afterwards visited Giacomo for the first time.

Louis, too, was homosexual. That evening, from work, he went directly to a bar where homosexuals went. The first time he had been into a gay bar from work, he worried that he was wearing a suit. Then he saw that there were other men in the bar who were wearing suits, and who had come from work. He realized that in every bar he had ever been in, there had been men in suits, from their places of work. It was simply that he had never noticed them. They had been swallowed by their offices, and their lives mattered less than their jobs, and the cloth on them. He no longer worried much about it.

The bar had a tiny door, so that the casual passer-by could not see the customers inside. There was something old-fashioned about this, and the bar was generally agreed, even by its patrons, to be absolutely awful because of it. Everyone who went there agreed that normally he would not be seen dead there. The gin was derided, and the staff of the bar were derided for their lack of glamour and rudeness, and the name of the bar, which was 'Brief Encounter' was derided 'One might as well call a bar "Quick Shag",' people generally said to each other.

It was crowded, but the loud music covered the quiet of the customers, most of whom were on their own. When each track came to an end, there was a strange airless hush. From the ceiling hung a large mirrored ball, the point of which was not clear even to the owners of the bar. One wall was lined with mirrors, but most of the customers in the bar were not the sort of tarts to stand and admire themselves, and they stood with their backs to it, and tried to engage eye contact with each other.

Louis bought a drink for himself and wondered how he was going to start a conversation. He knew that there were formal opening moves, such as offering to buy a drink, asking another man's name, mentioning the awfulness of the bar, or more less contrived jokes. He used none of these, and was on the whole one of those men who waited to be talked to. Fat but appealing, he did not often have to wait long.

'Hello,' said a boy. 'Do you mind if I talk to you?'

'No,' Louis said.

'Only my friend's gone, and I don't want to go just yet, and I don't like standing and talking. I mean not talking.'

'No,' Louis said.

'I'm not the strong silent type, see.'

'No,' Louis said. 'What on earth are you drinking?'

The boy had a bottle of pale yellow beer, with a quarter of lime pushed down and floating in the inch at the bottom. This was in the year 1990, and no one had ever seen such a thing before.

'It's called Sol. It's Mexican. I'm just going to get another one,' the boy said. He did not come back.

Louis bought another drink. He read a free newspaper for homosexuals and wondered who read it. Time passed.

'Do you come from London?' a boy said. 'Hello.'

'Yes, I do,' Louis said. 'Where do you come from?'

'Brazil,' the boy said, and laughed loudly for no reason. Then he made a strange noise.

'What did you say?' Louis said.

'Belo Horizonte,' the boy said. 'I come from Belo Horizonte.'

'What is that?' Louis said.

'It's a city,' the boy said. 'In Brazil. It means beautiful horizon.'

'What does it mean?' Louis said.

'Beautiful,' the boy shouted into his ear. 'Horizon.'

'Is it near Rio?' Louis said.

'Near Rio?' the boy said, laughing strongly. 'No, no, not very near.'

'I'd like to fuck you,' Louis said.

'Oooh,' the boy said. 'Oooh.' Then he pinched Louis's

face fiercely, and, still grinning from his laugh, went to the bar. He came back with one beer, which he gave to Louis, and, laughing, went out of the bar.

'Hello,' another man said after half an hour or so. 'How elegant you look.'

'Thank you,' Louis said. The man was a little older; perhaps thirty-five; in a jacket and a checked shirt, as if planning to go to the country, or if he had just come from there. He was blond and formerly good-looking.

'Do you work near here?' the man said.

'I work in the House of Commons.'

'How fascinating,' the man said. 'What do you do there?'

'Nothing much,' Louis said, unable to give a coherent idea of his job. In later years, when asked this question, he would answer that he was a man in a wig. This satisfied most of his questioners.

'How fascinating, though,' the man said. 'You must see all sorts of famous people.'

'Yes,' Louis said.

'Can I buy you a drink?'

'Thank you,' Louis said.

When the man handed him the beer, Louis saw that the man was wearing a wedding ring.

'Do you often come here?' Louis said.

'To London?' the man said. 'Or this pub?'

Louis had not thought of it as a pub, but as a bar. 'This pub,' he said, slightly stumbling over it.

'When I'm in London,' he said. 'It's really rather awful, isn't it?'

'I like it,' Louis said, although he did not.

'I don't find it *sympathique*,' the man said, and, trying to simper, succeeded only in appearing to wince. His manner was put on in the train and would be left at Charing Cross, Louis thought.

'Thank you for the beer,' Louis said.

'Oh, I shall go now, as well,' the man said.

Later on they went to bed together. The man gave him a false name and telephone number afterwards. Louis gave him his real name and a false telephone number, since he did not like him one bit, had fucked him out of politeness and did not want to be troubled by part-time heterosexuals. The man left in time for Louis to have dinner on his own before going to bed.

Louis's childhood was a matter of great gloomy houses. At home, he walked down the stairs quietly, so as not to disturb his father, who, elderly, slept in the afternoons and often in the mornings. At school, he clattered down the stairs with the other boys, and egged other boys on to shout rude words outside the headmaster's window. University was exactly the same, and the year off spent in London working in an art gallery shop, and in a dull little town in the Italian Marches teaching English to nine-year-olds. He did not remember his mother.

Louis came to work in the House of Commons in this manner. He saw an advert in a newspaper which advised the readers of the newspaper that, if they wished to become civil servants, they should write to the following address. Louis did not wish to become a civil servant, and could imagine few less desirable fates, but he knew that this was the way in which one became a House of Commons Clerk. His father had died by then; there was no need for him to work. But he feared solitude, and aimlessness. All his life he had known what he would do for the next five years, and all his life he had been organized by others.

In due course a form arrived, asking Louis many impertinent questions about his past life, his many qualifications and his few interests in life, and asking for the names of three respectable people who knew him well. Louis told the truth about his qualifications and lied about his interests (weight-lifting, solo sculls, poetry reading) and primed his tutor and the two friends who had agreed to tell lies on his behalf what lies precisely they should tell.

In due course an invitation arrived for Louis to go and take an examination. So in a large dusty hall in Wimbledon he sat with thirty other people. There was an aged invigilator who kept leaving the room to urinate and, on returning, said to no one in particular, 'Everyone all right then?' The rest of the candidates passed notes to each other. Louis did not, nor, during the coffee breaks, did he speak to the other candidates. The other candidates gathered round and agreed with each other that it was terrible, and that they didn't stand a chance. Louis did not find it hard; he went on his own to a sandwich shop, and read the newspaper; he came back and found the patterns in the dominos and identified the pieces of information required to come to a designated conclusion. A chance was what he stood.

Later a letter arrived informing him that he had been successful in the intelligence test, and inviting him to take an examination and interviews lasting two days in London. He bought a suit and went. There he found forty people, most of whom were patently unfitted for any kind of purpose. He took more intelligence tests; he engaged in group discussions on burning issues of the day, in which, observing the habit of others to agree out of nervousness, he disagreed with everyone on everything. He took care, in all the discussions, to begin half his sentences with the words 'on the one hand' and the other half with the words 'on the other hand'. He noted that the other candidates all began their sentences with the word 'Erm'. He wrote essays on fictitious problems of man-management and sewage control. He was interviewed, and took care to disagree tactfully with one of the interviewers, and to inform another interviewer that the question she asked him was none of her business.

On the whole he considered he had done rather well.

In due course, he went to the House of Commons to meet the Clerk and others and to have the work explained to him. He understood quite well that this was to ensure that he was not drunk, female or spoke with a Birmingham accent, and he behaved himself. In due course he was interviewed again, by ten people, and was asked questions of a staggeringly foolish nature. 'If you were able to introduce a private Member's bill,' one said, 'what would it be?'

Louis found it hard to answer, and sat for a long time before answering. He did not wish to change the world in which he would shortly find himself.

Two days later he had a letter from the Clerk informing him that he had been successful, and wishing him a long and happy career in the service of the House, and suggesting that he might wish to drop in to meet the chaps, perhaps on the fifteenth of July. He did so, and met several of the chaps.

'I'm pleased to say,' one of them said, 'that we've managed to keep the women out for at least five years now.'

Louis smiled with all the others.

'We won't be here a frightful amount once the House rises,' the same man said. 'Drop in from time to time, if you like, but otherwise I would just spend the summer keeping up with the cricket. I certainly shall.'

Louis did not feel that he could ask what 'from time to time' meant, and on the first of August turned up in his suit to the office which he had been told would be his. It took him some time to find his way up. He sat there for a while, in the empty office in the empty building for two hours, reading a novel; the telephone rang once, but it was a wrong number. All that time he did not see anyone else, and after two hours he went home with some randomly chosen books with parliamentary connections, including some novels by Trollope on what he later discovered was Henry's desk. Three weeks later he turned up again, and sat for a whole day, but he did not see anyone, nor did the telephone ring. On the first of September he received his pay cheque. On the twenty-eighth of September he was sitting at home when the telephone rang. It was the man who had been pleased that the women had been kept out for at least five years.

'Having a good summer?' he said, and then, without waiting for an answer, went on. 'Frightfully sorry to disturb you at home. I simply wanted to make sure you knew the House was returning on the sixteenth of October. There might be a need to come in the day before, I'm afraid. I understand the Clerk of the Journals is planning to be in then, actually.'

Louis reassured him that he had not been disturbed, and that he would not mind going to work as much as was necessary. He'd spent two and a half months sitting on his balcony reading novels and drinking in afternoons in gay bars.

This, it was later explained to Louis, was a typically long

and happy summer in the service of the House. He never discovered, in fact, if the two friends he had commissioned to lie on his behalf had done so.

'Hello, Henry,' Francesca said, opening the door, already brilliantly smiling. 'How nice to see you.'

'Oh, hello,' Henry said. He knew he was not smiling brilliantly back; he knew that a slight panic was on his face. However, Jane was nowhere to be seen.

'I knew someone was coming for dinner,' Francesca said. 'But no one said it was you. How nice. Sit down. Can I take your coat? What would you like to drink?'

'Oh,' Henry said. Things were disposed of for him. 'Nancy sends her love.'

'Good,' Francesca said. 'Tell her the same. We don't really see enough of her. Nor of you, come to that.'

'No,' Henry said, looking round as if for an emergency exit.

'Father's upstairs,' Francesca said. 'He'll come down soon. Now, about that drink.'

'Yes,' Henry said.

'Wotcher Henry,' Jane said. She was hanging from the door frame and looking relatively clean. Her hair stood up and out in clumps. She had changed her clothes again. Her flowery dress – an unpermissioned borrowing from Francesca, but oddly un-Francesca-like on Jane – and respectable cardigan consorted oddly with the way her thin ankles had been put into heavy-soled black boots.

'Hello,' Henry said.

Jane went to the table and poured herself a glass of sherry

before, as an afterthought, pouring one for Henry, and then, as another afterthought, not pouring one for Francesca. Conversation flowed stiffly, like papier mâché.

'Henry,' Francesca said when John was down, and they had begun to eat. 'Do you think we're like the Bennet sisters?'

He strangely knew what she was talking about.

'Not all of them, I hope, dear,' he said.

'Which ones, then?' Jane said.

'Well,' he said. 'I think you're Elizabeth, and Jane is Jane, but there are only two of you, of course.'

'I'd rather be Lydia, to be honest,' Jane said. 'I'd love to be a deplorable slag in an eighteenth-century novel.'

'Nineteenth-century,' Francesca said.

'I know,' Jane said. 'I don't mind Jane Austen. It's better than all that Emily Brontë. Francesca when she was fifteen, you know, used to go out on Clapham Common in the rain and run about shouting for Heathcliff. Went on for months.'

'I don't see why it was so funny to go for a walk on Clapham Common.'

Jane was choking on a bit of flaky pastry Francesca had made for the pie with excessive care, or possibly laughter. '*It's the way you do it*,' she said eventually. 'If we were all in *Lolita*, who would we be?'

'Jane,' John said. 'I do wish you'd behave yourself. You're not thirteen years old.'

'I can do it for myself, anyway,' she said, lighting a cigarette before carrying on eating. Henry refused to look at her, or at Francesca.

'Would you like some coffee?' Francesca said after a time.

'No,' John said. 'I ought to go and do some work. I've got to draft a note for the Speaker.'

'Why do you never say write?' Jane said.

'What do you mean?' John said.

'You always say draft, when you're writing something.'

'Well, it's not my responsibility in the end,' John said. 'I do have to go, actually.'

Jane stayed at the table and picked at fruit in a desultory and unhungry way.

'So,' Henry said to Francesca, on a sofa.

'So,' Francesca said. 'I must apologize for the food this evening.'

'No, no,' he said. 'Honestly, it was lovely.' He had hardly noticed it.

'No, you needn't be polite,' Francesca said. 'It really wasn't.'

'Please, don't,' Henry said. 'Dinner was delicious, I thought. You don't need to apologize for it.'

'I'm not apologizing,' Francesca said, with faint outrage. 'I'm complaining. It was terrible.'

'Well, I'm sorry yours was bad, then.'

'It all came out of the same pot. It can't have been just mine.'

'Well, all right, I'm sorry if it was all bad, then,' Henry said with an air of finality.

'Did you hear that?' Francesca shouted to Jane. 'Henry is complaining about the food.'

'No, no, honestly,' Henry said. 'That's just too bad.'

Jane didn't bother to raise her head, but Henry was just smiling as if he were being teased.

'How old are you, Henry?' Francesca said.

'Thirty,' he said immediately.

'How clever of you to be able to remember,' Francesca said. 'Most people over a certain age can't remember at all how old they are.'

'What age is that, precisely?' Jane said.

'That depends,' said Francesca, not seeming to direct her voice or her gaze away from Henry.

'And do they really forget, or do they find it convenient or amusing to forget?'

'No,' Francesca said, annoyed at having brought Jane into the conversation at all, 'they really forget.'

'How old are you?' Jane said.

'Oh, let me see.'

'You're twenty-eight, and I'm thirty, and Henry's thirty as well, or nearly thirty-one. Not so hard to remember.'

'If you've nothing to think about all day, of course it isn't,' Francesca said. Jane said nothing.

'Actually,' Henry said, 'one reason it came readily to mind is that it's my thirty-first birthday tomorrow.'

'I know,' Jane said.

'What are you doing to celebrate?' Francesca said.

'Well, nothing,' Henry said. 'I'm actually on duty. But I don't mind.'

'Oh, we ought to turn this into a celebration,' Francesca said.

'I thought we had,' Jane said, examining a plum.

'Well, I don't feel much like celebrating,' Henry said. 'I'm quite old now, but I don't feel as if I've achieved anything. I mean I haven't really achieved anything on my own or passed any of those big landmarks like buying a flat or getting married or anything.'

'Don't you live in your own flat?' Francesca said.

'Well, no,' Henry said. 'I never left home, you see. The

flat I live in is the flat my parents used to use when they came to London.'

'Do they still use it?' Francesca said.

'No, they live in Sussex the whole time, more or less. Well, to be perfectly honest, they come and stay rather too often. They worry about the garden, of course.'

'The garden?' Jane said.

'Yes, at least my father does. I mean, can you imagine me messing about with mud and seedlings? And my mother doesn't care a fig for it. But my father likes it.'

'It doesn't matter, not being married, does it?' Francesca said, making a leap of thought.

'No,' Henry said. 'Not really. I meant not having done anything other than be somebody's son and somebody's employee, do you see?'

'Oh yes,' Francesca said. 'You see, my main ambition in life at the moment is simply to leave home. Be a bit more independent. That would be so wonderful at the moment, just to have something or someone to be responsible for. I shouldn't complain about having your garden to look after at all.'

A silence fell which neither Jane nor Henry was inclined to break. Henry finally asked for some more coffee, and Francesca got up to set the machine to pop and fizz.

'What would you like to do then?' Jane said.

'What do you mean?' Henry said. The telephone was ringing somewhere; it was quickly answered.

'You said you wanted to be someone, not just someone's son or husband.'

'Yes.'

'Well, what do you want to do? Who do you want to be?'

'I'd really like to do something; I'd really like to write a book or something.'

'What sort of book?' Jane said. 'What about? We'd all like to be famous, you know. It's just that most of us realize the sort of hard work you need to put in first.'

'I don't think I want to be famous,' Francesca said, coming in from the kitchen and going back again abruptly.

'Not Francesca, at any rate,' Henry said. 'I think I know the book I'd like to write. I think I'd like to write a novel.'

'What about?'

'Oh, really, I don't know, I haven't thought about it,' he said, appealing to Francesca as she came through the kitchen door.

'Stop it,' she said as she set down the bomb-like fizz of the percolator. 'It's not something shameful, writing a novel. You shouldn't be so rude.'

'I wasn't,' Jane said. 'I was being interested. You should look at father if you want to see rudeness in action. He was yawning all through dinner.'

'I don't think I was,' John said, coming from his study. 'But I'm not sleeping very well. That might be it.'

'I don't think anyone is being the slightest bit rude,' Henry said, desperately.

'That was granny on the phone,' John said. 'She's frightfully ill, or so she says.'

'Oh dear,' Francesca said.

'Oh, granny and her illness,' Jane said. 'She phoned yesterday to get some sympathy out of us. She must be trying it on with you now.'

'What's wrong with her?' Henry said.

'Oh, a cold, I think,' John said. 'Though that's not what she says. She must have picked it up at the funeral.'

'It was quite a warm day, though,' Jane said.

'No, but all that standing around on damp ground,' John said.

'I don't remember it being damp,' Jane said. 'It hadn't rained for weeks, as I remember.'

'Well, it was damp,' John said, almost shouting. 'You don't remember.'

A silence fell.

'I must go and see her,' John said. 'What do you think of this new chap. Louis Cobb?'

'He seems rather shy, actually,' Henry said. 'And shockingly fat, of course.'

'Yes, he is fat,' John said, vaguely. 'But it seems to suit him, being as fat as that.'

'I see what you mean,' Henry said. 'I simply supposed that we were hiring Clerks by the pound these days.'

'How's the coffee?' Jane said. She got up and went up the stairs without waiting for the answer. She did not care what the answer was; she just wanted this to stop; and she did not know whether she could make it stop by being with Henry, or being without him. She just had to go.

'Delicious, thank you,' Henry said, with a moment of unsurprised irony. He wasn't being entirely honest with them, about his novel. He wanted to write a novel; he was trying to write one; but he was unable to do so. He went home each night and sat in front of his computer like Francesca. Unlike Francesca, he wrote with the light turned up, with the letters in throbbing green neon. He looked at the top of the page, where the words Page 1 were written in light. He sat with a cup of tea and a cigarette in front of him and listened to an opera and without thought wrote for an hour. Then he returned to what he had written the night before, and read that, and generally erased what he had written. Then he read what he had written that night. He finished the cup of tea, now cold, and smoked a last cigarette, and went to bed. He did not think of Francesca, and what he wrote had no connection with the things he met with in his day; it was a separate life, and it did not occur to him to think of anything while he wrote except what he wrote. What he wrote was not his novel, and now he wondered whether he would ever be able to make a start on the novel, for which a folder stood on the book-case, firmly labelled Novel. What he wrote was a letter to his father, which he doubted his father would ever receive, or look at, or read, or want.

'I wish you'd learn to treat Henry as a completely different person to the Henry he used to be,' Francesca said when the clearing up had been decisively left to the morning, and Jane had come downstairs again. 'It would make everything much easier for us all.'

'I would treat him as a different person,' Jane said, 'if it weren't for the fact that he is so utterly changed.'

The Cabinet Secretary was standing there when the Minister for Agriculture, Fisheries and Food came into the ante-room to the Cabinet room.

'First, I see,' the Agriculture Minister said, with a spasm of *bonhomie* and a quick genial hand-rubbing which made the Cabinet Secretary wonder if he imagined himself to be talking to a constituent. He inclined his head with a small smile.

'Ah well,' the Agriculture Minister said. He held a file of papers. He suppressed an urge to look at their deeply unfamiliar contents, and thought for a moment about his wife, for a moment about an argument he had shortly before been having with his Permanent Secretary, in which in his mind he now got the better of the man, and then at greater and more comforting length about the latest iniquity of the Church of England. In his head was a little tune from a psalm setting, when, together, the Secretary of State for Trade and Industry, the Leader of the House and the Secretary of State for Health came in.

'Splendid,' said the Health Secretary, with regard to nothing in particular. He had the air of a fashionably tousled novelist of the post-war years. He seemed to walk in black and white. The Cabinet Secretary acknowledged the comment with a tiny movement, the descendant of a bow, and a smile. It was as if he were ignorant of their pasts, their crimes, their wrongs, their names and their futures; he paid more attention to their roles, and seemed to hide his ignorance with a show of knowing.

Quickly, giving nothing away of their grandeur, the Cabinet assembled in the little room. In their faces, confidence and cheer blandly showed. As they came in, and as they stood, however, the stiffness and rage and fear showed itself, and they did not try to keep it apart. Sometimes they talked generally, but today they talked little, and to their associates, looking about them. The Prime Minister came into the ante-room almost sideways with the last member of the Cabinet, her grand strut unlike his confident rapid slouch. When she walked, she seemed to extinguish a cigarette beneath every pace; in her walk, it could be seen that she was in the right.

They followed her into the Cabinet room, and went quickly to their places, opening their files and speaking to their neighbours only. Some were grand and some were intelligent, and some were well dressed, but only one was beautiful. The Cabinet Secretary, who had not spoken and would not speak, took up his pen and waited. The real note-taker, behind him, practised her shorthand. The Prime Minister placed her papers on the table, looked at the pile, squared off the papers with the palms of her hands, looked more slowly around at the silent table, at her acolytes and enemies, and finally spoke.

'Gentlemen,' she said.

The Cabinet ran its course. Agreement was sought, and achieved, on three issues. The Cabinet was waiting, with the minimum of disguise for its eagerness, for the fourth item.

'Europe,' the Prime Minister said, 'and the Council of Ministers.'

She spoke for nearly ten minutes. If the Cabinet was more restless than it seemed, it was partly due to the discipline of not revealing its multiple disloyalties. It anticipated disagreement, and it was hungry for it; it wanted its meat. The Chancellor of the Exchequer looked around, with what appeared a likeable half-smile on his face. He had no need to sit on his hands, as the Chief Secretary to the Treasury was doing, and would not fidget, like, unmistakably, the Chancellor of the Duchy of Lancaster. He waited.

The Prime Minister finished setting forth her view. The Foreign Secretary stopped tapping his nails against a huge pile of documents. The Cabinet was suddenly aware of the silence in the room, like a fog, and the two pens, scratching. He turned slightly sideways to face her.

'Foreign Secretary,' she said. He started to speak, in his

harsh, noble voice. It took a while for the import of what he was saying to reach the rest of the Cabinet, most of whom knew what he would say. He appeared to be agreeing with the Prime Minister, and to be saying what the Cabinet expected him to say. He finished, and drank from a glass of water. The Chief Whip, distant, itched to doodle. The Secretary of State for Energy, his ruined good looks like an emaciated Buddha, smiled, or grimaced. They could wait for the notes to understand what had just been said. Not needing to, he did not look at the Prime Minister.

'Prime Minister,' the Leader of the House said. He was sitting at a point where he could not easily see her without turning sideways. He did not turn sideways, but spoke directly forwards, without looking at her.

'Deputy Prime Minister,' the Prime Minister said, carefully.

'What the Prime Minister has been saying, and the Foreign Secretary too,' the Leader of the House said, 'I think we will find on reflection to be, in general, correct. But there are some points where some possibilities of difference may be seen to emerge. I think I might outline these. First, and most importantly, the Mechanism.'

He spoke for a while longer. He was disagreeing, but he had lost the Cabinet's attention. They surreptitiously consulted their watches, glanced at the window, made notes for what they were about to say.

'Secondly,' the Leader of the House went on, 'the proposed Treaty.'

He continued. He could see that what he was saying seemed unimportant. He was disagreeing strongly with the Prime Minister's position. He was arguing with her; he was virtually denouncing her; but it seemed as if no one was noticing. His voice might as well have been inaudible, and soon, perhaps, someone would start to speak over him. He could not turn and see the expression on her face, though he knew what it would be like, but he could see the expression on the faces of those facing him, and they were bored faces. Anger was somewhere in him, but he kept it from his voice.

'It's not clear to me what, if anything, the word subsidiarity would mean in such a context, which seems such a crucial concept, or to what degree, even if we could establish its precise meaning, it is a serious proposal, or what role it would take, even if these things could be established with any degree of certainty, in a number of possible future Europes. It appears to be a concept which may in the eyes of our partners form a transitory state – what 'transitory' in that sentence means in terms of years or decades is not, and never could be fully for us to decide – and it would not be right not just to acknowledge that, but not to act on that assumption in our attempts, which ought, it seems to me, to be quite dispassionate, to discover whether that might be a good or a bad thing.'

He finished, with his characteristic baffled air, and glanced sideways at the Prime Minister, serenely gazing, as he knew she would, to her front.

'Thank you,' she said. 'Energy Secretary?'

John's mother-in-law had retired to bed. It wasn't that she had given up; but sometimes you had to admit defeat and just go to bed until the whole thing was over. She sat in bed with a book, a comforting book, she had read many times before, and a box of tissues, and a box of chocolates, and a white angora bed-jacket, which is what she wore when she was ill, and waited for her friend who had kindly popped in to see if she was on the mend to pop up with a cup of tea and a chat. She might well accept any casual offer of help and send her down to the kitchen again, to make some beans on toast. That would be rather nice. She was terribly tired. She thought, not for the first time, that really Fanny Price had been quite a fool not to accept Henry Crawford when she had the chance.

'Wretched, wretched cold,' she said out loud. She wiped the sore papery skin of her upper lip with a paper tissue.

Giacomo stood at the window of his flat and looked out. The fog's wet, neither descending nor ascending, had turned to rain and cleared itself. People wore clothes of grey and brown, sheltered under their own umbrellas or those of their companions, walking. Gloved, wearing coats, under umbrellas, they hunched, and it was difficult to imagine flesh of any sort in the street.

Giacomo stood at the window of his flat and looked out. His flat was heated to the point that he worried that his neighbours might complain. Certainly they rarely needed to use their own central heating systems. He was almost naked. He wore only a pair of shiny red shorts, by choice a size or two too small. This was what he usually wore when in the flat, when he was waiting for a man to arrive. Today there were no men, and would not be. But he still wore his uncomfortably gripping red shorts, as if there were someone to please. He looked out at the street, waiting for someone.

From time to time the telephone rang. There were two

telephones in the flat. The one that was ringing was the line that men rang if they had seen his advert in the press. Giacomo had not known what prostitutes write in their adverts, in English. His first attempt had been returned, with his cheque, by the magazine he had sent it to as unsuitable. He was a little ashamed, not that it might have been offensive or obscene, but that it might have been returned as ungrammatical. After that, he copied out an advert in the magazine, changing the personal attributes that seemed to be unlike him, and writing his own telephone number and his brother's name. And that was accepted. The telephone now rang once or twice an hour, and more often in the evenings or on a Saturday or Sunday afternoon. These cold Sundays, incubative of a warm desire in the solitary flats of men with fifty pounds to spare.

The telephone was ringing now, but he did not answer it, or move to answer it. The answering machine began to play, with a message which made him feel quite hot whenever he overhead it. It sounded both professional, and, because it was his voice, unappealing. And many, perhaps most men who rang the number and got the answering machine listened to the message and then rang off. It didn't really matter too much, not today. One telephone was ringing from time to time, but the other telephone never rang, and never would.

Giacomo was thinking about money. He charged fifty pounds for an hour of sex, or in practice forty-five minutes. In two hours he could earn enough to pay the rent on the flat for the week. In the drawer where he kept money there was seven hundred and fifty pounds he had earned in three days. It seemed a lot, and it seemed to have amassed very quickly, without too much effort. But, though Giacomo liked money, like most people he liked sex more. If a man came who was unclean, or very ugly, he would turn him away, quite simply, not politely. These men seemed to accept the refusal as they would a lover's refusal, and nobody had ever suggested that it was Giacomo's job to put up with anything that arrived on his doorstep.

He wondered if this rejection had happened in the past to the man he liked best, who seemed to like him best. He thought of him as his regular. He had sex with men that he found attractive, and who he enjoyed, and even if they weren't particularly pleasant or intelligent people, they would always pay him. The man he liked best was not a man many other people would have found attractive, and Giacomo wondered why he looked forward to his visits. He had been coming once or twice a week or so for a month or two, and they seemed, honestly, to get on. He was rather old; he had a small hunchback, which clearly occupied his thoughts a good deal. He was kind and trusting. He once told Giacomo that he had been married, and had two grown-up daughters. It didn't surprise Giacomo as much as he clearly thought it would.

Giacomo needed money. He needed a steady stream of income. What if this man, or someone like him, bought him a flat and visited him from time to time? A monthly allowance. There would be only one telephone, and there would be no silent telephone. The man would come; but finally, he would stay.

Giacomo's fantasies were all like that. They began with thoughts of money, as he felt they ought to, but quickly turned to thoughts of love and devotion. To thoughts of moving in with a man, who would love him. He turned and looked at the telephone on which he was waiting for a call from his brother Luigi, whose name he had, for the moment, taken, and listened to his own mechanical voice on the other telephone, saying to a stranger on the other end, 'Hi, this is Luigi, I'm sorry, I can't come to the telephone . . .' Then the telephone was put down, and the tape stopped, and scrapingly rewound. Giacomo looked out of the window, almost naked, and waited for a man whom he could give his telephone number to.

The next day it stopped raining. And, in that strange autumn, it was almost hot for a while. At almost the same time two days later, John was standing at another window. He thought, not about Giacomo, but about men in general. For John, men constituted two sexes. There was a sex that was sexless. That he worked with; whom he exchanged quiet guarded comments in corridors with, who came to dinner, inhabited rooms and houses that their restricted personalities filled. There was a second sex, that he talked freely with, about money and sensation and happiness, whose names he never fully knew, who inhabited streets, cafés and bedrooms. Their nature and their voices never seemed to impinge on their surroundings, never seemed to need much expression. John didn't know which he was; didn't know which he preferred to spend time with. He didn't know which he would prefer if he had the choice, was glad both his children were girls.

'Not busy?' Louis said, coming into the office from his morning cup of coffee.

'No, not at all,' John said. 'I was just wondering what those chaps were doing over there.'

Louis looked over at the parapet from which fit brown

men in shorts and tool belts were teasing and throwing things at each other. He paused for a moment before speaking.

'I don't know what they're doing now,' he said. 'But they're supposed to be patching up the decrepit fabric of the building.'

'Yes,' John said. 'You sounded just like Henry for a moment there. The way he speaks. It looks as if they've had enough of that.'

'I don't blame them,' Louis said, stifling the tremor of lust in his voice. 'I should hate to be stuck up on a boiling hot roof all day like that.'

'Oh, I don't know,' said John, slightly surprising himself. 'They seem to be having quite a lot of fun at the moment.'

'Lead in Ducks and Geese,' intoned the Senior Vote Writer, entering the office like a one-man colonnade, holding the proof of a list of statutory instruments before him. Louis went back to his desk and began to write something. John knew he had nothing to do, but didn't ask what he was writing. He carried on looking out of the window at the workmen, for the moment.

'What have you been up to?' said Henry's father Richard. It was their weekly telephone call.

'This week?' Henry said.

'Of course.'

'Working quite hard,' Henry said stiffly. 'This and that. Also I went one night to a colleague's house for dinner.'

'A man?'

'Yes.'

'What's his name?'

'John. His wife died, a month or two ago. He's got two daughters.' Henry was aware that most people found him camp, and presumed him homosexual, and could not exclude his father from making this judgement. He could not go on to point out, however, that his father had met one of the two daughters, years before, and had found her drunk and forward, and a disagreeable trial to have in the house for a week.

'How's Nancy? Hasn't phoned for a while.'

'She's very busy, I know,' Henry said. 'I haven't seen her since the funeral of this man John's wife.'

'Your mother's not very well.'

'No?'

'Not really. Wretched cold. Blasted weather, that's what it is; can't make its mind up.'

'I suppose so. It's like the weather in Shakespeare when there's some murder going on and all the seasons get mixed up.'

'Garden's a mess. Hate it. Your mother's too old to do anything much of any use.'

'No?'

'How's the garden getting on down there? Get any time to work in it, do you, at all?'

'Not much. It looks all right.'

'Good. Important to keep it up, you know. Shouldn't leave it to us to clear up the whole mess, now that your mother's getting on. How old are the daughters?'

'Which daughters?'

'Your colleague's, that you went to dinner with.'

'Twenties, I think.'

'Good. Your mother wants a word. No, she just wants

to know if Nancy's all right and I've just asked that. Phone me next week.'

He rang off, leaving Henry to think about Jane, who had disgraced herself years before and been obliged to leave their house five full days early. 'That beastly drunk girl,' his father would say. He looked out of the window at the brown tangled mess of wood and leaves that his father called the garden. It was one of the many fictions of their relationship that Henry was fascinated by gardening and had a native ability with any kind of plant. When he was a child, Richard had given him a pot geranium to look after, which mysteriously flourished for some time. After that, he regularly tried to enlist him to help in the garden, and, once he left home, even asked his advice on plant matters. Henry would say, 'Sounds as if you might be over-watering it,' or, 'I think the earth must be sour.' Richard might even take the advice. If the plant died, he never seemed to blame Henry for it.

Henry despised himself for not talking truthfully to his father on any subject whatever. This was why he was writing a letter on his computer. It was a letter to his father. It was a letter on the subject of himself, and in it, every day, before he erased what he had written, he tried to write something absolutely truthful. He tried not to lie; he tried not to say anything deceiving or dishonest, and he tried to say, in this letter which he had been going over and over and erasing and starting again and changing and revising until he had a blank sheet which was the final version of a thousand revisions, he tried to say, not everything he felt for his father, but just one thing, just one single solitary true thing about himself or about his father, or anything at all. It was quite hard, actually.

When he and his father and his mother all lived in the flat where Henry now lived, every so often his father took Henry on a tour of the garden, and showed him the stage various plants had got to. 'Philadelphus out,' he would say. 'Oh yes,' Henry would say. Then they'd walk for a while. 'What's that?' Henry would say, to simulate interest. 'That's the blasted philadelphus,' Richard would say.

When flowers came out in the spring or the summer, it took a while before Henry noticed them. Sometimes it would be the next visit of his parents, and Richard would say, 'Garden looks well; untidy, though.' Henry would look out, and see that there were flowers crawling like slow, gorgeous beasts over everything. He enjoyed looking at them, and when his father wasn't there, not having to ask what they were, and not having anything much to think about. He liked the comfort of looking at complicated gardens through windows.

Richard was never surprised by flowers as Henry was. After all, he planted them. But though the flowers were always a pleasant surprise, Henry kept thinking that plants had other surprises they could spring. When his father died, who could say if the roots of some plant or cherry tree or something neglected wouldn't reach down as far as a drain and crack it? Who would be there to tell him if this was about to happen? Not the succession of offensive acid-house-playing nineteen-year-olds who rented the house next door, or his academic or raffish colleagues, or Jane or Francesca. Maybe Francesca, but he wouldn't ask her. It was always a source of great and impending pleasure to Richard, to see a formerly well-kept garden going to ruin under a new owner. 'They're letting themselves in for ten thousand pounds,' he would say of the garden next door, as they let a dwarf spruce spread horizontally without check, like a hovercraft, unaware that all the time its roots were stretching down and around the vital pipes and arteries of the house.

There was certainly, it is true, never any great catastrophe of pipe-breaking. But Henry still thought of gardens as rather like children. For him, they were a source of worry by the fact that nothing was done to them; they occasionally surprise you by pleasant things; but, at the end, they might behave so badly and destructively that everything else seemed trivial by comparison. In a way Henry looked forward to his garden's ultimate tantrum.

When he had first lived in the flat on his own, the guilt of inheriting a good garden and not adding to it came to him. He went out, with the vaguest of ideas of a plant to buy. Something tall; with big white heavily perfumed flowers. He came back with a pink hydrangea, squat as a tortoise. For a morning he sat with a book about plants and the hydrangea in its pot at the kitchen table. When he finally turned it upside down and, tapping, managed to get it out of its pot, the thick white worms of roots forming a phantom pot around the earth called a forgotten word to mind: *pot-bound*. It reminded him of the pathetically crippled feet of Chinese empresses; he could not see how it continued to live in such a state.

Eventually he took it outside and scooped out a hole for it in the earth. He watered it, and then forgot about it. It might still be there; there was no way of knowing. Now Henry's attention to the garden was limited to watering it. He knew when to do this because there was a dove-grey bush near the back door which quickly wilted for lack of water. When he noticed the wilting, he went out and threw buckets of water over everything. Some things survived; some things died; and some things – a comforting thought – could look dead for years but just be waiting for the right moment to spring back to life.

His garden would spring a disaster on him one day. He enjoyed the feeling of letting go; he enjoyed his irresponsibility. He felt that he had been too responsible for everything as a child, too stiff and well behaved, too forced to say the thank-you-for-having-mes of unhappy afternoons. And now he neglected his father's garden. He felt that he had gone too early into a job which made him take responsibility, and only three years of silliness had intervened. Had he enjoyed that either?

The thing which gave him most pleasure, which he had invented all by himself and took care to hide only from his father, was his manner. He discovered, late in life, that he liked to say 'My *dear*', and to flap his hands a little. He liked to sit comfily with girls on sofas; and he found, when he did so, people liked him better than when he behaved as he did with his father. An extraordinary thing. He didn't calculate it; indeed, practising it tacitly with Nancy, he fully expected to lose friends through it; but that was how he was, and he felt happier. Occasionally people assumed he was homosexual. He wasn't, and he didn't mind it.

Richard telephoned once a week, and the garden, on which he had spent so much love and attention, was the main subject of the conversation, often. Henry wondered what else they could, or should, talk about; love and attention, maybe? He wondered if Richard loved anything else. If he had been asked, he would have said, 'Of course I love Henry,' or, 'Of course I love your mother.' But that isn't the same thing. Though he talked about the garden for most of the time, there was another subject which always cropped up. Richard, too, like an acquaintance, was patently concerned that Henry might be homosexual, and always asked whether men Henry had dinner with were married. He also wondered, Henry thought, about Henry's marrying. No hints were made; none needed to be.

Henry wondered himself about marriage. He didn't think he was homosexual; no hard-bodied swimsuited emperors came looming unsmiling through his night to master him; he would never ask men for sex, and would never accept an offer; although, as he would say to his intimate women, who loved him for it, who could be sure? He was all right looking; his skin was perfect and his eyes were clear; his general appearance almost excessively – was this a recommendation? – natty. His touch of imperviousness. And that was, perhaps, just the problem. When he looked at himself in the looking-glass, whether in his exquisite, groomed day wear, or the careful, soft weekend outfits he thought about in shops, he couldn't imagine himself asking anyone to have sex with him, or them agreeing. He never had. That was his secret, and it was a secret Jane kept for him.

He could imagine a proposal of marriage, of excruciating embarrassment, which would end with a woman melting in his arms. 'Oh Henry,' she would say. But then his imagination failed, and he couldn't see what she would say, or what he would say, or what she would look like, since she could only look like Jane, or not like Jane. Nothing more, until the wedding. With doves, and white silk, and morning coats, and children being good as gold in matching tiny military coats and miniature ballgowns. Nothing before, and nothing after.

In some moments he thought he would be destined to marry literature. Sometimes this pleased him; sometimes this seemed a little sad. He would write his book, which would be printed in a few heavy, expensive beautiful copies, and be romantically unread by the masses, and change the lives of a very few. Perhaps he would marry late, for companionship, and for walks in parks in autumn. His father had married late; a child had been a bonus. He felt himself a bonus, and he wanted to be an exquisite bonus to his wife. He looked forward to telling all, or any of this, to his father, in a letter, perhaps. There are so few virgins, and they do not know each other.

The business collapsed. No one knew why.

'They're not interested in the Chamber,' Henry said. 'It's all much more interesting outside.'

'Surely the Whips can keep it going for the sake of appearances,' John said.

'Apparently not,' Henry said.

A girl in the Tea Room asked a Member if the House was really going to rise before seven.

'A nice early night for you, my dear,' he said. She concentrated on slightly burning his toast.

'All over,' the Clerk of the House said to his wife, knitting. She smiled but cursed slightly; the telephone would have to wait for another evening.

The Prime Minister had no idea that the House was rising, and it would be of no interest to her. No one thought to tell her.

The whips shrugged.

Upstairs, the Clerk Assistant and the Clerk of Public Bills

stood over Louis as he read their approximate minutes to the Senior Vote Writer, who corrected the proof of what he had sent to the printer. It was shortly before seven.

'Is that it?' Henry said.

'Looks like it,' Louis said. 'Why are you still here?'

'Oh, nothing better to do,' Henry said. 'A bad habit, I know. Fancy a drink?'

'Of course,' Louis said.

But when they got down to the bar the bar staff had packed up and gone home.

'Oh dear,' Henry said. 'Well, there's nothing to do but go to Soho.'

To Louis, Soho suggested vice and degradation; he was slightly nervous that Henry would suggest one of his regular homosexual bars. But the taxi drew up outside a quite unexceptional sort of place. Henry explained that it had been exactly the same for years and years, and this was why it was still worth going to.

The light bulbs had one-third gone, and dividing up the bar were two purple-faced sots of indeterminate sex and hunched appearance, holding court, as, all afternoon, they had clearly done, to three or four cronies. Louis sat down at a table and Henry went to the bar to get a bottle of wine.

There was no one there, and he stood, waiting patiently, for someone to arrive.

'Do you mind if I sit here?' a girl said. She was glamorously groomed from a distance, but her edges were untidy; her fingernails unpainted and a little grimy; the sole of one stiletto slightly worn and flapping. 'If you sit on your own here, you get pestered.'

'Of course,' Louis said. 'I won't pester you.'

'Pester away,' she said. 'Have you got a light?'

'No,' Louis said. 'I can get one.'

'I can get one too,' she said. 'No, I can see you're not the pestering type.'

'No, not at all,' he said. 'At least not you.'

'Thanks.'

'Nothing personal,' Louis said, bantering.

'Just women,' she said.

'Yes,' he said. A strange giddiness came over him; this accelerated conversation, this woman who, so impervious, told him what confidences he would give her, and then sympathetically listened to him saying Yes. 'I'm with a friend, actually.'

'Oh, a friend.'

'No, not that sort of friend. It's just that.'

'Oh, is that your friend at the bar?'

'Yes,' Louis said. 'In the suit.'

'I know him,' Jane said. 'At least, I used to.'

Henry came back with a bottle and two glasses.

'Hello, Jane,' he said. 'I didn't know you were coming.'

'No,' Jane said. 'Neither did I. I just sat down here with – what's your name?'

'Louis.'

'Louis, and he said he had a friend. But I didn't know it was someone like you.'

'Shall I get another glass, or are you going?'

'No, another glass would be rather nice. I hadn't really any plans, frankly.'

'Nor me,' Louis said. 'How do you know each other?'

'From university,' Jane said quickly. 'We both studied Russian.'

'No,' Henry said. 'I didn't.'

'Oh, it was me that studied Russian,' Jane said. 'I forgot.'

'How can you forget?' Louis said.

'Easily,' Jane said. 'When you get to my age. Or to Henry's, I suppose.'

'Or to mine,' Henry said. 'Have some more.'

'Thanks, I shall,' Jane said. 'And you. Have you got a light?'

'No,' Henry said.

Jane fixed him in her murderous glare for one second, before getting up and going to the bar to buy some matches.

'Look,' Louis said. 'Shall I go?'

'Christ, no,' Henry said. 'I don't want to be alone with her.'

There was a little silence.

'Come to that,' Henry said. 'I don't want to be with her at all.'

'Well, do you want to go?'

'Yes, I rather do,' Henry said. 'I think I'll go. Are you going to come?'

'No,' Louis said. 'I don't mind staying and making an excuse for you.'

'Say I'm feeling sick or something.'

Jane came back.

'Gone, has he?'

'Yes.'

'I knew he would. That's why I went to the bar. Do you want me to go away too?'

'No,' Louis said. 'Of course not, I've got no one to drink with if you go.'

'And I've got no one to drink with if I go,' Jane said. 'But I'm used to drinking on my own.'

'You look well on it,' Louis said. 'Have you been stood up?'

'Oh no,' Jane said. 'I just came out to get away from my sister. We've been cooped up all day like some nightmare existentialist play.'

'Is she so bad?'

'Yes, of course. Did you say you were queer?'

'No, I think you said I was queer.'

'Oh right,' she said. 'So I did.'

'You don't mind?' he said.

'Christ, no,' she said. 'No one seems to know for sure, least of all Henry. It's nice meeting someone who does.'

'Some people do, you know. Mind, I mean.'

'Not me,' she said. 'You're terribly fat.'

'I know,' Louis said. 'It doesn't seem to matter, really.'

'What do you mean?' Jane said. 'Do you go to gay bars?'

'Yes, sometimes.'

'But you prefer bars like this?'

'No,' he said. 'I prefer gay bars.'

'I imagine,' she said, 'gay bars as being full of people trying to pick each other up in a drunken sort of way.'

'No,' he said. 'I wish they were. Come and find out some time.'

So they made a date.

'Do you like being gay?'

'Sometimes I do,' he said. 'And sometimes I just hate having to spend all my time with men. Men smell more than women, you know.'

'But presumably you like the way men smell,' she said. 'If you're gay.'

He looked at her. 'Yes, I do,' he said. She saw him begin to like her. 'To tell the truth, I like being queer, and when

I'm not liking it I'm not thinking about it. It's just that you're supposed to agonize a bit. Let's go.'

So began the first of a series of rather long evenings.

It was two days later.

'Yes,' Henry said. 'I really ought to see more of her.'

'I don't really know what to do with her,' John said. They were talking about Jane. 'She never seems to do much, or want to do much. You saw the other night. She just loafs around insulting her sister.'

'Well, she always did that,' Henry said. 'But doesn't she have any friends she sees?'

'I don't think so,' John said. 'Only people she never sees, like you.'

'I see her from time to time,' Henry said. 'I adore her, you know that. But you know how busy we are at the moment.'

'We are busy,' John said. 'Whenever I leave the office there always seems to be a great pile of mail and messages waiting for me when I get back.'

'Well, there is an answer,' Henry said. 'You must simply stay chained to your desk and do every scrap of work and read Erskine May from the first to the twenty-first edition from cover to cover ceaselessly in your spare moments, and end up as Clerk of the House and going half-mad, like Gavin. Just a sec.'

He got up and left the room. John wondered briefly what Henry thought he was doing when he left the office in the morning for no reason, and then asked himself why he wanted to drop these hints, these preliminaries to confessions. He didn't answer his own question, just for the moment.

They were in Henry's flat in Pimlico. They drank; four floor-level lamps cast pools of light, luxuriously, upwards; an unbelievably ancient Edith Piaf record was playing. It was a flat few came to; Henry was not willing to be dropped in on, and did not issue standing invitations. He was conscious of the danger of late-night drunks and those on the way back from the supermarket, just calling for a cup of coffee. It was the disadvantage of living too close to the centre of the city. Henry lived very near the House, claiming that it was necessary to live so close if you found it difficult to get out of bed in the mornings. Others put it down to a lack of imagination, a lack of sympathy with other parts of London; and sympathy, Henry thought, was exactly what other parts of London needed.

So his life was not separated out like the parts of an egg. Work and not-work were close to each other, and mingled. The common notion was that where Henry lived was a glamorous sort of place; it was not; it was elegant, but rather seedy. Henry might have chosen to live somewhere else, but his parents had lived in this flat long before Henry had lived there alone. There were two bedrooms, a kitchen, a bathroom and the garden. The other room, which in other flats would have been called the drawing room, was just called the Room. Like Henry, it served all other purposes indiscriminately and not quite adequately, and, if the garden was untidy and riotous, the flat had, like him, an immaculate nattiness.

'I think the room needs decorating,' Henry said. 'People will keep smoking in here. Do you think we can expect another challenge this year?'

'I wouldn't have thought so,' John said. 'Isn't there a specific date they have to issue a challenge by?'

'I haven't the faintest idea,' Henry said. 'I simply don't know. It's not as if, though, her position is that secure, she's so unpopular in the country –'

'Always has been,' John said. 'The ones they love are never the ones the country loves. They're not going to start worrying about that now.'

'Oh yes they are,' Henry said. 'And they do. If Mr and Mrs Electorate are going to start hurling bricks through Argos's window to protest against taxation, they must be getting concerned a little about her unpopularity. For a start, they think she'll lose them the next election; and frankly, they don't like her, even if they know her, which half of them don't.'

'They're scared of her,' said John. 'That's all it amounts to. Take my word for it. Anyway, who is there?'

'The Honourable Member for Henley, for one.'

'Oh, come on. His day's come and gone. If anything, he's more unpopular than the Prime Minister. Besides all this, did you see the reception she got at the party conference last month?'

'Thank you, I have much better things to do with my summer than that. It isn't up to them, is it? I'm sorry, do smoke if you want to. I didn't mean that.'

'No,' John said. 'I'm trying to give up. It's not so easy when your daughter smokes. You know Jane smokes?'

'Yes, I know,' Henry said. 'Actually, Jane taught me to smoke. I only gave up fifteen months ago.'

'Do you need to be taught?' John said, refusing to be embarrassed.

'Well, it isn't natural,' Henry said. 'Oh, we have to stop talking now for *La Vie en Rose*.'

'For what?'

'The song, *La Vie en Rose*,' Henry said. He crooned slightly. 'Mmm, mmm, mmm, *la vie en rose*, mmm, mmm.'

It was apparent even to John that Henry did not know the words to the song. He looked dispassionately at the well-dressed man with his glass of whisky on a table by him, with his eyes closed and his head tipped ludicrously back, making an extraordinary noise. The song was dimly familiar to him, but he would have been unable to identify it.

'Do you mind if I tell you something personal?' Henry said when it had come to an end and Edith Piaf started on another song of woe.

'That depends, of course, on what it is,' John said. He said what he meant, when he said anything.

'I don't think you should wear cufflinks with that suit,' Henry said.

'I hadn't honestly given it much thought,' John said. 'Why on earth not? And what am I to keep my cuffs together with?'

'Well, I think you should perhaps keep double-cuffed shirts for double-breasted suits,' Henry said. 'That's a very nice suit, but I think you probably ought to wear a single-cuffed shirt with it. The shirt looks more formal than the suit.'

'I dare say,' John said. 'Do you suppose I spend much time thinking about the clothes I wear?'

'Why not?' Henry said. 'I'm sure when you buy your suits you think about them quite hard.'

'Up to a point,' John said. It was now that Henry noticed that John was getting quite angry. 'It doesn't seem to me – I may be wrong – but it doesn't seem to me a subject a grown man should spend his time thinking about.'

'Perhaps not,' Henry said, nervously.

'It doesn't seem to me to be of the slightest importance what one wears, so long as it conforms fairly minimally to what people expect you to wear.'

And yet John was generally immaculate.

'What happens when people have no expectations of you?'

'Well, people always have expectations, and there's always a correct thing to wear, all the time.'

'What you want to wear comes into it, of course,' Henry said.

'No of course about it at all,' John said. 'I have no opinion on the matter. I like to think I have better things to think about. Could I have some more whisky?'

'Of course,' Henry said. He got up and went to the kitchen thankfully.

'Why don't you take Jane out for lunch, some time?' John said, as Henry came back into the room, where in any case the whisky was. There was a pause which might usefully have been filled by one of them lighting a cigarette.

'Well, it's very kind of you to think that she would like to have lunch with me,' Henry said. 'But you saw what she was like the other day. I don't really think she would want to.'

'She would be fine if she weren't showing off in front of Francesca and me,' John said. 'You don't need to worry about that. She often talks about you, you know.'

'Maybe I will,' he said. 'I don't think it ought to be lunch, though; it's a bit of a sentence, you can't decently leave before pudding if it gets a bit difficult. Would you like some water with that?'

'No, I've had enough,' John said. 'Maybe you're right. Help me up, will you?'

It was the sort of conversation that Clerks only had with each other when they were very drunk, late at night. John left, with the minimum of *bonhomie*. Henry cleared up and washed the two glasses. He put away the bottle, thinking for a while about his own clothes and about whether he was right to think what he thought, that double-cuffed shirts, when worn with single-breasted suits, were a trifle reminiscent of pimps in 1970s movies. He picked a book off his bookshelves, more or less at random. On his bookshelves there were two hundred novels. He bought no books that he did not read, and he bought no books which ended happily. He liked tragedy, and he liked to be moved by cleverness and slaughter. He read for a while, kicking the shoes from his feet, forgetting the glass by his side. He did not think of his anger, and he did not think of Jane, or of John, angrily or otherwise. His thoughts wandered, when they wandered, on to clothes; he thought of a heavy sweater, with a thick rolled neck, the colour green-tinged black olives could be. He resolved to go and look the next day for such a garment in the ten shops he habitually went to. Then he noticed that it was nearly one in the morning, and, as was his habit, he went to the bathroom, washed his now unshaven face, masturbated into the sink and went to bed, falling asleep within three-quarters of an hour. This was better than usual, though he realized on waking that this was because, on going to bed, he had felt completely fucked. He did not think of Jane, angrily or otherwise.

THE CHILDHOOD OF HUNCHBACKS

JOHN SLEPT FROM time to time in the afternoon, and when he fell asleep, as a child in his room, or as an adult in his office, or in recesses, on his bed, he had always felt that he should not give his habitual afternoon sleep too respectable a status. So he did not draw the curtains before falling asleep, and certainly he did not change into his pyjamas. He removed his shoes, and lay on his bed in his day clothes, and fell asleep in the, sometimes, bright light which fell on his face.

These many rooms in which he had slept; the eight offices he had occupied since he was not more than a boy in the House of Commons. The bedroom with his wife's idea of décor in his house now, and the bedroom in the previous, smaller, house; bedrooms in holiday homes, and once or twice, Helena's idea, in expensive hotels in cities she wanted to go to, but the hotel was the point. And beyond that, beyond those domestic rooms, there were rooms in which he had fallen asleep, not for long, for several minutes only, and quickly dreamt, and woken to find a simulacrum of the nude boy he had dreamt of beside him, nude, or dressing, or once, dressed, and rifling through his things. And beyond that, there were the bedrooms of his childhood; his room he had kept for himself, the room he had at his grandparents' house in the country, the room of infancy, before he knew what rooms could be like. He slept in them all. He slept in these bedrooms, fantastic now, and some existing only in his mind, in the afternoons.

He dreamt strange dreams, when he was lying in the sun. When he woke, he knew to ascribe them to the bright light which struck his eyelids and, depriving them of dark, made his sleep orange. His usual dream on these afternoons went rather like this. He was handed a document, by a woman in an official capacity. She looked at him without expression and, for reasons which varied, he was expected to read it. He was expected to understand, and he was expected to be the same as the others. But as he looked at it, a terrible tiredness made him close his eyes, and he could not force them open. The document stayed unread, and expressionless, the woman looked at him, at his failure, and he condemned himself.

A dream which was never got rid of, this terrible dream about the relief of exhaustion, when exhaustion was not there. His childhood was rather like that. There was one overriding fact about it. Something which was now surprising, although it was not surprising at the time, and there was no way to overcome the terrible fact. But all the time, all through his childhood, and in retrospect, he felt that there was a single document, a single awful fact which he was put on earth to explain, and to read, and never could, and never would.

The strange thing about John's life was that the one thing everyone who ever met him noticed was also the one thing that no one ever commented on. His parents never talked about it, except in the context, when he was very young, of doctors he was to go and see. Doctors discussed his hunchback, up to a point, but no one he knew. And after he was a little older, there was no point in their talking about it either, and they stopped. Children he knew talked about it, when he was a child, but after a while, they too stopped. He wondered sometimes whether it was tact or fear. He wondered sometimes why he never talked about it. It was as if truthfulness about it resided only in his childhood, and now he was old, no one would ever mention it. Truth had been lost, and deformity remained. He did not know even how to begin to talk about his physical pain and his physical shape.

And when he was grown up his wife never mentioned it, all the time she knew him. Only in the sympathy in her eyes, shining, did he see that she had noticed it at all. His daughters, too, had never seen it; never thought of it as part of anything but their father. Only once had his wife mentioned it, in all those years, only once. She was talking to Francesca.

'Oh,' she said. 'My parents never wanted me to marry your father. They said all your children will end up hunchbacked.'

John was not meant to hear, and he went on without responding. But the strange fact that she had ever noticed registered with him, and he had a strange unclassifiable anger. He loved his daughters, but whether it was because they had never noticed his hump, or whether it was because they saw him, and they saw his hump, and they did not distinguish, he could not tell.

But his hump. What did he think of his hump? He

thought it was not part of him, and yet it was something he could not get rid of. If he had been a more whimsical sort of man, it is conceivable that he might have given it a pet name. But he was not whimsical, and he only recognized that it was something quite different from him, quite apart from him. All through his childhood, he had seen something crouched murderously on his back; and as he walked the streets, people looked at him. They were the audience at the pantomime, and he, in the Quasimodo costume he could not take off, was the villain, or the object of pity. But to him, the hump had no meaning, and when the people in the streets looked at him, as if to say Behind you, behind you, he could not respond.

He knew that other people turned suddenly and did not see a great lump of flesh hanging between their shoulders, and he knew that when people glimpsed part of their body, they did not think of it as alien, or obscene, or a strange involuntary addition. But as he went through his life, John took to thinking of it as the repository of everything vile and murderous and poisonous that was in him; and, like the vileness and murder and poison in everyone which one never speaks about, it seemed to him natural that no one ever mentioned it, except the young in the street, who knew no better, and could see nothing but the truth.

For instance. Once. He was about fourteen, and for some reason he became interested in clothes. It was an interest he never lost, in a way, and an interest he never quite admitted to, and even, sometimes, denied. It was at a time when the young, who had previously dressed as their parents largely did, began to dress in quite different ways. John had seen photographs of the French and American young, in *Picture Post*, and coveted their freedom, their fun, their clothes.

He did not want the charcoal grey for the week and the lighter grey for weekend; he did not want the neat press and the flannel and the shirts in piles. But it was not until long afterwards that he realized, when he looked at the pictures of the French and American young, that what he coveted was not their zooty bags, or tight hipless black wool numbers, or even the extravagant swirling flow of the girls' skirts. He did not covet their clothes; he hunched over the precious magazines, and he coveted their flesh.

But you could become anything you wanted to be by changing the clothes you wore. Surely you could. Clothes were what one saw. All one saw. And the will of men was such that a transformation could be achieved. He believed this, and what he did not know was that clothes and flesh are alike only in their temporary state.

At that time he was not intelligent, not intelligent as he later became, and he genuinely believed this. He went and did his best, against the problems of money and the province of the country in which he lived, to find an outfit which would approximate the outfit he, and *Picture Post*, held in wide-mouthed appreciation. He assembled it, but he could not think of any occasion on which he might wear it.

He was lucky. A friend introduced him to his sister, a girl called Anne, and her best friend, a girl called Eleanor. James's sister was sallow and thin, and, though faintly but unmistakably stupid, she had the reputation of being sharp as a knife. She appeared intelligent at first, but she merely had a knack for a cynical comment and a frank insult. This was, and is, good enough for most people; John had never voiced his doubts. Eleanor seemed to John more glamorous. She had been expelled from her previous school.

Her present school had taken her, but she was there on trial. Once or twice he had asked her opinion on something, or asked how she felt about her life. 'What do you think?' was her response. She was impervious; she threw comments back; she enchanted John, up to a point.

For a few weeks – they were remarkable golden weeks – James and he had sat with Eleanor and Anne in parks and teashops, and seen no one else, and laughed a good deal. Eleanor had smoked. She said her parents didn't care; or rather, when asked if her parents cared, she had merely replied, as if amazed, 'My parents?' All of them understood that her parents would probably care a lot. Any parent would, they supposed. But they did not challenge her, or ask what she meant. Once his father had said that he hoped John wasn't falling into bad company, from which John understood that he had been seen, laughing, with James and Anne and Eleanor, who had been smoking. He made allowances for over-protectiveness. Perhaps too much.

John's parents did not go away much, or, if they did, they generally took him with them. So it was unusual when they decided to visit John's aunt for the weekend, and told him that he was surely old enough to look after himself for three days. John's mother spent Wednesday and Thursday frantically cooking things which would keep until Sunday and could be safely reheated, and easily. A fruitcake for emergencies; a box of biscuits; bowls of hard fruit. A neighbour was briefed, and asked to look in from time to time. John was invited to ask some friends round for tea, or even for lunch, on his own account.

He planned to do so, anyway. He mentioned the fact that his parents were going away to James, Eleanor and Anne, and suggested that they should come round for Friday evening, which was the first evening his parents were away. As well to allow plenty of time to clear up afterwards, he thought hopefully. He described the evening as a decadent evening, and suggested that they should drink whisky and smoke cigarettes in his parents' drawing room. He tried to sound knowing and amused when he said decadent, as if he were accustomed to hold such parties. 'Decadent?' Eleanor said. The girls looked at each other before accepting. He knew he had not succeeded in his pose of sophistication. But they had accepted.

Anne pointed out that, although the evening would be fun, it would not do to return to their homes smelling of whisky. John thought briefly and saw that she was right. So it was agreed that James and his sister and Eleanor would come to stay overnight, and that Eleanor's parents should be told that she was staying with Anne. Anne's parents would be led to believe that not only was James staying at John's house, but John's parents would be there. Subterfuge seemed a reasonable way of arranging a party, when they were sixteen.

John calculated the beds. He did not want to use his parents' bedroom. The first guest bedroom had a double bed in it, which the girls could use. The second had a single bed in it, which James could sleep in. There would be women in the house, sleeping. He tested himself against this knowledge. Or he and James could sleep in the double bed. That was also a possibility.

He bought the whisky for the evening, and three packets of Rothman's. Then he put on his zooty clothes and waited for them. He was hot with embarrassment when he thought of the morning he spent buying them; but they were bought. They did not quite make the impression he had thought of, but they fitted, and had a certain something. They were better than usual. He thought suddenly of the way James's dark hair was always too long in front, and the way it fell over his forehead, the way in the sun it shaded his face, the way he looked up and his eyes fixed yours. He wondered what James would wear.

He carried on dressing, after a while.

When they arrived, he wondered if he had made a mistake. They arrived together, dressed in their usual day clothes, and, though James commented favourably on the clothes he had put together, Eleanor looked him up and down frankly, and said nothing. They sat together for a time, and talked about their respective schools. John offered them drinks, but only James accepted the offer. John put on a record of some jazz music; he was enthusiastic about it, but they did not respond. When it came to an end, he turned it over. There were only one or two records, and he hoped they would do. After a time, Eleanor and Anne, looking at each other first, agreed to have a glass of whisky, and after a little more time, Eleanor asked him to light her cigarette.

John leant over and lit her cigarette, and then took his cigarette case from his pocket. Though it was his father's second cigarette case, the cigarettes it contained were those he had bought. He placed a cigarette in his mouth and lit it. He was aware that the other three were observing him, and they stopped talking. For a while he thought that he was doing well, and they began their conversation again. He had never smoked before.

'You don't inhale at all, do you?' Eleanor said suddenly.
'No?' John said.

'No,' Eleanor said. 'You're supposed to inhale. Watch me.'

She leant back with her cigarette in her mouth, and sucked at it, the tip burning up. She took it from her mouth, and looked at the ceiling for a time. Sated. Her hunger for fire was visible; they were silent in the face of her.

'Change the record,' she said. There was only one more record; a record of a French singer. John put it on and the strange wail began. Eleanor pulled on her cigarette again. After a while, she breathed out, theatrically, but no smoke at all emerged. John was impressed.

'I see,' he said.

'I can see why you were expelled now,' Anne said, a little enviously.

'Not for that, darling,' Eleanor said. She would swallow anything, that one, John found himself thinking in his mother's voice; and just as he did so, Eleanor began to sing, with the record. *'Quand il me prend dans les bras et me parle tout bas je vois la vie en rose il me dit des mots d'amour les mots de tous les jours.'* A silence fell in the room, a silence which surrounded her voice and the scratching record, and, her eyes shut, they looked at her. She broke off. *Les mots de tous les jours.* Her heavy lashes opened, and she looked, she conferred her gaze on John, and forever afterwards, he could never decide whether her gaze was fond, or if it were terrifying in its hunger and kindness. Was she mocking him by showing him how to smoke? Had she been kind? Did he like her, and did the mother's disapproval he had constructed for himself make him like her still more?

Oh, the rest of the evening went as planned. It was a success. But even when John, after the immense contraption of explanation and apology and seduction had been assembled and dismantled, was lying beneath the beautiful rutting boy, and feeling a thing never imagined accurately, never known before and never forgotten afterwards, the feeling of being fucked by a beautiful rutting boy with a man's dick, what he thought of was not James, but the moment when the girl swallowed the smoke and turned to look at him with her great eyes. And after then, John knew what he had never before known, that secrecy and fear are things which are always stronger than desire.

It took a day and a half with the windows open to clear the smell of smoke from the drawing room. John could never remember wearing his fashionable clothes again. Perhaps they were absorbed into his ordinary wardrobe like ink in a jar of clean water.

For months afterwards, John was preoccupied with two thoughts. The first was that she would have allowed herself to be seduced that night, but not afterwards, just as James had. He also believed, however, that the reason she was kind to him was his deformity. He was right both times. Only later did he come to think that he did not mind being loved and pitied for his hunchback. At that time he felt that he would prefer someone who did not pity him at all.

A year later, or two, a packet came for him in the post. There was a note in it, which said, in letters cut out of newspapers, From your decadent admirer. With it was a single Rothman's cigarette, crumbling from the post. He recognized it; there was half a packet still mouldering at the back of his sock drawer.

The next time he saw Eleanor she had changed her name, and he carried on thinking of the packet as evidence of her love. He was middle-aged before, cursing his egotism, he saw the mockery in the gift.

Not a year later, or two, but many years later, when they had had two children, when people asked Jane what she thought about her father, it always took her a moment to see that they were asking her what she thought about her father's hump. 'I don't know,' she would always say, because it would be too absurd to say, 'I never noticed it,' which was the truth. It had always been there, and always part of him, the beloved father, and not something to be commented on, especially. Because Jane was the first one who loved him without condition and the only one who trusted him, even where he warped. And even where he was not perfect. Because somewhere Jane was always within earshot of her dead mother, saying, 'My parents never wanted me to marry him, because the children would be crippled,' and in response, Jane nodded, and said to herself, They are, they are. She loved him even where he was not perfect; she wondered what the perfected, after all, were like. She thought of her mother, and shivered.

JEALOUSY, EVEN OF THE AIR,
IS DANGEROUS

S HE HAD HALF an hour to spare. This was unusual. It was a Friday afternoon, and everything had been done. There was so much to do, and for the moment it had all been done.

Her life was extraordinary. She was an ordinary person, she said to herself. She understood ordinary people, and her life was not ordinary. There was no time to spare. There never had been time; time spent eating seemed a waste, if business was not advanced in the course of eating. From time to time, at a dinner, she might be talking to someone who knew as they spoke that they would remember this conversation all their lives, though she would not remember it the next morning, and a sudden pleasure would descend on her. These moments; it took her a moment to locate the source and the origin of the pleasure, and then it came. The food. A quick intense burst of flavour – never quite warm, never quite enough. People had worked for it – she thanked them at least every three months – and she noticed what they produced once a fortnight.

Unimportant. If she could rid her life of these things,

these things which used her time, which seemed to be using her for ends of their own; if she could live without the hours spent asleep; if she could turn every ingestion of food into a meeting; if the minutes of ablution and dressing could be done away with; what might not be done. What ends might not be achieved, and what perfection descend. But there was a weakness in her soul. It was a weakness which seemed to want not to achieve, and not to reform, and not to work, but simply to potter. Somewhere in her head there was a point which forever urged her to stop. She would kick off her shoes, which were always new and never comfortable; in her stockings she would pull herself up on a sofa, and with an apple and a piece of cheese and a glass of whisky and a record she would relax.

No one whatever knew about this weakness. Many people who actually knew her would flatly disbelieve it. A long record might last an hour. She did not have an hour, and for a decade and a half had not known what an hour was like. When did she last see a film, or read a book for pleasure, or sleep in the afternoons, or call up a friend for a conversation with no point, or have sex in the day? She could not remember.

She took her shoes off, anyway. She had half an hour. For a moment her mind was blank, and then she realized with pleasure that her mind had been blank. There was a paper on the desk that had been there since lunchtime; not important, not urgent, not even official, but a private letter from the Chief Whip about the state of the party. She picked it up and began to read. It was extraordinary; it was something he could not put in a paper anyone else would read. She carried on reading. It was pleasure, too.

✳   ✳   ✳

Louis took everything that was in the fridge out. One piece of cheese he threw away immediately. He examined three slices of bacon closely, and then put them back in the fridge. He sniffed at a loaf, and put it on one side. Everything else – some ham, a small plastic tub of a colourless paste, another piece of cheese, an apple and some milk – he took to the table. He could hear his flatmate getting up. He switched on the kettle and waited for it to boil. It was a quarter to nine on Saturday morning. He began to eat his breakfast, standing.

'What are you doing?' his flatmate said, coming in.

'Nothing,' Louis said, sitting down. 'Breakfast.' His mouth was full.

'Oh christ. I don't know how you can.'

'It's got to be eaten.'

'You mean, you might as well eat it.'

'Yes,' Louis said. He looked at his flatmate, eating nothing and looking repellent. Louis resented his flatmate, for a number of reasons. When he had bought the flat, he had considered that it would be good for him to have a lodger. It would give him a certain amount of income, and it would introduce him to a large circle of people whom he would otherwise not meet. He therefore informed a telephone service for homosexuals in London that he was looking for a lodger.

The prospective lodgers who had visited him were three. The first was a man who propositioned him before he had been shown the whole flat. It was impossible to determine whether the second came from Newcastle or Albania, but in either case he spoke in his native tongue, and could not be understood. The third was extremely thin and dressed entirely in lycra, through which it could be seen that both his nipples were pierced. He spoke of discotheques he had visited and lovers he had taken; he asked Louis if he knew friends of his, which Louis did not; he commented not on the flat, but on the bottle of cologne in the bathroom. Louis agreed to let this third man move in.

Since then, he had wondered idly, approximately twice every morning, why this flatmate, whose name was Joey, was so thin, and he was so fat. He wondered idly, now, for the second time that morning, why Joey was so thin and he was so fat. Then he remembered, for the second time that morning, that before he got up to eat breakfast, he had just finished eating a sandwich in bed, which he had bought the day before for lunch. Something better had come up, and in any case it was enjoyable to lie in bed on a Saturday morning eating a sandwich in bed.

'What are you doing today?' Louis said.

'Nothing. Thought I might troll on down the Fridge tonight.'

'As usual. Didn't you have an interview for a job on Thursday?'

'Yes,' Joey said. It was quite common for Joey and Louis not to see each other for some days, although the flat was not large, and each resented sharing it with the other.

'You didn't mention it,' Louis said.

'There was no need to,' Joey said. 'I've got no qualifications to be a merchant banker. When they asked me if I was prepared to work for twelve hours a day seven days a week I said no. I don't know why they even interviewed me.'

'But why did you think you wanted to do it?'

'I thought I wanted to make a lot of money,' Joey said.

'Well, don't you?'

'Of course, but I'd rather sell my arse in Harvey Nick's window than do that. So boring. What did you do last night?'

'Nothing,' Louis said. He was unable to think of a way of making standing in a horrible bar trying to pick up men sound interesting and funny. These were the two qualities Joey generally demanded in a story.

'Have you heard any scandal recently?'

'What sort of scandal?'

'I thought the point of your job was to be as close as possible to all the scandal,' Joey said.

'Not really,' Louis said. 'I don't really know anything much. There's supposed to be some trouble brewing over Europe.'

'That's not scandal,' Joey said. 'I meant mistresses, rent-boys, murder. I would never have told you to take it if you never picked up any gossip. Is it true about . . . ?' He went on to ask whether two Cabinet Ministers were having sex with each other.

'No idea,' Louis said. 'Anyway, you'd only try and sell it to the newspapers. And you didn't tell me to take the job. I wouldn't take your advice about anything.'

'Do you think the newspapers don't know all the gossip already?'

'Do you think I'd tell you the gossip even if I knew it?' Louis said, rather belatedly.

'Yes, of course you would. You can't keep your trap shut about anything, you. I'm just going to sit and watch telly all morning.'

'You watch too much television.'

'And I eat too much, everyone says, and I know I sleep too much. But the palace of excess is built with bricks of law, or forgives the plough, or something. Christ, you'd never think I had an education. Maybe I will do something constructive.'

'Clean the flat.'

'I said constructive. That's not constructive; destroys the dirt. Do you know what Quentin Crisp says about dust?'

'Yes,' Louis said. 'You're always quoting him.'

'You can never have too many of the eternal verities,' Joey said. 'I think you could do with losing some weight.'

'I dare say I could,' Louis said.

The flat seemed different to Joey and to Louis. To both of them it was in a part of south London which might be becoming more respectable, or might have become quite as respectable as it ever would, and now would start to become less and less respectable. To both of them these possibilities seemed more or less equal. To other people, although not to each other, they said that the area resembled a village, which it did not. They often described the friendliness of the people who served in the greengrocer's, and the butcher's, and the delicatessen. They mentioned the green space which was convenient, and pleasant to go for walks on. They did not mention that five hundred yards from the place they lived in were streets where men were killed with guns; where women fought with knives over drugs; where children were robbed for five pounds; where suffering was. If these things were mentioned to them, they said merely that nothing had ever happened to them. Nothing had ever happened to them.

For Joey, the flat was principally a room which he was passing through, in which one day he might achieve something. In romantic moods, he said to himself that nothing else mattered, but just to sit and do nothing until he was sure he could achieve something. He didn't know what, and in depressing moods he wondered what would happen if he ever did. He talked about what he might do sometimes; he might write a book. He might learn the piano – there was no piano in the flat – and become a cocktail pianist on a cruise ship. He might learn Spanish and get a lover who might last beyond the end of the month. He might become a management consultant, or get some other job which would supply a pay cheque which would last beyond the end of the month.

Or he could continue to do nothing. He did not need to do anything. He did not need to work to pay the rent, since the dole did that, and the money he had left over from his last job was more than enough for food. He could stay in the flat, and eat from time to time, and that would be perfectly all right. The only clubs he went to were clubs that friends of his ran, and he was on the guest list, and the only drugs he ever took were drugs which friends of his gave him. If he thought about it, he liked the flat, and didn't mind Louis, really.

If Louis took the trouble to think about the flat, there were some parts of his life which seemed quite compatible with the flat, and other parts which he could not imagine ever introducing to it. The shy christian girls who were his friends at university seemed to go with it quite well. They came and they drank tea, or ate their lunches, and they looked around them with a fondness and a nesting in their expressions. None of them had ever met Joey. That was deliberate. They wanted to clean, to tidy, or, failing that, they enjoyed the bachelor squalor of the shared parts of the flat. They never saw Louis's bedroom, which would have shocked them. Dusted twice weekly, with bed made within minutes of his getting up, with three watercolours hung quite straight, a tidy desk, and four bookcases with books ranged in alphabetical order, it had no taint of bachelor, no suggestion of solitary viciousness or lack of care; no invading looseness from the rest of the flat.

Was this quite fair? Was that what Louis was like, in his secret inside? Or, when you got intimate with Louis, was that when he was at his most secret, his most hidden? After all, he could have been like Joey, had he wanted to. He could have been relaxed. And Joey brought men home, though Louis never did. That was a part of his life which was never there, didn't have a place there. No men were ever brought by him. He rationalized it by thinking about how Joey would size up the man he brought home, and talk about him shamelessly, the next day. The neighbours. But it wasn't that. He knew what it wasn't, though he didn't know what it was. He always went with men to their flats, their spaces. And each time he experienced a tiny tremor of fear and lust, the knowledge that *no one knows where I am*. They shut their doors behind him, and he would ask the man, looking at him with unspecific desire, what his name was. And the response was always the same; the response was to carry on looking at him. Just that.

Dear Father, Henry wrote, and then stopped. He had nothing more to say. He wanted truth in his life, or something.

'I don't know how she could bring herself to fall in love with him,' Jane said.

Nancy looked at Jane nervously. They were talking about Francesca.

'He is my brother, you know,' Nancy said in the end.

'He's not very physically appealing,' Jane said.

Nor are you, Nancy thought. It was twenty to three on a Tuesday afternoon. Jane seemed to have forgotten that she had asked Nancy to call round to go shopping, and she ate her breakfast without apparent embarrassment. She was in her pyjamas, which were a week away in either direction from the laundry. Her hair stuck up and was plastered down in more or less equal amounts. 'In any case,' Nancy said, 'she's obviously not that interested in what her men look like.'

'That's absolutely not right,' Jane said. 'She's very interested indeed. They always look exactly the same. They always have glasses, and dress incredibly badly, and are five feet eight, and have hollow chests, and blush and giggle like schoolgirls are supposed to. And they've always been exactly eight years older than her.'

'Henry's not.'

'Minor detail.'

'And he doesn't look like that at all,' Nancy said. It was true, though Nancy was being loyal. Henry was on the whole an elegantly dressed good-looking man.

'He does,' Jane said. 'In his soul. Anyway, that's what she likes them to look like. They always look almost exactly the same. It doesn't matter if they're brainy or not, she just fancies weedy men. Or,' she said, dropping her spoon into her cornflakes, 'men who are weedy in spirit. She just likes the type. After all, what does she know about Henry?'

'What do you mean?' Nancy said.

'I mean, how well does she know him?'

'Presumably,' Nancy said, 'she knows him very well indeed. After all,' she said finally, 'you used to go out with him.'

'True,' Jane said. 'Do you think she's got any idea whether he's intelligent or not? I'm not sure I do.'

'Well, of course he's bright,' Nancy said. 'You're just being deliberately annoying. He got endless O levels and endless A levels and a First and prizes coming out of his ears and he got this high-powered and very brilliant job at the House of Commons. You're just trying to wind me up.'

'Of course I am. The awful thing is that he used to be a proper person and now he's just like all those Clerks. They all go on about how bright they are, but it's like the Princess of Wales's sex appeal, there's no point to it. Really, what have any of them ever achieved in life, really?'

'Well, what have any of us ever done?' Nancy said, quailing a little.

'Nothing, but we don't pretend to be brilliant,' Jane said.

'Henry's supposed to be writing a novel, isn't he?'

'Did he tell you that?'

'No, you did. Henry wouldn't tell me something like that.'

'I'll believe it when I see it. He told Francesca fast enough. I don't suppose you've asked him. But the Clerks – I know there's supposed to be someone my father works with who's produced some incredibly important new version of some poet or other, and someone else who writes about music, but none of them have ever finished anything or achieved anything worth mentioning.'

'But they're brighter than you or me,' Nancy said.

'They're brighter than you,' Jane said. Then she remembered what was left of her manners, and said, 'At least, if they are brighter than I am, I'm not admitting it.'

Then she shut up like a clam. She went to the kitchen to light a cigarette from the stove. Nancy picked up a magazine from the sofa, called *Hello!* She had not seen it before; she flicked through it. It seemed to be awful rubbish, and to be filled with people she had never heard of. Jane's friends understood that the subjects of Henry and unrequited love had to be avoided in her company. That was what they described as the great bore about Jane. She was interested in other people's frustrate passions, and recommended cures confidently – 'Try masturbation,' she said once, over dinner, to Francesca. But when she was reminded of her own affairs, her own single love, she made it apparent that she was offended and wouldn't accept an apology.

'Isn't that your father?' Nancy said, fed up with talking about her brother. John was on the television screen, sitting in front of the Speaker in a wig and gown and a white bow tie, yawning his head off, while Members of Parliament insulted each other in the third person.

'I do feel sorry for him,' Jane said. 'I can't imagine what he thinks about, sitting through all that.'

'Most people just switch off when anything disagreeable happens,' Nancy said. 'Still, it must be a bore, listening to all that, all that venom the whole time. I suppose he just thinks it's quite a separate thing, that part of his life. Does he talk about it much? Henry never does.'

'Not about sitting there, no,' Jane said. 'He once said the chair was uncomfortable. He enjoys the whole thing.

He just likes keeping it to himself, I think. Turn it off, will you?'

'How's your granny?' Nancy said.

'Not very well, actually,' Jane said. 'She's got a horrible cold, or worse. She had the doctor out, and he just said that she should stay in bed and get plenty to drink and call if it was no better.'

'How old is she?'

'Eighty-five,' Jane said. 'She's one of those women who are always said to be marvellous for their age. Well, she is; she's like a marvel that people ought to go and gawp at, like an Aztec pyramid. She'll be all right.'

The streets were filling. It could be seen by those who could see that there were more people in the streets, every month there were more. There were those who came to the city from outside; those who spoke no English, those whose parents had always lived in quiet or ugly English cities. These came and stood in the streets, and looked about them, and thought deeper about what they saw than anyone. And, after a time, some of them went, and some of them, as best they could, tried to make a living with what was at their disposal. There were those who had no need to stand in the streets; those who said to each other that they would not go in the street, that it was no longer safe, that they would now lock their doors, and the doors of their cars, against the street. And yet they stood in the street and walked, and talked to each other on their mobile telephones, and their money was, they hoped, on their faces, like fame. There were those who tried to make a living on the street; some of them succeeded. Some stood and sold things, some tried to sell themselves, some tried to entertain, and some were ordinary one-man businesses, trying to become something else, something more. And below that there were more men than ever before, more men month by month, who lived on the streets, who were always on the streets, because that was where they had to go.

Never before had people lived on the streets of London; never before had people been asked for money; never before had people asked for money. And it was as if shame had disappeared from the sky which had so shaped the city, and the people in it would now do anything. Out there it was Africa. There was a wildness which was made up of individual men, and was driven by the will of many men, but the will of no man was enough to touch it. No one could change it; no politician, no initiative. Because the men on the streets had found a street in themselves, and it was something which had always been there, and nothing, no shame, no fear of being found out, was there to hide it once more. And the streets continued to fill.

'What do you think of Ivy Compton-Burnett?' Henry said to Louis. They were in the Journal Office on a Tuesday afternoon.

'Advanced, forthright, significant,' Louis said.

'Seriously,' Henry said. I'm a great fan of hers, you know. Read them all.'

'I can't believe anyone's read all of them,' Louis said. 'I've read three. I liked the first one but the other two were exactly the same.'

'What have you read?' Henry said.

'*Manservant and Maidservant, Present and the Past, Father and his Fate*,' Louis said.

'They're not remotely the same,' Henry said.

'Yes they are,' Louis said. 'What do you like about them?'

Henry was caught out by this. Not many people questioned his taste; not many people actually wanted to know anything about what he liked. It was the sort of thing Jane used to ask.

'I have favourites,' Henry said, but just then a Member came into the office.

'Can you help me with a Petition?' the Member said.

'My colleague is the expert on Petitions,' Henry said, gesturing with his head in the direction of Louis. The Member took the Petition over to him.

'It's been signed by thirty-two thousand people,' Henry heard the Member say confidentially.

'Henry,' John said. 'Can I have a word or two?'

'Of course,' Henry said. 'Fire away.'

'I have to go out this afternoon, I'm afraid. The Clerk Assistant wants me to talk to some schoolmasters for some reason.'

'You *are* unfortunate, being stuck with these hideous tasks all the time,' Henry said. 'I don't mind at all, unless Louis has some unavoidable invitation to tea or something.' He didn't speak directly to Louis, who was reading the Member's Petition.

'That's all right,' Louis said, with his head down over the Petition. 'I'll be here. No, I'm sorry, there's a problem with this.'

'Why?' the Member said.

'It's not addressed to the House,' Louis said. 'It's asking the Government to take action.'

'What's the problem?' the Member said.

'The Petition has to be addressed to the House as a whole,' Louis said, 'not just the Government. It's asking the House to act, or ought to.'

'So, okay, what needs to be done?' the Member said. 'If I just cross this out, and write –'

'No,' Louis said. 'You'll have to send it back to your constituents and ask them to rewrite it by hand, addressing it to the House.'

'But,' the Member said, 'thirty-two thousand people have signed it.'

'Well,' Louis said, 'perhaps they should have checked the form of words before they started to collect signatures. There's nothing else I can do, I'm afraid.'

'I'm going to raise this with the Serjeant at Arms,' the Member said in a fit of pique, walking out.

'She really is the most ghastly woman,' Henry said. 'You did quite well there, though what she thinks she'll achieve by raising anything with the Serjeant at Arms I can't imagine. Complete waste of time, Petitions.'

'Oh, an utter abuse,' John said. 'Wish we could get rid of them. Louis, I wondered if you would like to come to supper at the weekend, perhaps on Saturday?'

'Yes,' Louis said. 'Let me see. Yes, I would, thank you very much. Saturday looks fine.'

'Would you like to come as well?' John said to Henry.

'No,' Henry said. 'I don't think – no, I can't, I'm seeing my sister.'

'Very well,' John said. 'Just Louis. I'll be going out about three. I may be back around five or so. Incidentally, Louis,

I should go down for Prime Minister's Questions if I were you. It might be interesting.'

He left the office.

'What was all that about?' Louis said.

'Oh, nothing,' Henry said. 'He wants me to marry Jane.'

'Jane?'

'His daughter. You met her.'

'Oh yes,' Louis said, not quite seeing.

'Perhaps he wants you to marry the other one. Don't bother going down for Prime Minister's Questions, by the way, it won't be interesting.'

'I enjoy it,' Louis said. 'And, anyway, everyone tells me all the time that I ought to go and listen to it, so I will.'

'You won't enjoy it in six months' time,' Henry said. 'You'll be bored with it, like the rest of us. We're stuck with this lot for years to come, and this daft old bat at the top of it. Nothing ever changes. You watch.'

'Maybe eventually it does,' Louis said.

'But there's no one else, and as time goes on there are fewer and fewer people,' Henry said.

'It only seems like that when something hasn't changed for so long. But things always have to change sometimes.' He stood up as the Clerk of the House came in. He was going to stand up anyway, but it did no harm.

'Hello there,' the Clerk said. 'I need to find something out a bit urgently. Debates of no confidence. The motion's always in terms of no confidence in her Majesty's Government, isn't it?'

'Always,' Henry said.

'Has there ever been a debate of no confidence in the Prime Minister?'

'I doubt it,' Henry said. 'I can't immediately see why not, but these things are always framed in the same terms, aren't they? And an ordinary no confidence motion would quite naturally turn to the conduct of the Prime Minister.'

'Quite,' the Clerk said, grinding his teeth novelistically. 'I simply wondered whether a debate had ever been conducted on other grounds.'

'There was an occasion,' Louis said, 'when the Government initiated a debate of confidence in itself.'

Henry and the Clerk turned and looked with surprise at Louis.

'Really?' Henry said. 'They must have been deranged.'

'There were special circumstances, I think,' Louis said.

'In any case,' the Clerk said, 'we know that won't happen. Just keeping a step ahead of the game.'

'Several steps, I should have said,' Henry said when the Clerk had gone. 'Though you seemed to be a step ahead of him. No one's suggested that there's going to be a no confidence debate soon. They'd be mad to try it. But how on earth did you know that?'

'Oh,' Louis said. 'I don't know. I suppose I'll have to go and read lots of Ivy Compton-Burnett now.'

'There are worse things in life. Like going to John's for dinner. Well, we live in interesting times,' Henry said, yawning.

The Prime Minister rose to her feet. She seemed to be waiting for silence, but it never came, and in a moment she raised her voice like a contralto and answered the question. That was what she did; treat the hubbub like the ritornello to an aria. Her appearance of patient waiting guarded her need for a moment to think and recall.

'If the right honourable Gentleman would recall the record of his own party in this matter between 1974 and 1979,' she said over the noise, 'he would not be so ready to raise the matter. I can, not for the first time, remind him that the overall burden of direct taxation has fallen significantly and consistently in the last eleven years.'

The Members facing her were beginning to force a chant out of the roar. What was it? 'VAT. VAT.' But they weren't asking questions, just yelling, and she ignored them.

The Leader of the Opposition sat back. He had missed his chance, somehow, he didn't know where. Somewhere between the second question, when she had seemed to be floundering, and the third, which she had answered with a frank neglect of the truth, he had not managed to ask the right question. What was the right question, what would have pinned her down? Even now, he didn't quite know. He grinned, anyway.

A Member from her side was asking a question. It was going to be about roads somewhere.

'I refer my honourable Friend to the answer I gave some moments ago,' she said.

'Order,' the Speaker said, and the noise died like a small noisy animal having its head cut off. 'I want to hear the Prime Minister. I might remind the House that the question is about Dover.'

She corrected herself. 'I last visited Dover three months ago, but have no immediate plans to visit there again.' It was something she never did, a mistake she never made. She tried not to appear thrown or give away her slight annoyance with herself. It just made her appear foolish, and they were already laughing, and it was the one thing she was not, foolish.

The Member, unpromotably boring, began his question.

'May I congratulate my right honourable Friend on the measures she has taken over the last eleven years to ensure,' he said.

She stopped listening, knowing what he was going to say. He sat down complacently and stopped listening to her answer.

'Indeed,' she said. 'My honourable Friend has hit the nail on the head.'

Afterwards, two Secretaries of State met in the tiny lobby behind the Speaker's chair, between the two division lobbies. A lobby no one stood in except doorkeepers; a lobby safe, because everyone walked through it.

'Got a moment?' one of them said.

'Of course,' the other said. They crossed the corridor, colliding with a group of nervous civil servants scurrying from their hole in the Chamber, passed the Foreign Secretary's office, the Prime Minister's office, and went down the staircase by the office of the Clerk of the House. They had both survived, over the previous seven or eight years, endless attempts by the newspapers to have them sacked, and slightly less frequent attempts by the newspapers to have them promoted. There was no reason for this except the boredom of journalists. In fact, they were now both more or less where they had been a decade before, and saw no futility in their histories.

'It can't go on,' the first said, when the door was shut.

'I know,' the other said. 'I know exactly what you mean.'

'Question time's a bit of a knockabout,' the first said. 'Always has been.'

'Not always,' the other said, better informed.

'But still,' the first said, ignoring this, 'it's absolutely no good standing up and telling lies. Not lies, but selective truthfulness, anyway. Let alone all that ancient history. Let alone pursuing all those obsessions in public. The press are bound to just carry on writing about it. Some of the press, anyway, I suppose.'

'Only the bits we're not worried about, who probably won't hit on any serious problems we want them not to know about anyway,' the second said. 'And how many people read those things anyway?'

'Not how many, that doesn't matter,' the first said. 'But who.'

'No, no,' the second said. 'That's precisely it. It is how many read it, or the staff newspaper of the Cabinet Office would be the most important paper in the world. But there is something a bit more serious going on. I agree that telling selective truths, your words, to the House is not exactly on, but I wonder if we'd be worrying about it at all if there weren't other things we were worried about. After all, we all put the best face on things.'

'Exactly,' the first said. 'It's symptomatic. There's this sense of going over and over the old ground and fighting the old battles without really thinking about it all the time.'

'What we have to decide is what exactly the bigger problem is,' the second said. 'There are members of the Cabinet who can see something, who are probably more worried about it than you or me. We all probably have a different diagnosis, but we all probably agree in general terms. As if we were all noticing different symptoms, but we all knew what the single cause of them was. Or most of us, I suppose.'

'I think we do all agree,' the first said.

'The second point we agree on,' the second said, 'is that, whatever the precise nature of the problem, and wherever we lay the blame, it's soon going to become a resigning issue. We've already had one bad one.'

'We've got over that.'

'Wouldn't be so sure. King over the water, that one. And the last thing we want is a mass resignation from the Cabinet, or a lot of junior ministers trying to raise their standing by resigning. But it's what we're heading towards. If there's more experience and talent out of the Government than in, then it starts to snowball. People start to think of throwing in their lot with the next Government rather than be tainted with having been in the last one in its last days. You know how these things work.'

'Yes, though I think that's easily overstated,' said the first. 'After all, what happened in seventy-five – that kind of witch-hunt – isn't remotely likely to happen now.'

'But if people think it might, then that's all that matters.'

'Oh, people, people, that's all crap, what people think. But beyond that, if we're going to start speculating on possible disastrous outcomes of the present situation, and I think everyone else is, so we might as well, we've got to start worrying about what this is going to do to the country. After all, the country hates her. They seem to be quite keen on Europe, keener than we are. But we're supposed to be the Europe-minded lot. She hates it, and she's making fewer and fewer bones about showing it. Imagine being Chancellor or Foreign Secretary, and having to negotiate with that kind of heckling going on the whole time, all that background noise.'

'I like that. I must remember that. Frankly, I don't much care about the country at the moment. We've got a while left. I'm just worried about the Party and the House. That's something we have a reasonable chance of controlling, by whatever means. The country is something we can't control, or not really.'

'So,' the first said. 'We're largely agreed on what the problem is?'

'Well, I think so,' the second said.

There was a pause. The clock in the room was suddenly loud.

'It's the Prime Minister, isn't it?' the first said.

'Yes, I think so. I suspect the whole thing will look completely different when the House comes back from prorogation. I have to go, I'm afraid.'

'Hello, Henry,' Francesca said.

'Hello,' Henry said. 'Francesca.'

'Can I come in?' she said. He gestured silently.

The feelings which Francesca induced in Henry when she stood, unexpected and uninvited on his doorstep on a Saturday morning, and the feelings she induced when he happened to see her at dinner at her father's house were quite different. Unexpectedly seeing her outside his house, Henry thought for a moment of pretending he wasn't in. He suppressed the urge – she might have seen him looking out – but he couldn't suppress the feeling her smile and forward posture induced in him, the scare he felt at her evident belief that he was a seducer, and perhaps her seducer. The feminine mysteries of her behaviour, her bags, her clothes, and the way her face looked beneath the make-up. Her echo, like a scent in the air in a lift, of Jane.

She came into the flat and stood for a moment in the hallway.

'So,' she said. 'I've tracked you down.'

'Yes,' he said. 'People never just drop in, do they? Not that I mind, of course.'

'Not in London,' she said. 'Though I should have thought that people did, here.'

'Not really,' Henry said. 'It seems central, but actually it's a bit of a wasteland.'

'I like it, though, don't you? People dropping in and out?'

'Yes,' he said. 'Yes, so do I.'

He felt as if he were talking to his father in his embarrassed lack of flourish.

'Where shall I go?' she said. All the doors were closed.

'It doesn't matter,' Henry said. 'They're all the same, really.'

'They're all the same?' she said, laughing in a silvery way. 'What do you mean?'

'Nothing,' Henry said. 'In here will do.'

What Henry meant, as he showed her into the room, was that all the rooms were the same. The room he showed her into could have been his bedroom, since it had a bed in it, or at least a sort of divan. But half a wall was covered in books, there was a desk, a sofa and what seemed to be a dining table. Most of these things were also to be found in the other rooms in the flat. Everything was recently dusted, sorted, and, in a sense, immaculate.

'Sorry about the mess,' Henry said. There was a book on the floor. 'I was doing some work.'

'I imagined you were writing your novel.'

'My novel?'

'Yes,' Francesca said. 'Had you forgotten you'd told me about it?'

'Yes,' Henry said. 'Yes, I had.'

'You didn't really,' she said. 'You didn't say much about it. I'd love to read it. When it's finished, of course,' she added.

'No, no,' Henry said. He couldn't remember what on earth he had said about his novel. 'How did you know where I lived?'

'You're in the telephone book,' she said.

'Am I?' he said. 'Aren't there rather a lot of H. Wrights in the telephone book?'

'Not too many,' she said. She looked at him, and a silence fell. He wondered what he would rather talk about.

'Do you get on well with your sister?' he said.

'Jane?'

'Yes.'

'Very well,' she said. 'She tells me everything. Do you get on with your parents? And Nancy?'

'Yes,' he said. 'We often talk. Of course, Nancy lives quite close to here.'

He was aware that the effect Francesca had on him was to damp down his campness. He was like a desiccated version of himself. He could think of nothing to say to her, and he said nothing to her, more or less.

'Good,' she said. 'I'd love to read your novel.'

'Is that why you came round?' he said.

'No, of course not.' She stood up, and went to a picture on the wall.

'It's by Patrick Procktor,' he said. Then he saw that she

wasn't looking at it, and said, 'The picture. You wouldn't really like to read my novel, would you?'

'Of course,' she said. 'Aren't you going to offer me a drink or anything?'

'Would you like a drink or anything?'

'What are you having?'

'Nothing. I mean, anything.'

'Then I'll have the same.'

'Then I'll have a cup of tea.'

When he came back she was running her finger along the shelf of books in the way women do in very bad French films.

'Is it autobiographical?'

'Is what autobiographical?'

'Your novel.'

'In a sense,' he said.

'In what sense?'

'In the sense that everything is,' he said. He didn't actually believe this; he felt he ought to say it, and felt it was expected of him. He wondered what interest Francesca would be showing in his novel if she didn't know him, and then realized how pointless his thought was.

'That's very true. Would you mind me reading it?'

'No, not at all. If I had a copy.'

'I'm flattered,' she said. 'I'm flattered that you trust me like that.'

'Francesca,' he said.

'Yes?' she said. He had no idea what he was going to say.

'Do you know anything about clothes?'

'Not much,' she said. 'I never think much about them.'

That's obvious, Henry thought, surprising himself with

his cattiness. 'I wondered,' he said, 'what you would think about the sort of man who would wear a double-cuffed shirt with a single-breasted suit. I don't know whether you've ever thought about it.'

'I never have,' Francesca said. 'Thought much about it, I mean. I didn't know it was such an issue.'

'It isn't really,' Henry said. 'I was just thinking about it.'

'Is it research for your novel?' Francesca said.

'Oh no,' Henry said. He had nothing else to say.

'I haven't read any Ivy Compton-Burnett,' said Francesca, as she came to the long line of yellow books. She put the emphasis on the last syllable.

'*Bur*nett, I think,' Henry said. 'She's awfully good. Why don't you borrow one. *Two Worlds and Their Ways* is good. You could have some cake, if there was any.'

Dear Father, he wrote later. *I had a girl to tea today. She took a book away with her. I lied and told her that I was writing a book. I am writing nothing. I am doing nothing; I am achieving nothing. When I die, I shall leave nothing to nobody and my friends will die and my children will not exist and I shall not be remembered. This is what the girl reminded me of.*

On her way home, Francesca bought food. It was her night to cook, and a guest was coming. A colleague of her father's. Before she left Henry, she extracted a promise from him to drop in for a drink before dinner. Her motives were not clear, even to herself. To herself she said that she was attempting to bring about a reconciliation between her sister and her sister's former lover. To Henry she said only enough to suggest that he might stay for dinner, if things went well. She decided not to mention it to Jane, in case she decided that she couldn't face him. Which would make things difficult all round.

Henry seemed to accept the invitation, and all the way round the supermarket Francesca tried to remember what he liked to eat. She thought about the odd time when he was so much their relation that they placed no value on him, and she couldn't remember what he ate at all. In Francesca's memory, he and Jane seemed to live on cigarette smoke, on air tainted with fire and mint, like gods.

What Francesca thought about as she walked around the supermarket was not what she would cook; she thought about what she would wear for Henry's benefit. When she reached the queue for the till, she found that what she had bought was the stuff for lasagne. Which was what she normally cooked on Saturday night. There was a tin of raspberries, and a large pot of cream in her trolley, and, in any case, the conversation was more important. In any case, he probably wouldn't stay.

In front of her there was a man who had bought seventeen iceberg lettuces, three watermelons and a tin of cat food. She stored it up to talk about amusingly later.

'What are you grinning at?' Jane said, recumbent with a novel as Francesca came in with her plastic bags. 'Where have you been?'

'To the supermarket. There was a man in front of me with seventeen lettuces in his trolley and nothing else.'

'Perhaps he was Korean,' Jane said, bafflingly.

'And I went to see Henry.'

'Why?'

'No reason,' she said. 'I just felt like seeing him.'

'Did he feel like seeing you, do you think?'

'Well, I think so,' she said. 'He gave me a cup of tea, and showed me his novel.'

'He's writing a novel?'

'He said so the other evening. You never listen to what people say.'

'I never listen to what he says. He never says anything interesting or truthful.'

'Well, he was today. And his novel is brilliant, I'm sure.'

'Everyone sooner or later tries to write a novel. I bet you've started a couple.'

'I don't see the point in telling you anything,' Francesca said. 'He's certainly writing one. He's half-way through it. I've seen it. It's a love story.'

'Is that it there?' Jane said.

'No,' Francesca said, going through into the kitchen and starting to unpack the plastic bags. 'That's a novel by Ivy Compton-Burnett.'

'How romantic,' Jane said. Francesca couldn't hear her, and after a time the dirty smell of supermarket mince frying started to come from the kitchen.

Jane showed no surprise when Henry arrived that evening. She levered herself up slightly, and put her book down on the sofa beside her. She didn't try to get up, or greet him in any way. She just looked at him reproachfully, with all her lack of the feminine signs of shyness and blandness and goodness. No one expected her to blush; Henry wondered why it was so clear to him that she was still in love with him.

'You're getting to be quite a regular,' Jane said. 'I didn't know you were coming. Perhaps I did. Perhaps I wasn't listening properly. Are you staying for dinner?'

'I don't think so,' he said. 'Francesca asked me to come for a drink.'

'You don't think you're staying? I think you ought to make up your mind before too long. It might be too late to get any food.'

'No, I meant no.'

'I'm going to phone Nancy,' Jane said. 'Have you seen her?'

'Yes, she's fine,' he said. He looked at her, and she looked back in a spirit of pure hostility.

'Oh, sod it,' Jane said.

'Henry,' John said. 'I didn't know you were coming. I was upstairs, actually.'

'Do you mind if I smoke?' Henry said.

'Not at all,' John said.

'I'm not staying for dinner,' Henry said. 'Just a drink.'

'Oh, do stay,' John said, 'so that Louis's got someone to talk to.'

'What, that boy in the pub?' Jane said.

'Yes,' Henry said.

'Do you know him?' John said.

'Yes,' Jane said. 'He was with Henry one night. A nice boy. I didn't realize it was him that was coming.'

'I wish you wouldn't read in that way,' John said.

'In what way?'

'You know quite well.'

'Very well,' Jane said. 'Let's start again. How are you, Henry?'

'Very well, thank you, Jane,' he said, joining in.

'You look as if you've put on weight,' she said.

'I don't think so,' he said. 'I will stay for dinner, actually.' He looked at John standing, with his unnatural posture, and he noticed again how he clenched his fists. It occurred to him for the first time that John's hunchback might in some way make this the most comfortable way to hold his hands. But his clenched fists seemed, nevertheless, to hold themselves, as if in panic; and to prepare themselves for the assault which at any moment might come.

Jane got up and went to the window, and was standing there looking at the torn up garden when Francesca came in with her unnatural happiness.

'Supper won't be long,' she said.

'It smells delicious,' Henry said.

'Oh, no, just something I was cooking anyway,' Francesca said. 'And I haven't had time to make bread, or anything.'

'I had no idea anyone still made their own bread,' Henry said.

'Francesca's boasting,' John said. 'I don't think she does either. Oh, the door.'

There was a little scramble to be first to the door. Jane opened it.

'Hello, Louis,' she said.

'What?' Louis said. 'How did you get here?'

'I live here,' she said. 'With my father.'

'Your father?'

'Yes,' she said. 'My father.'

'I had no idea,' John said, 'you knew Jane. Don't keep him waiting there on the doorstep, what must he think of you? Come in, come in, Henry's here already.'

'Oh, is Henry here?' Louis said, already scarlet.

'Yes,' John said. 'First he wasn't coming, then he was. You never quite know with Henry. Never mind. Give your coat to Jane.'

'Don't panic,' Jane said, once her father had gone. 'I'm not going to say anything.'

He muttered an abrupt thanks, and dashed into the drawing room. Jane followed him, more slowly.

'And this is Francesca,' John was just saying. 'My other daughter. How funny that you should have met Jane.'

'Yes, isn't it?' Louis said. The evening went on, in its way.

'Are you married, Louis?' John said at one point.

'He's hardly old enough,' Henry said. 'How old are you?'

'Twenty-five,' Louis said. 'So quite old enough.'

'But you're not,' John said. 'No plans to?'

'No,' Louis said, going scarlet again. It was embarrassing, after all, to be quizzed by John, whose wife was dead, about wives.

'Good,' John said.

'I nearly married once,' Henry said.

'But you didn't,' Jane said.

'No, I didn't,' Henry said. He looked at her. She looked at the table cloth.

'I'll get the pudding,' Francesca said.

'No, I will,' Jane said. She got up and went into the kitchen. Her father followed her, shutting the door.

'Are you all right?' he said to her.

'Yes,' she said. 'Thanks for asking.'

'I was worried,' he said. 'If you just want to go to bed I won't mind.'

'No,' she said. 'I'd rather stay and get it over with. Don't worry; I'll behave.'

'You don't have to behave,' John said. His laugh, when it came, always surprised her.

'Do you live here?' Louis was saying to Francesca when they went back in.

'We both do,' Francesca said. 'We like it, really. It's far nicer than living in some bedsit somewhere.'

'Do bedsits still exist?' Henry said. 'They have a sort of period sound to them, as if people lived in them thirty years ago and don't any more. I can't remember the last time anyone described themselves as living in a bedsit.'

'Perhaps they're called something else,' Louis said.

'Or perhaps,' Jane said, 'you move in too elevated a circle to know anyone who would live in a bedsit in any case.'

'That must be it,' Henry said, not giving way.

'Do you have a job?' Louis said to Jane.

'Neither of us do,' Francesca said. 'I don't know why. I did once.'

'What did you do?' Louis said.

'Well,' Francesca said. 'When I left school I didn't really know what I wanted to do. I thought for a while I wanted to do something creative, but I don't think I knew then what I wanted to do exactly. I do now, of course, but I know now you don't get jobs in the arts, exactly, not creative ones. I didn't know that then.'

'Did you think you became a poet by getting the Job Centre to send your CV in?' Henry said.

'More or less,' Francesca said.

'Do you know now how you become a poet?' Jane said.

'I think so,' Francesca said.

'I don't think anyone ever knows how to become a writer,' Henry said impressively. 'I think you never know how to do it until you've done it, and then you have to learn how to do it all over again.'

'Why?' Jane said. 'What do you know about it?'

'Nothing, of course,' Henry said. 'I wasn't speaking from experience, I was just repeating what I've heard.'

'I hear you're writing a novel,' Jane said. 'Francesca told me.'

'Did you always know what you were going to do as a job?' Louis said suddenly to John.

John went on with his apple for a moment.

'I don't know,' he said eventually. 'I enjoy my job.'

'That isn't really what he asked,' Jane said.

'Still, I do enjoy my job,' John said. 'I was just getting round to answering him. You do interrupt, you know. I honestly can't remember what I wanted to do, or even if I applied for any other jobs when I got this one, it's so long ago. I remember I wanted to be a train driver, I think, when I was a small child.'

'Really?' Louis said. 'That just sounds like the sort of thing people say – what one was supposed to want to be when one was a small child, I mean.'

'And didn't one want to be one?' Jane said.

'No,' Louis said. 'I suppose some small children might conceivably have wanted to be a train driver.'

'I did,' Henry said.

'So did I,' Francesca said.

'Well, that is improbable,' Louis said. 'I wanted to be a dress designer. And I can't imagine you, even if you were eight years old, wanting to be a train driver at all seriously.'

'Actually,' John said. 'I think you're right. I don't think I ever did want to be a train driver, not seriously. I just said it because it's the sort of thing people say, even if it isn't true.'

'So what did you want to be?' Jane said.

'Oh, something quite, quite different,' he said. His usual half-smile broke up into a quick surprising laugh.

'What do you want to be when you grow up?' Jane said to Henry.

'I thought I was grown up,' he said.

'I thought you were, too,' Jane said.

'We never found out,' Louis said, 'what Francesca did as a job.'

'Oh, she worked in some shop or other,' Jane said. 'How dare you treat me like this.'

'I don't know what you're talking about,' Henry said.

'You know quite well,' Jane said.

'Which shop?' Louis said.

'Harvey Nichols,' Francesca said in a rush. 'Upstairs in the women's department. Jane, don't go.'

'I'm only going to the lav,' Jane said, over her shoulder as she left the room. 'I want,' and she turned and she looked for one second, and it was quite enough, at the whole silent table of them, looking, 'to piss.'

'The thing,' Francesca said after a moment. 'The thing was, I wasn't very interested in clothes, and I didn't know much about them. I managed somehow to get myself dolled up in smart outfits and look reasonable – at least, reasonable in Harvey Nichols terms, I thought, to be honest, I looked rather awful – but after I'd got myself dolled up and stood around on the second floor, some customer would come up and say, I like this dress, but do you have something very very similar but with a more A-liny sort of skirt, and not so many tucks. And then I was completely lost, and had to go off and ask some-body else.'

'It's just a matter of getting the right vocabulary,' Henry said.

'Yes, that's very true,' Francesca said. 'No, I just don't think clothes are a very serious sort of thing to think about.'

'Oh,' Henry said. 'They're the only serious thing in the world, I sometimes think.'

'What do you mean?' Louis said.

'What do you mean, what do I mean?' Henry said.

'I mean, what do you mean?' Louis said.

'You always say that, and I never mean anything by what I say, except what I say,' Henry said. 'I mean, clothes are the only serious thing in the world, they are, really they are. Because they're the only thing we can use to show what we're like to people who don't know us. Which is everyone, really, in statistical terms. The number of people we don't know makes the number of people we do know statistically negligible. And they're the only thing we have to understand people we don't know, until we meet them. Which is everyone. And when they wear out –'

'Clothes, or people?' Jane said, coming back.

'Clothes, clothes, we're talking about clothes,' Henry said. 'When clothes wear out, and when you have to throw out some favourite pair of trousers or something, they just remind you that nothing is for ever, and everything comes to an end, and everything has to be thrown out in the end. Not just clothes.'

'Except these shoes,' John said. 'I've had them since 1967 and I just have them resoled every now and again and they're perfectly all right.'

'Your trouble is,' Henry said, and then he faltered, and he faked a cough, and he would not finish the sentence, because what he had been about to say was that John's trouble was that he could never accept the fact of death.

'Whatever are we talking about?' Jane said.

'Clothes,' Francesca said. 'Though I can't imagine why.'

'Oh, I love clothes,' Jane said. 'Not this shirt, it wants a wash. But I like clothes. I don't understand why people think clothes are a silly subject of conversation. There's something really magical about a whole row of coats in a shop, waiting for all those people to come and take them away, and all looking exactly the same for the moment. I have to say I can't often be bothered with them. I mean I can't often be bothered to get dressed, not seriously.'

'Or at all,' Francesca said. 'That's exactly what Henry was saying.'

'Not exactly,' Henry said.

'What are you doing tomorrow?' Jane said to Louis.

'Er, nothing,' Louis said.

'The thing is,' Jane said. 'The thing is, I don't know what I'm doing tomorrow. I mean not exactly.'

'No, nor do I,' Louis said.

'Do you want to go out for a drink or something?' Jane said.

'Yes, why not,' Louis said.

Afterwards, when he got home, Louis ran a bath and thought about the evening. Joey was entertaining a noisy bodybuilder; their cries of ecstasy could be heard in the hallway of the block of flats. John had spent most of the time asking Louis about his girlfriends, his fiancées, his wives. He seemed obsessed with this imaginary harem, and didn't stop until all possibility of women in Louis's life had been excluded. 'Ah,' he had said. For Louis this demonstrated that, if Jane had now no intention of telling her father he was homosexual, it was because she had already done so.

'You just want the different parts of your life to stay apart,' Joey had once said. 'But life is always coming together in unexpected ways. Look at that boy I used to work with who ended up at the Fridge that night you came.'

'That's not surprising,' Louis said.

'No,' Joey said. 'You can't separate people in the way you want to. You can't separate the way you treat people like that.'

'Oh, I know,' Louis had said, not minding.

Now, waiting for the bath to run, he took the middle pages out of that day's newspaper on the kitchen table. He never understood why Joey got it, since he never read it; he did not understand that it was a small piece of kindness on Joey's part, to get the sort of newspaper he thought Louis would like to read. Louis started to read; he read the pontifications of celebrity columnists about their husbands, their children, their curtains, Northern Ireland, the state of the world, the state it was in, and the certainty that the resignation of the Leader of the House would have absolutely no effect on the personal standing of the Prime Minister.

He read about all this while his bath ran. Alone, with the noises of sex in the next room, he put his hand inside his dressing gown and felt his stomach. He had never taken enough of his clothes off in the open air in the summer to become brown, and his flesh was pastry-grey and abundant. He took a handful of his stomach's flesh and pulled at it. It seemed to move quite away from his bones, and he imagined what it would be like to scoop away at the flesh, dropping great ice cream dollops of flesh and lard on the floor, and leave nothing but skin and hair and effortless beautiful bones behind. Like a haircut, the jellied waste would lie on the floor, and the good would come behind him, and sweep it up, and burn it.

The strange thing about Louis's fatness was that it did not make him less physically attractive. He had never had any difficulty persuading strange men to go to bed with him. He could not account for this, and neither could the men who went to bed with him. They said, often, that there was something mysteriously appealing about Louis; about his eyes; about his evident desire; about his passivity. They said that there was something about him which suggested that he would be a tremendous fuck. It was not clear that they were correct, and, even as they said it, they often wondered what had led them to this belief.

There were a number of things Louis thought about when he had nothing in particular to think about, which was usually. His weight was one of them. He knew he would do nothing about his weight but complain about it. He knew, though his weight shocked him unceasingly, that it would take the onset of a serious wasting disease or the development of a drug-taking habit to rival Joey's before he became very much thinner. The second thing Louis thought about was his money. When his father died he had been left with twenty thousand pounds a year. When he had been an undergraduate, and a graduate, this had seemed like an enormous sum of money. Most people he knew had the student grant to live on, which was a tenth of what he had. His money made him hugely popular, but it just filled Louis with dread. Unlike his friends, he could see that his money would not stay as it was for ever; could see the limits to it; could see that he needed a job to make the money last. And this is what he had. The third thing, of course, he thought about when he had nothing else to think about was his hair.

Louis spent a great deal of time and money looking after his hair. He had a collection of shampoos and conditioners and hair oils and hair waxes and hair putties and hair reconditioners. They were scented with fruit and flowers and herbs and nuts and cactuses, whatever they smelt like. They were to be used once a day, twice a day, twice a week, once a week, once a month, once a year. Some were for greasy hair, some were for dry hair, some were for normal hair, and some were for combination hair which was greasy at the roots but dry at the ends. Louis bought a new hair preparation every week, or whenever he felt unhappy or bored. He looked after it, and he felt that it was beautiful. He often felt his hair, felt its silkiness and its high polish and finish, like a racehorse. But the only person who ever commented on its beauty was the handsome Cypriot in Covent Garden who, once a month, cut it, whom Louis, for this reason, loved a little. It was as if Louis were aware of his appeal, and the way men found him attractive, and because he was incapable of accounting for it, sought to bring one part of himself to such a pitch of perfection so that he could blame that for his futile desirability. Sometimes he thought that, though no one ever commented on it, his hair's beauty and perfection were somehow influencing them, without their knowing. That they could not sleep with him for no reason, or for an intangible reason, and the reason they slept with him was his hair.

So he lay in the bath with a new hair putty on his head, and listened, and tried to think of the dark Italian man, a *marchegiano*, of his Italian dreams, and not to think of the dinner, or his body, or to assess his beliefs. They were nonsense, of course, his beliefs. There is never any reason for one man to make himself vulnerable by offering himself to another man.

The day before, the Leader of the House had written to the Prime Minister. She stood and she read his letter of resignation, and, although she was busy, she read it again. She thought and she read it again. She thought she was happy, perhaps, and she thought she was right. Her private secretary came into the room.

'Prime Minister,' he said. He knew before she did. Elsewhere, journalists were sitting in front of black screens, writing down the views that they were formulating as they wrote, for Louis and Joey and Jane and Francesca and John and Henry to read, though not all of them did read their views, or remembered them when they had read them.

Jane came to the huge thick doors of the public entrance to the House of Commons. There was a policeman there who looked at her. There was a queue to get into the galleries to watch the debates, and there was another queue just to get into the central lobby to try to see a Member of Parliament to complain about your life. But Jane didn't queue, and when the policeman looked at her, she just said, 'I've come to see Mr Wright,' and he let her through, as if she hadn't made a joke.

Inside, there was a huge contraption of airport security in the cold medieval hall, through which everyone had to go.

It would detect metal weapons and plastic explosives, but not much else, and many things which people habitually use to kill or hurt each other would have passed through it without electronic comment. Jane observed the machine drily, but it didn't object to her, and she had no bag for it to object to.

She had almost never come to the House of Commons. John never asked his daughters to dinner there, and Jane was not a girl who would push in order to suffer, unlike Francesca. And since Henry started working there, she would not have wanted to go there. Much.

In the central lobby, she spoke to a man in a black coat and white bow tie, who telephoned Henry. He asked for her name, and then, after a moment more, told her that Henry couldn't come down for fifteen minutes. She told him that she would wait, and he relayed this information. They nodded at each other, and she sat down in the lobby to wait.

The lobby seemed to her like a nightmare in which the normal variety of humanity, the ordinary differences between people had been erased in favour of a uniform and crippled nature. There were one hundred and twenty people on crutches. They dragged themselves between two poles like terrible avenging water birds. The effort was too much for some of them, and they sweated. Some of them smiled, and were cheerful, and that was too much for Jane. She watched them walk and stumble as she waited for Henry.

'Is it always like this?'

'No,' Henry said. 'Some days it's tramps, and other days it's miners or pregnant women or Tibetans.'

'Why are they all here, anyway?' she said.

'Well, they want to see their Member, to put their case.'

'Does it achieve anything?'

'I suppose it must, or they wouldn't do it. Maybe they would anyway. It's hard to say. It's nice to see you, you know, but what can I do for you?'

'You could always give me a cup of tea,' Jane said. 'Preferably somewhere I'm allowed to smoke.'

They walked away from the crowd of the crippled. They were not allowed to leave the large octagonal room; they were not allowed to do anything but stand there. It was not Jane's habit to admire any building – to admire anything, in fact – or comment on her surroundings, and it was left to Henry to comment on the pictures in the corridors and the glimpses of the outside walls and protuberances of the famous building. Jane said nothing; she may have nodded.

'It's Francesca, actually,' she said. 'You've been seeing quite a lot of her, haven't you?'

'Well,' Henry said. 'I don't know why, really. I've seen her a few times recently. She came round on Saturday. I see her from time to time.'

'That's quite a lot,' she said. 'You see, I know she wouldn't tell you this herself, so I think I ought to tell you.'

A familiar feeling of nervousness was evidently coming over Henry, judging by his fingering of his tie. Jane observed this, as she took advantage of it.

'Tell me what?'

'I don't think you should take it too seriously,' Jane said.

'Well, I don't,' Henry said. 'If you mean what I think you do.'

'I do,' she said. 'She's already got a boyfriend, you see.'

'I see,' Henry said. 'I think you're making a bit of

a mistake telling me this, if you don't mind me saying so.'

'I was worried about that,' she said. 'But, you know, if you have brothers and sisters – I don't know how you feel about Nancy –'

'No, you have no idea,' Henry said, blushing.

'If you have brothers and sisters, you actually want to act for the best for them. Sometimes it seems like a bad or stupid way to act – to other people, anyway – or clumsy. I'm just telling you something so that you know what the situation is so that you won't hurt her. I just don't want her to be hurt.'

'Well,' Henry said. 'That's all very well. Do you want me to thank you?'

'No,' Jane said. 'I don't expect anything at all. I'm just acting in the way I think I ought to. I'm just acting in Francesca's best interests.'

'Well, I'm very seriously annoyed,' Henry said. He got up. 'Just think about it. If we can't behave better than this to each other, I don't see the point in carrying on talking to each other. It's that way to the way out.'

Jane was walking along the street outside the Palace five minutes later with her head back when Louis stopped her.

'What's so funny?'

'Funny?' she said. 'Nothing, why?'

'Why are you laughing?' he said. 'Do stop it, people are staring.'

'Oh, I don't care,' Jane said. 'They always stare at you, anyway.'

'No they don't. But why are you laughing?'

'Telling lies always makes me laugh,' she said. 'I've just

done the funniest thing. I love it. Anyway, I thought you weren't speaking to me after the dinner from hell?'

'Not at all,' Louis said. 'It wasn't your fault.'

'Well, we were supposed to go out for a drink the next day and you never called me.'

'No I didn't. I'm sorry. I thought you'd forget.'

'I never forget anything. I've just seen Henry.'

'Now, I did think you weren't speaking to him.'

'Not at all, we spoke just now, and the other night, and in April I spoke to him on the telephone, for some reason. There was some other time as well, since April.'

'Do you want a cup of tea?'

'No thanks,' she said. 'I've just had one. But you could ask me out for a drink, not now, but just so long as you mean it this time.'

'All right,' Louis said. 'Six o'clock tomorrow, central lobby?'

'No,' Jane said. 'I'm not coming here again. I can't stand all those cripples, if you want to know. I hate waiting there. Seven o'clock, Dome. Can we go to a gay bar?'

'All right,' Louis said, looking round in case there was anyone he knew. 'Cripples? Look, I've got to go now.'

'All right. Why are you all so immaculate?' Jane said.

'I never used to be,' Louis said. 'But I've changed.'

'Well, I change my clothes from time to time as well,' Jane said, beginning to laugh again at her own joke, and at Henry, so cross at her act. She looked forward to a good lie down and a drink and laughing herself sick.

Henry walked up the stone staircase which echoed with his angry step. He listened to it as he stomped, and he felt a little detached from his rage. In the office, there was only a note on his desk from John. All it said was

'I shall be out of the office until late in the afternoon. I am talking to some visiting Clerks.' Henry observed to the Senior Vote Writer that John was often talking to visiting Clerks, but then noticed that he was asleep. He wondered about John's daughters, who seemed to be making a habit of visiting him uninvited for cups of tea. For a moment he thought that Francesca was worse than Jane since at least a cup of tea with Jane only lasted until the insults grew too much to bear, which often wasn't long. A cup of tea with Francesca, on the other hand, might well last until she fell out of love with him. But Francesca was nicer, ultimately, probably; she deserved the chance to be not as bad as her sister, he thought penitentially.

And John was at that moment sitting on Giacomo's legs with a bottle of oil. Face down, Giacomo dreamt of men, of beaches, of the sun and sand and tired inexhaustible props of the usual mind's eye pornography. John dribbled the cold oil down the soft straight spine. Down the involuntary, delicious shudder, and Giacomo, to his mild surprise, found it not difficult to incorporate John's face in the mind's movie; not an imagined straightened version, but John himself, with all his kindness. It was not always possible to do this with his other clients. There was something about this pleasant, considerate, attractively clean middle-aged man which suggested that he was not thinking of his own pleasure all the time, was in fact that rare and unexpected thing, a sexual partner.

John pressed the tender palm of his hand against Giacomo's shoulders. He placed the two palms around the latex softness of Giacomo's neck, and left them there, as if to allow

Giacomo to trust him. In him there was no rage; there was no suppressed anger; just for once. He knew what he could do now. He knew he could do the worst thing in the world. And he knew Giacomo would trust him to do it, and he knew that he trusted him not to do it. His hands around the soft warm throat. He let the nervous tense grip move away down his arm, its tightness like the feeling of love in the depths of the stomach. The hand moved over the dark smooth skin, down the back, the impossible narrowness of the hips, the secret and trusting parts, and he moved away. He noticed a small blemish on the left arm, like a purplish flaking spot. It made him perfect, and if John had known what it meant, he would have felt just the same, that moment. He thought the word, LOVE, and, with one finger on Giacomo's broad shoulders, he wrote the word LOVE, four letters, between the armpits.

'What are you doing?' Giacomo said.

'What would you like me to do?' John said.

Giacomo told him.

Afterwards, they lay together, naked. A dream, or a memory, or a thought, came to John. What came into his mind was an afternoon. It came all at once, the hours and minutes compacted, as if into a box. It was an afternoon he spent with his wife, a year or two before she died. It wasn't the best time, or the worst time they ever spent together. It would be difficult to pin those down, isolate them from ordinarily good or awful times. They happened – they must have happened – but they happened at an end of a series of not very good or not very bad afternoons; just like this one.

'I can't believe you've never been to Chiswick,' she said, raising her voice, although he was just there.

'Well, I haven't,' he said. 'I don't know why. I know it's supposed to be a beautiful house. I never seem to be going near there, somehow. When did you go there?'

'I go there all the time,' she said. He didn't believe her; he knew she didn't spend the afternoons in the week going to art galleries and beautiful old houses. She just thought she did, and she thought other people believed her when she said she did. But although he knew she was lying, it reminded him that he went to work in the week, and then, what did she do?

It was a Saturday afternoon. What she called 'the girls' were out. Or one was out and the other sleeping upstairs. They were alone together after lunch, and talking about Chiswick.

'It's unusually beautiful,' she said exaggeratedly, 'and so tiny. We must go there some time.'

'Let's go now,' John said. 'Why not? We never go anywhere.'

'I don't feel like it now,' she said. 'I don't know why. And we do go to places. We went to Kenwood, for that concert, only the other day.'

'Last summer.'

'Perhaps it was. I'd love to go to Chiswick, I really would, but next week.'

'That would be nice,' he said. 'I have nothing to do, this afternoon. We could do anything you wanted to. We could go upstairs.'

'No,' she said, her customary refusal of the customary euphemism. 'I don't really feel like doing anything.'

What was that tone, that voice she used then? It was incredible how well memory conveyed a tone of voice, a slackness or tightness in the vocal cords only, a speed of speaking. He couldn't remember with any exactness the words she used; but as he lay here waiting for Giacomo to move across him, he heard the noise of her civil scorn, her showing him, unplanned, how little she relished his company, his body, his desire. Not that he felt like going upstairs either. What he wanted was something he did not feel he could ask her. He wanted her Chiswick. He wanted, not to go to Chiswick with her, but for her to talk him through it. He wanted to lie next to someone building a palace in words, a beautiful tiny one, in beautiful tiny grounds, in the words they spoke. As they spoke, the tiny palace in its tiny grounds would expand like a Japanese shell flower dropped in water, would expand in his mind. He could never say that to her, now; and he could never have told her this, told her his definition of love, not then.

The afternoon went on, he supposed. Perhaps one daughter woke up, and the other came back in a red cloak with cheeks red from the wind. The washing-up must have been done; the cooking for the next meal must have been embarked upon. And in the gap between these daily acts, now forgotten, was desire, which they then forgot. What remained was a moment's lapsed tone of voice and the way it would not stay in the moment. It would not be separated from the love and warmth he must have felt. It spread like salt in a stew, until his marriage seemed to him, now, one long revelation of her boredom. His inability to ask her to talk to him in a way they would both have enjoyed.

'You fell asleep,' Giacomo said.

'For a moment,' John said. 'I'm sorry. I've been here for over an hour. You should have woken me up.'

'That's all right. I like looking at you when you go to

sleep. You're so quiet. I like having you here when there's nothing else to do.'

John was embarrassed and could not look at him. He did not know what he meant.

'You know what I mean,' Giacomo said.

They lay back together. Giacomo's hand along John's side. Happiness. The noise of soft flesh stroking against soft flesh. Quiet.

'Will you talk to me?' John said.

'Of course.'

'Tell me about a place I don't know.'

Giacomo puffed histrionically, as if at an unreasonable demand. For a moment, John thought he would not say anything, then he started to tell him about the town he came from.

'I don't think you could know the town I come from. No one does. No one goes there. My father and mother live in a flat in the town centre. You can see the volcano from one window in the flat, and from another you could see the sea, except there's a building in the way, and you can only see that wall. My brother the boxer, I told you about, he lives in a flat where you can see the sea but not the volcano, and he says he wants to see the volcano, to see what it's doing. But he's crazy. I like to see the volcano, too. It's everywhere. The building we live in is black like coal, and it's made out of stone from the volcano. I don't know the word. When you go out of town into the country, all the earth is black from the volcano, and it looks like earth, it looks soft, but if you fall down you cut yourself and hurt yourself pretty bad. It's sharp like metal. There's a church next to where they live, my parents, and it drives my parents crazy sometimes, but then they closed it three years to mend it, and the bells shut up, and my father's crazy because there's no noise. My mother, she's gone crazy too, with my father complaining about everything, and she's right.

'It's so quiet. I thought London was quiet, but it's noisy. Only now it's quiet. But in Italy there's always silence. And outside the window there's a big tree, so big you can't see the sun in the street, and there's this beautiful smell in the summer from it, like I don't know what. No, I mean, not all summer; but when in the summer it rains, at the end of the summer, there's this wonderful smell from, like, nothing. And in the courtyard on the other side of the flat, there's a lemon tree and two orange trees. I never smell that smell you get from trees, not here.'

He had stopped for a moment. Perhaps to think.

'Do you speak to your family?'

Giacomo shrugged.

'They know your telephone number?' John said.

'Yes,' Giacomo said, puzzled. Then he laughed, in a small volcanic uproar, realizing what he meant, or perhaps only thinking he knew what John meant, and recognizing a thought of his own. 'You mean the message on the machine, the Hi, I'm Luigi, you can fuck me, message. No, I've got another telephone they know the number of.'

He couldn't say 'a number they ring,' and it was as if he saw something about himself, or about John; that he wouldn't lie to John about the silent telephone, or about anything else.

'Why have two telephones?' John said.

'One for people I love,' Giacomo said. Then a flicker of cruelty crossed his face, and he said, 'And one for people like you.'

John accepted it, deserving no better, and, since it was

only a flicker, Giacomo regretted it before he had finished saying it. They recognized goodness in each other, and, lying there like lovers do, they waited for each other to speak, and, as they waited, they listened to the surprising whispers and rustles and noises another body made, when it was next to them. Neither of them had known about it, before. It was the ninth time John had been to Giacomo, and they had given up pretending that they had never met before; that John was not one of Giacomo's regulars; that Giacomo was not John's only regular.

'I don't know why I did it,' Louis said. 'But it's too late to get out of it now.'

Henry and Louis were leaving the Palace at the same time. Their briefcases were under their arms, and they had a swift head-down semi-trot. They talked out of the corner of their mouths, and they did not look at each other as they walked. From time to time, a colleague or acquaintance walked by them. In accord with a doctrine of Clerks, they did not greet them, but simply looked quizzically at them. A bald man with a beard, a Clerk of great self-esteem and smooth expensive vulgarity, now approached them and, like a smooth investigating shark, veered away.

'Who's that?' Louis said, recognizing the deliberate non-acknowledgement of the Clerk.

'Roger,' Henry said.

'What's he like?'

'Unusually silly,' Henry said. 'You'll regret it, getting to know her. Sometimes I see her and she seems just the same as she was when I first knew her. If she was like that all the time, I would see her all the time. But she isn't. She was so offensive to me this afternoon. What do you think I should do?'

'I'm sure it will be fine,' Louis said uncertainly. He was not used to these kind of confidences; he was not prepared to exchange confidences in return. He did not believe Henry; he thought it was more likely Henry had changed than Jane. He disliked being asked for his advice on a matter he knew nothing about. But it was part of Henry's manner to ask advice on his personal affairs, on a bank to use, on the desirability of a tie he was wearing. Some people thought this was a way of eliciting compliments; others had already been put off by the scrupulousness of his person; but a third group of people would perceive a likeable vulnerability in Henry. This is what he thought. But he was wrong. Henry was not vulnerable, and Louis was right not to go along with it.

'You see, I was close to marrying her once,' Henry said. 'But she just seemed to change so much, there was no point to it. And I suppose once that sort of thing happens to you, you never really trust anyone again.'

'I see,' Louis said. 'How has she changed? In what way?'

'Just after I started work here.'

'How, I meant.'

'Oh, in every way. You saw her the other night,' Henry said. 'That's what she's always like now. She used to be great fun, you know. I remember when one of us had a car once, she was always saying Let's go to London or Let's go to Cambridge, and we would, just for the evening. You've no idea how fast that seemed then. She was quite a ringleader. But now I think John is right to be worried about her. She just sits at home with Francesca and they just sit and never do anything.'

'I don't know,' Louis said. 'I don't really know her.'

A bus arrived just then and Henry got on it without quite saying goodbye. Louis thought about Jane walking along the street laughing. She had not, really, changed, it seemed; it was just that Henry was no longer shown a side that was fun. But Louis wondered if the side that was fun was altogether worth the candle. It meant being scared of what Jane would do next; what insults or food she would throw. It meant walking in the street with someone making quite a spectacle of themselves. Jane had not changed her undergraduate manner; it was Henry that had changed.

The bus Henry was on was only going to Trafalgar square. Louis really was going to Trafalgar square, but he walked up Whitehall. The bus moved so slowly in the thick traffic that from time to time Louis overtook it, and saw Henry sitting downstairs with his stiff bag on his lap. Around him, in their cars, men tapped their hands on the steering wheel as they did not move; others were more frustrated, and shouted; others were still more frustrated, and hit their heads on the wheel, and wept; and they did this every day. Louis did not vent annoyance. From time to time the bus overtook Louis, and Henry saw Louis with his head-down, already Clerkly stride. They did not wave or acknowledge each other, as people with less of a sense of shame might have done, and they moved forward and back past each other with an assumed innocence of each other. Louis didn't think that he might not have asked the right questions; he didn't think for one moment about Henry and Jane, although these were the things which Henry imagined him to be thinking about as he walked.

He was deep in thought and didn't at first hear when John, who had returned to the office for half an hour before leaving again, hailed him from behind.

'Hello,' he said again. 'Hello.'

'Oh, John, hello,' Louis said. 'I was just thinking.'

John was not someone to ask what Louis was thinking about.

'You've certainly arrived at an interesting time,' John said. 'When I started work, the most interesting thing that happened for years was the Secretary of State for Defence having to resign. He lied to the House, of course, you know.'

'Really?' Louis said. 'Is it really more interesting than usual? I assumed it was always like this.'

'Oh yes,' John said. 'She might be in serious trouble.'

'I've always assumed that she would be there for ever,' Louis said.

'Everything changes,' John said. 'And they remain the same, in a way. But when things change for ever they always change much more quickly than you expect. I think she'll probably get through this. We all thought she was holed below the water over that helicopter business, and she just sacked a few people and the Opposition didn't seem to understand what the issue really was, and she came through all right.'

'But when she does finally go, won't it be something like this?'

'Maybe,' John said. 'I don't know really. I can't see her resigning under any circumstances whatsoever, to tell you the truth. Or what would force her to resign. I think if they lost an election she'd probably refuse to go, hang on to the seals and squat.'

'Do you think they're going to lose the next election?' Louis said.

'Haven't the foggiest,' John said. 'Really, that depends on the electorate, who have no idea at all why they vote or for what reasons, and in any case the whole thing is completely beyond speculation. General elections are interesting when they're actually happening, but speculation about them, other than speculating when the Prime Minister might decide to set one, is utterly boring. It's really not something we know anything about at all.'

'When do you think the next one will be?'

'Haven't the faintest idea.'

They walked on in silence for a while.

'Or rather,' John went on, 'I suppose there might be a war, a little one over this invasion, and then she'd be hugely popular and she'd call a shameless khaki election. I suppose.'

'Thank you so much for dinner the other night,' Louis said.

'That's all right,' John said. 'Glad you could come. Sorry Jane was misbehaving.'

'Oh, I didn't notice,' Louis said. 'I like Jane.'

'Some people find her difficult,' John said. 'Of course, I don't.'

'Look,' Louis said. 'Is that man waving at you? That very good-looking man?'

On the other side of the road, there was a tall, muscular, dark man waving in their general direction. He looked delighted to see whoever he was waving at. He was beautiful and happy; it was incredible to both of them that such a man could be waving at either of them. It was Giacomo.

'It's someone I know,' John said, waving back. 'Do you think he's very good-looking?'

'Yes, of course he is,' Louis said. John did not look embarrassed or cross, or shocked. He looked pleased to see Giacomo, and that was all. He was pleased; pleased at his breach of confidentiality, his lack of professionalism; he was pleased Giacomo was pleased to see him, in the street. He almost lied, and then, he did not.

'This is a young friend of mine,' he said. 'And this is a colleague of mine. It's very nice to see you.'

'Where do you come from?' Louis said, not knowing Giacomo's name.

'I come from Italy.'

'Do you live in London?'

'Yes,' Giacomo said.

'Where are you going?' John said.

'I left the flat for a walk,' Giacomo said. 'It was such a nice day; a pity to be stuffed inside.'

'Oh, I quite agree,' John said. 'A very nice day.'

'Do you work here?' Louis said.

'Oh, no,' Giacomo said. He looked at Louis with his strange intense unaverted gaze. Both of them saw this, with different emotions.

'Are you on holiday? Oh, you said you lived in London.'

'No, I'm a student.'

'What do you study?'

Giacomo seemed not to understand.

'He's here to study English,' John said. 'He knows Jane. That's how we know each other. She talks to him once a week in English.'

'Is Jane improving your English?' Louis said. 'She might not be the best model.'

'Oh, nonsense,' John said, looking at nothing except the pavement and speaking at top speed. 'It's perfectly good, the way Jane speaks, when she makes an effort.'

'Well, I'm actually on my way to meet Jane now,' Louis said. 'Perhaps you should come along and have a drink and practise with her. Although perhaps she might object to talking to you for nothing.'

'Oh,' John said, to stop Giacomo saying anything at all, 'she doesn't do it for money, she doesn't mind. But it's best to keep to one hour a week or soon they'll just sit in pubs and giggle, they have to have a regular time and not start meeting each other outside that. Isn't that right.'

'Yes,' Giacomo said. 'I can't come and say hello to her, I'm afraid. Give her my love.'

'Where are you going?' John said.

'Nowhere,' Giacomo said. 'Just walking.'

'Well,' John said. 'I'll see you soon, I imagine.'

'Come round soon,' Giacomo said. 'Next Tuesday at four o'clock.'

'Won't you be at work?' Louis said, liking the way Giacomo overdid the whole thing. He had understood almost everything, from the way they looked at each other.

'Yes, of course,' John said. 'You mean Saturday.'

He turned quickly and crossed the road, expecting, perhaps, Louis to come with him. But Louis went on walking, and did not even see John go, until he had gone. And Louis was walking with the most beautiful man in the world, just for the moment. The flesh and blood and skin and smile of perfection was walking by him, with apparent contentment; when they passed men, they would gaze at Giacomo. And he deserved to be gazed at.

Giacomo looked after John, crossing the road, with a strange absentness. Louis had to stop to let him catch up. It was the next five or six sentences which Giacomo spoke which Louis would remember for the rest of his life; and remember as a chance he should never have missed, and remember as five or six sentences attached inseparably to the unforgettable, belovable face.

'Would you like to go for a drink?' Giacomo said.

'Yes, of course. I think that I would like that,' Louis said. 'Do you know where there is a bar near here, perhaps?'

'I think I can show you.'

'Do you want to come for a drink with Jane?'

'He,' Giacomo said meditatively, 'is clever. But maybe he isn't clever enough. No, just with you. Let's go. Forget about your Jane.'

'I can't,' Louis said. 'I promised. Tomorrow let's do it. Call me. I just can't now.'

He was driven by fear, as we all of us are. He was afraid of Jane, and afraid of a man he did not know, and he was afraid of John, and the heavens knew what. Giacomo looked at him in no surprise, and agreed. At the look, in his eyes, as he took Louis's telephone number, Louis saw that he was wrong; he saw that Jane would forgive him this; he saw that Giacomo was a good man; he saw that Giacomo was the best man; he saw that he was going to make – had already made – a mistake which could never be put right. He turned left, where Giacomo turned right, and walked to Piccadilly Circus and back, until it was time to meet Jane. He had no choice; his choices had supplied him with none.

They did not go to a gay bar, Louis and Jane. They met in a bar where heterosexual couples went, and they looked quite like a heterosexual couple, quite like. They had dinner, which Louis, flushed with largesse, paid for. All the evening he thought from time to time about Giacomo – all the rest of his life, from time to time, he thought about Giacomo, whose name he did not then know, whose name he only found out when everything possible had changed, who was too perfect a fulfilment of, not his every desire, but his sexual desire only, too perfect to be followed, to be spoken to, to be fucked by, to live with. He thought of him, perhaps going to a bar, on his own, with two beers before him, drinking one, and then the other, alone. Then going home, unhappy.

In this he was quite wrong. Giacomo waited on the pavement as Louis walked away.

He was not surprised, and he did not take it as a personal rejection. He knew that he was a good man, and that he would be the best man for many men, and not just Louis, and perhaps not just John. He also knew that John was the best man for him. He knew these things calmly, without conceit. He rejected men himself, although not from fear. He knew the gradations and degrees of rejection well.

But that was it.

That night, that weekend, many men said in the course of it that it would go down in history. They had the sense of something momentous happening. There was a series of telephone calls between Members of Parliament; between Ministers; between Ministers and civil servants; between parliamentary private secretaries; between journalists; and between all these people. They talked about something they had anticipated for many years, some of them. The impending departure of the Prime Minister.

Some of them looked forward to it; the comment of one Member, an earl, that the Prime Minister was an old cow, was revealed and discussed in newspapers, even newspapers which thought the comment to be true and justified. Some thought the departure of the Prime Minister would be a terrible thing, and talked of it in terms of her murder, or her helplessness.

None of them considered that, if she went, the Prime Minister would still exist, and would still live where the Prime Minister had always lived. Nor did they consider that those who, for a time, had occupied the offices and been referred to by the titles of those offices would continue to live, would continue to be guarded in their big houses. Only the Clerks knew that, whatever happened, what they wrote in their big green books at the Table of the House would not change; that between the departure of one Prime Minister and another no alteration would occur, and, when at the end of a motion, the name of the mover appeared in its incidental parenthesis, on the first day, it would read (*The Prime Minister*); and on the second, it would read (*The Prime Minister*); and they did not waste time telephoning each other to discuss the matter, much.

The Prime Minister sat at her desk while all this was going on. She had a box of papers in front of her like a barricade, and a telephone which never rang. The power of her; she never needed to answer the telephone, and she never did. She would not telephone anyone to beg for support. It was an absurd notion, that they should oppose her, and nothing needed to be done. She would not trawl the tea rooms begging for respect from people she barely knew. There were Members whom she would never have given a job to, and Members who had had jobs, who had betrayed her trust, and had to be sacked. There were Members who should not be in the party, with their lack of merit, and their lack of loyalty, and their lack of anything which could be seen as an understanding of what they were all trying to achieve. They all perhaps had reasons to betray her. But they were trivial reasons, and she knew they would not. Fear and trust would keep them loyal. They knew her record. They would support her. She thought of the whole thing with scorn. No. She did not think of it at all. In the meantime, there were papers to be gone through. There was a country to be run, and to be saved. She fingered a button on her suit, which appeared to be coming loose.

Outside the door, grown men like schoolboys stood as if they would like to kick their heels, and waited for her. They would wait for hours. They knew what would happen to her, and they knew what would happen to them. It was not yet the time to talk about it, but they all knew that the time to talk about it might soon arrive, might already have arrived, unrecognized, and have passed, unsaved.

'Nineteen seventy-eight to nine,' one said.

'Nineteen seventy-five,' another said.

'But nineteen seventy-nine,' a third said.

'And nineteen eighty-three,' a fourth said.

'And nineteen eighty-seven,' the first said.

'And nineteen ninety-one,' they all might have thought. 'Or maybe ninety-two.'

The moment, the crucial moment might have come, and gone, and left unnoticed, unsaved. But all moments, at the pitch of government, are crucial, and none are left unsaved. *Every second counts*, they all thought. They had all, at some time, said it, and wasted time by saying it, and most had even thought it true. They carried on waiting, with their pretence of business.

'Are you really homosexual?' Jane said.

'Of course,' Louis said. 'Why do you think I'm not?'

'You might just have said that.'

'But why?'

'Girls are supposed to say they're lesbian if a man is pestering them. It puts them off.'

'Do you do it?'

'No.'

'And you weren't pestering me.'

'I am now,' Jane said.

They were in a bar with every appearance of fashion. There were posters pasted to the walls for events which took place seventy years before, in a different country. The waiters were offensive and slow, as if they could afford to be. Behind the bar was a coffee machine which, despite the fact that it was gigantic, made terrible coffee. These appurtenances did not vary from branch to branch of this chain of urban cafés. They were profitable; even the coffee was profitable. Jane obviously knew about the things to avoid here, since when Louis arrived she had ordered a bottle of white wine and two glasses. She was almost halfway down the bottle by that time, although, after his long walk around central London, he was absolutely prompt.

'I was glad you turned up when you did,' she said. 'They were starting to look askance at me, as if I were drinking a lot on my own, or something.'

'Well, you were,' he said. 'On your own, I mean. Don't

you love that expression, to look askance? What does it mean?'

'I've no idea, though I use it too.'

'Honest of you.'

'But have you got a boyfriend, or anything?'

'No, not at the moment, no,' he said. Or ever, he thought, thinking about the Italian man who fucked her father. 'Have you?'

'No, not since Henry.'

He liked her for that.

'Do you see him?' he said. 'I mean, do you see him often? I know you bump into him from time to time, of course; at least, that's what he says. He mentioned it today, in fact.'

'He mentioned it today? Did he tell you about yesterday afternoon?' she said. 'That's exactly the sort of thing I meant.' He didn't understand what she meant. 'He really is quite different, you know. For a start I just turned up to talk to him, and immediately, he just started jumping down my throat and saying it was none of my business. He would never have done that before.'

'What was none of your business?'

'Oh, Francesca.'

'Your sister Francesca?'

'Of course, yes. You know she's a bit in love with Henry.'

'I didn't know.'

'She often falls in love with unlikely people. She hasn't told me, of course – she wouldn't – but I've seen it all happen before. I'm just putting up with it. And because I never see him – not properly, not any more – I didn't know how he felt about it. So I came into the building to talk to him about it. As you can imagine, he didn't respond very well.'

She looked straight at him and poured the rest of the bottle into his glass.

'Did it not strike you that you might not be the person that he would want to talk to about all this? I mean, what would he think if he really was in love with your sister, or if he didn't know, but thought she might be in love with him? What would he think about what you were doing? Didn't it maybe seem like evidence that you were still in love with him whatever he thought?'

'Of course I'm not in love with him,' she said. 'That's just ridiculous.'

'I'm not saying you are. I know you're not. I'm just saying what he might have thought. I know you were only acting for the best, and you wanted to do what was best for her and for –'

He stopped at the amazing sight of Jane laughing and laughing. Her guffaw, like a howl of rage in a play, silenced the tables around them. If they had been standing, the possibility of moving away would have existed. If he had been standing, he would have pretended not to have been with her at all. Her laugh like lunacy went on until, quite abruptly, her arms and shoulders collapsed on to the flimsy table. He held on to the bottle and his glass; her glass shook but did not fall. It was after some time that she lifted her head up, and, around them, conversation began to resume, cautiously.

'You're amazing,' she said in the end. 'You know quite well I wasn't. I can't believe how polite you are. I just came in to torment Henry and make things difficult for Francesca, and if you want to know why, I'll tell you why.'

'I know why,' he said. 'It's because you're still in love with Henry. I know that. I'd behave in exactly the same way if it were me.'

'I've got to make a telephone call,' Jane said, not dissenting. She got up and, weaving between tables, made her way to the stairs down. She ran her fingers down the banisters, singing a little private song, and past the unoccupied telephone. She went into the lavatory and examined her reflection. Laughter made her eyes as red as weeping did. She splashed her face and with the communal comb pulled back her hair. She carried no bag, never did; and she either carried what she needed in the pockets of her consequently out-of-shape clothes, or needed nothing, and borrowed, bought and threw away things as she went.

When she left, a little more in order but feeling oddly drunker, a woman was using the telephone. Jane rapped on her shoulder. 'I need the telephone now,' she said.

The woman simply hung up immediately, a thing Jane would never have thought of doing. Jane dialled without thinking, and Francesca answered.

'Oh christ,' Jane said. 'Francesca, I dialled the wrong number without thinking. See you later.'

She hung up and started again. But as she dialled, she realized that she had made no mistake, that she had dialled the number she meant to dial, which was Henry's number, by heart. It rang eight or nine times before Henry answered.

'Henry, it's Jane,' she said. 'I've got to talk to you.'

'Not now,' he said.

'Is she there?' Jane said. 'Is my sister there?'

There was a pause.

'Yes she is,' Henry said.

'Why is she there?' Jane said. 'I've got to talk to you,

Henry, I must. You must tell me what you think about her, it's most important.'

'I can't talk to you when you're like this, and I don't want to,' Henry said. But he didn't ring off.

'Why did she answer the fucking telephone?' Jane said. 'What are you doing?'

'Nothing,' he said. An admission of something could be heard in his voice; no guilt, just the sound, like a click of a telephone ringing off, of an admission. Fuck you, she said to herself, and for five seconds she stood in silence holding the telephone.

'Jane?' the voice said.

She put the telephone down.

When she got back to the table Louis had ordered another bottle. She composed herself, walking.

'You know,' Louis said, 'I almost didn't come tonight.'

'I wouldn't have been very pleased,' Jane said.

'I thought you were used to being stood up,' Louis said.

'People often stand me up. That doesn't mean I like it. Why did you nearly not come?'

'An Italian boy tried to pick me up and I almost let myself be picked up,' Louis said, looking at Jane. He was sure she was the kind of girl that would like the story, and, perhaps later in the evening, he had a feeling they would be discussing the types and orders of men that pleased them, like drunken taxonomists. 'He was remarkably good-looking.'

'Why didn't you?' Jane said.

'It wouldn't have been very nice to stand you up.'

'Now you're lying again to be polite.'

He laughed, but didn't contradict her.

'Do men often try to pick you up?' Jane said. She knew the expression, *fag hag*; she wasn't going to let it be used of her.

'From time to time,' Louis said. 'Look, I know this is a stupid thing to say, but you're not going to mention any of this to your father, are you?'

'You're right,' Jane said. 'It is a stupid thing to say. Of course not. Do you ever let them pick you up?'

'All the time,' Louis said. 'Have some more.'

'Does anyone you work with know about all this?'

'No, nobody, as far as I know,' he said.

'No reason why they should,' she said. 'In fact, I'm quite surprised that anyone should know that you're there to be picked up. You don't seem very obvious to me.'

'I'm not. No; I suppose I am. But it's like dogs and whistles. When two men that are available to each other meet, they always know, even if no one else can see it. Like a pitch above everyone else's hearing. I can almost always tell even if someone's walking down the street. Something to do with body language or the way someone walks or eye contact. Yes, eye contact, definitely. Or a way of talking or a particular sort of well-dressed elegance. Or a certain sort of shabbiness. Or mincing or walking upright or maybe even the way people are built.'

'But homosexuals are all so different.'

'Yes, but you can tell them. I don't know how.'

'Nonsense,' Jane said. 'You make it sound like a conspiracy or a secret life or something. You can't possibly tell.'

'Not always, but mostly. It might not be secret, it might be that it's a stranger or someone who hasn't needed to mention it.'

'Who is there in here?'

He pointed out two waiters, a man sitting with a woman at a nearby table, and one of two men just entering at that moment. Jane saw immediately what it was about them. Each of them was imitating the pose of the other. The waiters stood next to each other, and from time to time they looked at each other, in the eye, and laughed; and in the meantime stood with one leg held slightly bent and their arms folded. The man with the woman had taken on her pose, her chin on her folded hands, her elbows on the table; the men entering took off their unnecessary sunglasses simultaneously, choreographed. She saw how, insecure, they took on the stance of other people, as if reliant on others even for the way they could stand. It set her to thinking.

'Do you think Henry is?'

'Henry?' Louis said immediately. 'No, he isn't. But you know that better than I do.'

'But he's so camp.'

'That's nothing to do with it. That's just how he is.'

'Don't you think –' she said. She didn't know; suddenly she didn't want to go on with it. 'This is fun. Who else? The Clerk of the House?'

'Do you know him?' he said.

'He came to dinner once,' she said. 'It was hell, like having a very well-behaved walrus at one end of the table, and all the time you wondering whether he was going to start eating the tablecloth. No conversation at all, and that beard.'

'It is horrid,' he said. 'No, I don't think so. He married late, of course, which is always a good sign of faggots who don't want their wives to be demanding. I just don't get any whiff of sex off him, if you see what I mean. It might be little boys with the Clerk of the House, of course.'

'What nonsense,' Jane said. He wondered for a moment if she wasn't shocked, or if she were merely determined not to let herself be shocked. 'What about my father?'

'Your father?'

'Yes.'

There was a moment suddenly between them.

'No,' he said. 'Of course not.'

He didn't convince himself even; he knew something he hadn't known before; or something he had known before. The second bottle, they both saw at the same time, was finished.

'Where are we going to eat?' she said.

'Fine,' he said stupidly. He hadn't known they were going to eat.

As soon as they reached the restaurant, she went to the telephone again. This time Francesca answered.

'What are you doing there?' Jane said immediately.

'Who is this?' Francesca said.

'You know quite well. What are you doing there?'

'It's none of your business. I was just talking to Henry.'

Henry came to the phone.

'I don't want to talk to you,' Jane said. 'I want to talk to Francesca.'

'Look Jane,' Henry said, in conciliatory mode, 'she came round at eight. It's now after nine. We were sitting here with a drink. She's on her way somewhere else. Where are you now? Shall I come and have dinner with you?'

'No, you swine,' Jane said. A thing she had always wanted to say. What she knew quite well was that Francesca was imposing herself on Henry, and that he would want to get rid of her. She knew this quite well; she would not admit it. 'Pass me my sister.'

'Do be reasonable,' Henry said, not waiting for her to answer.

'I'm not going to talk to you,' Francesca said, taking the telephone over, 'when you're obviously drunk and don't know what you're doing. You realize that you're making Henry's life a complete misery.'

'I can't be. I never see him.'

'Rubbish,' Francesca said. 'You see him all the time. I'm not going to talk to you like this. If Henry and I fall in love, that's completely our business. It's nothing to do with you.'

There was an awful silence at both ends of the telephone.

'You've done it now,' said Jane cheerfully, and put the telephone down.

'My theory about menus,' Louis said, 'is that the most delicious things on the menu are always the ones which sound unbelievably disgusting.'

'What happens if they really are disgusting?' Jane said. 'Yes, a bottle of red Rioja, thank you. No, no water.'

'Then you're not disappointed by a florid description, anyway.'

'What are you going to have in that case?'

'Dried and salted pig's liver,' Louis said.

'It does sound terrible,' Jane said. 'But if it sounds as bad as that, isn't there a risk that no one will ever order it and when you finally turn up, the bit of liver you get will be four weeks old and straight out of the freezer?'

'I don't suppose dried pig's liver spoils even in four

weeks. Anyway, if we're having Rioja that minimizes the choices.'

'Well, I like it, anyway, and I'd rather have that and food I might not want than food I want and a wine. No, a wine I don't want and food. You know what I'm trying to say.'

'How drunk are you?'

'Awfully,' Jane said. It wasn't really true. She said it to be sociable.

'I met your pupil,' Louis said, giving in to an impulse he could not quite understand.

'Oh, my *pupil*,' Jane said, disconcertingly. 'Fancy. Are you drunk?' She wondered what on earth Louis was talking about.

'Me too,' he said. 'I mean, yes I am. Do you think Henry might be queer?'

'I said I've no idea,' she said. 'He could be.'

'You're in the best position to know, of course.'

'I'm not,' she said.

He wondered what stage in the evening they had got to.

'In what way?' he said.

'Well, we never had sex,' she said. 'Does that sound extraordinary?'

'No,' Louis said, although it did. Louis often had sex with men whose names he did not know. He could not imagine what it would mean to love someone and not have sex with them.

'I think it is fairly extraordinary,' she said. 'Not many people over the age of sixteen go out with each other for three or four years without jumping into bed with each other. It just never came up.'

'It never came up?'

'No, that's exactly right, it never did. We necked and all that but I've never seen him without his clothes on. Once we went swimming.'

'Once you went swimming?' Louis said, and began to laugh. 'Oh christ, here it comes.'

The salted dried pig's liver and whatever Jane was having arrived. They stopped talking and began to eat. Neither had realized that they were so hungry until the food came, and once it came, they gave themselves up to it. The perfection of dried liver; the impossibility of describing it in a way which would convey its deliciousness. It was like leather and piss and sweat and perfume, and yet rich and sumptuous and velvet.

'I feel vindicated,' Louis said finally.

'Is it good?' Jane said, finally. She had no idea what he was talking about, at first. 'No thanks, I'll take your word for it.'

'Why are you telling me all this?'

'What, about the swimming trunks, and the no-sex-please-we're-Henry? Because I'm drunk, of course. You know, it wasn't just Henry's fault that we didn't ever go to bed together. I never asked him, either.'

'I'm drunk too. Do you think we're friends?'

'I've no idea,' Jane said impatiently. She wasn't so drunk she didn't recognize things people only said to each other because they were the sort of things drunk people said. She wanted to talk about Henry, and – it wasn't true, what she said – she felt that she would have talked about him if she had been more sober. 'I just want to know if I was wrong and if we should have gone to bed together.'

'In a way it makes the whole thing more extraordinary that you didn't.'

'You mean I wouldn't now be going on about it in this way if we'd had an affair in a normal way?'

'Yes.'

'Do you ever not have sex with people?'

'Yes, I don't have sex with people all the time,' said Louis. 'I don't know what you mean.'

'You know quite well,' Jane said. 'It's just like talking to my sister. She's always claiming not to understand what I say. You could be my pupil, too.'

'Yes, I could. Perhaps you're difficult to understand,' Louis said.

'I am now,' she said with a parody drunkard's drawl.

'But no,' Louis said. 'I have sex with everyone I know. I fuck men in the street and I fuck men I know and I fuck men I've just met at dinner parties, and I fuck waiters.'

'Another bottle, please,' said Jane. 'And can you bring me some of that dried liver too.'

The waiter nodded with impressive politeness and left.

'You've eaten,' Louis said.

'So I have,' Jane said. 'It wasn't memorable. You haven't fucked him, at any rate.'

'No,' Louis said. Their conversation for the moment was gone. The evening continued and, with a flash of clarity, Louis saw the restaurant they were in. Tiny, fashionable, a middle-evening rumble of accumulated well-bred converse somewhere, it seemed, above them, and lit, as if from pools, from marsh-gas globules of light, by candles placed in glass globes and illuminating. Too dark to see anything that mattered, and the food, the lists, the drink might have been anything, even their opposites, but upwards, as if from unseen sources, the faces over their food were lit flatteringly, impressively, like handsome healthy demons in a gas-lit pantomime. Unrecognizable they were, like the food they ate; and only the waiters could be identified, and only as waiters, in their white-aproned clean bottle-plucking perfection. And all over the tall dark room, men, who could not be recognized by their wives in the light, hailed waiters who had not served them, and the waiters, like priests, passed on, and sent back other waiters, who like them seemed tall, and beautiful, which they were, and sleek and rich, which they were not.

They were abashed and shy and they ate.

'What are you going to do?' Jane said.

'What, now?' Louis said. 'Nothing.'

'I think you were right about this,' Jane said. 'It is good. It's surprising that it could be good, but it is.'

'I know,' Louis said. 'I was surprised, too.'

'I don't really want to stay here and have a cup of coffee. Let's go home.'

'What?' Louis said. 'Where?'

'My house,' she said. 'It's all right. I've got a little sitting room and I doubt if my father will be there anyway. You won't have to talk to him.'

'I like your father.'

'I doubt if you really know him. I think he's quite odd in some ways. Your parents seem quite normal when you're a child but later on they do seem peculiar. No, I've changed my mind, I don't want to go home just yet, I want some figs.'

'You want what?' Louis said. She was aware for a moment he wasn't used to her.

'I want figs,' she said. 'I don't want a pudding, just figs. That would be really rather nice. You.'

A waiter who was standing idly amazed Louis by his

responding to her impolite demand with a polite 'Madam'.

'There are no figs,' he said when the request had been made. 'There is a selection of fresh fruit, but I do not think that in the selection there are any figs.'

'And I have no doubt whatsoever that you will bring me in your selection of fresh fruit some which I have no desire whatever to eat even if I were more sober than I am now, such as that exemplarily repellent fruit the pear.'

'Pears are included in the selection of fresh fruit this evening, madam.'

'And I have no desire to eat pears. Tell me, would you eat a pear?'

'I am fond of pears, if they are not quite ripe, madam.'

'Then you are mad. Can you bring us figs?'

'No, I cannot, madam.'

'Tell me,' Jane said. 'Is this a good restaurant?'

'It is a good restaurant,' the waiter said.

'Is it the best in London?'

'It is among the best in London.'

'Is it the very best?'

'No, madam,' the waiter said, with a fit of honesty at odds with his professional manner. 'It is not the very best restaurant in London.'

'In that case,' Jane said with her mother's grandeur. 'Bring us the bill. We are going to the best restaurant in London, in order to eat figs.'

'Certainly,' the waiter said, and left.

'My goodness,' Louis said.

The bill arrived and Louis paid it. Jane made no comment; she had done grandeur, now, for the evening, she felt it was Louis's responsibility if he wanted to pay, and not hers to have gratitude imposed on her.

The best restaurant in London admitted them without question; they claimed they wanted dinner. Only when they were seated and a man appeared with a menu, did they admit their slight lie. The man took their order for two plates of figs and half a bottle of Sauternes without questioning it; and it was, after all, the best restaurant in London. Louis was qualmed by the restaurant.

'Do you like it here?' Jane said.

'You're like a dog too,' Louis said. 'You can tell when people are nervous. Like the dog and the whistle. And homosexuals.'

'Are you nervous?' Jane said, following what he was saying. 'You do give that impression, you know, anyway.'

'I am now,' he said. 'I'm not like that all the time.'

'Why are you nervous here?'

'I'm a bit afraid of being found out.'

'Found out as what? Can you not pay for a plate of figs and a bottle of wine?'

'Well, I hope I can,' Louis said. 'I mean, I think I'm going to be exposed as a fraud. I mean in general. I don't think I'm clever, and people seem to think I am, or deserve to have a job, and someone once thought I did, and I'm not heterosexual, and I think people are going to find that out as well.'

'People have found out that you're homosexual,' Jane said, as the waiter put down the two plates of figs. 'And no one seems to mind too much. The thing is, that being afraid of being found out is what makes you human. If you knew there was nothing wrong with you, that there was nothing at all short of perfection in you, then what sort of person would you be?'

'Not a nice one,' he said. He thought of Jane's father, running across the road with his heavy briefcase and his twisted back. 'And now one more person knows I'm homosexual.'

'What, the waiter? Who cares? Do you think he cares?'

'No, of course not.'

'And don't you think that even though being afraid of being found out isn't such a bad thing, once you are found out that's not such a bad thing either?'

'I can't tell whether that's true or not or if there's some kind of paradox there or anything. You've stopped telephoning.'

'Christ, so I have,' Jane said, getting up immediately. She knocked over her chair as she did so, but, wise, made no attempt to pick it up. It would only have made things worse. She made her way steadily to the telephone.

It was now of the utmost importance to Jane that she dial the number correctly. She did not have the confidence that she could do this unassisted, so she took out a pencil and began to write Henry's number on the wall. After three digits, she found that she could not remember it, so she took the telephone from the hook and let her fingers make the familiar pattern over the keys. When she had discovered what the remaining four digits were from her fingers, which were not drunk, she wrote them down, as well, on the white wall. She then hung up for a second, took the receiver from its hook and dialled the number she had written on the wall.

'She's gone home,' Henry said.

'You're lying to me,' Jane said.

'It's after eleven,' Henry said. 'Why would she still be here?'

'Because you're going to fuck,' Jane said. 'That's why. I'm under no illusion.'

'Jane,' Henry said. 'Do yourself a favour. Go home and stop drinking. Where are you now?'

'The Ritz,' Jane said.

'The Ritz?' Henry said.

'No, I don't think so,' Jane said. 'But it's some very fancy place I've come to to eat figs. I wanted figs and at the other place they wouldn't give them to me. And it was good and I wish they would have done because I'd much rather have stayed there than come here. Is she really not there?'

'No,' Henry said.

'Why can't you come and pick me up?' Jane said. 'You could come and have a drink as well. It would be really nice. It would be just like it ought to be, and you could eat all my figs. I wish I knew where I was and then you could come. I could find out. And you could come and –' She stopped. She heard herself for a moment. She knew exactly what she sounded like. She knew exactly how drunk she seemed. She knew she was letting herself be found out, just as Francesca had let herself be found out by simply saying the word *love*. That had been enough for her; but Jane had not even needed to say it.

There was a long silence; there was a terrible noise, the noise of a telephone being replaced, and Jane had nowhere to go but back into the restaurant.

When they were at Jane's house, as they somehow were, and coffee was somehow being made, Louis said, 'You know, I think he might have waited until we had finished eating before he brought us the bill.'

'Do you think he wanted to get rid of us?' Jane said.

'Yes, I think he probably did.'

'But it was such a good restaurant.'

'Which is why they wanted to get rid of us.'

'Do you think they found us out?'

'Do you think they discovered us?'

'I think they did.'

'And it wasn't too bad, after all,' said Louis. 'You were right. It doesn't matter at all, being found out.'

'Maybe it does matter,' she said. 'If it mattered I wouldn't know now. I can't think straight. I don't want coffee.'

'What do you want?'

'I don't know what I want,' she said. 'Just come here.'

He did. She was on a sofa, her curled worn body like a sofa itself. He went into it not knowing what was there. Why? he thought. They lay there for a while. He was like a favourite book of hers, one she had read before and liked in the way she liked things when there was nothing else to know and everything else to enjoy. She was like something very new to him and at the same time immensely old, like a mother or the earth he never thought much about, or velvet.

'Phone him again,' he said in the end, when it was all, or seemed all to be over.

'Why?' she said, knowing why.

'Because you want to.'

'Do you think I should?' she said.

'It makes no difference what I think. You're going to phone him anyway.'

She did. But this time she knew what she was going to say, and when the voice at the end of the telephone had turned into a silence, and she was shrieking at it about her sister, and her sister, at the top of the stairs in a nightgown with frills and ribbons no human being would buy for themselves, was looking down at her with all her apparent knowledge, all her arm-folded sureness that her life was ruined, then Louis looked at her and felt his tooth break. In his mouth, a sudden fragility; a back tooth breaking (and he had always thought of his teeth as good, as reliable) and a gap and a sharpness for the tongue. Thoughts of vulnerability; of his own innocence; and into his head like a charm for snakes came the word *friable*. The evening. And then it was morning. Outside.

Dear Father, Henry wrote. *I am writing to you after a strange night. I was telephoned by a girl I used to love and don't love any more, and while she was telephoning me, I was sitting with a girl I don't love yet but am going to. I am concerned about what happens to the girl I used to love, which perhaps means I still love her, and I have no interest in what happens to the girl I am going to love, which perhaps means not only that I do not love her but never will.*

I am bored by speculating about myself.

I want to be nothing in particular.

What I want to be is air. I want to be a thing that can't be done without but can't be felt or seen or smelt or touched. I want to be indispensable and invisible. I want to be without personality. I am jealous of air, and I am jealous of nothing.

I want to talk to you, and to everyone, without bringing my personality into it. I want to talk without boring myself, and to be heard without the consideration of my history. This is what I want. I want to leave evidence of myself behind me, and never to be apparent myself.

*   *   *

Henry slept. Somewhere there between eye open and eye shut, floating (into sleep? out of sleep?), in that place he saw something. A phrase, bright and blue and banal as neon. His lips moved, in sleep or out of it, with the letters in light, in his head. *Free as air*, his mouth said, and again, *free as air*. I avoid clichés like the plague, he thought, and then, a third time, a charm for luck, *free as air*.

What it meant and what it would mean troubled him in his bed. He rolled over with difficulty, and continued rolling, into the empty half of the bed, a half he used and never thought of. Free as air, who was free as air? What was he free as? As nothing? Was nothing air, or was air a thing? Like stilled wind the air surrounded him, and if he floated – he felt himself floating – it would quite surround him. Like water it supported; it did not feel what it touched, and it could be felt in return. Henry's mind again turned to the bodies he had never touched, poised as if they were falling through the air they existed in, unbreathing. It turned to jealousy.

He thought of the freedom to act, not to act, and not to be.

In his room, full of air, he was like a limp dry shirt in a hot electric drier, moved by winds which went nowhere and came from nowhere. Either falling into sleep or coming out of it, he thought in his own silence about air and freedom and jealousy. He thought of things he had never thought of before, and which were not truly there, but only as he thought of them, and the truths he would send to his father.

They all woke up in their own beds. It was a surprise to some of them; and it was a surprise to some of them that others of them were in their own beds. It was only not surprising one bit to John, who was used to it, and had long ago stopped thinking of how things might be different. Boys were for afternoons, and wives were dead.

He walked down a street which led to Giacomo's house. He had no plan to visit Giacomo, but he felt like a walk, and it was a street which might be walked in. As good as any other. He looked at the houses. All quite the same. They differed in their degrees of shabbiness, and in their degrees of whiteness. He did not consider what might be contained by them; goodness, or murder, or song. He did not wonder how many of them contained men who differed in no sensible respect from Giacomo; it did not occur to him that such men existed. For him there was Giacomo, who was paid, and who was separate.

When he walked in the street John feared one thing and it was not the thing that happened to him that day, or the thing that happened to anyone around him, but the thing that had happened to him the day before. He feared recognition. He feared, if his daughter had been there to say it, he feared being found out, and, unlike her, he did not think that his fear made him human.

'Have you got any money?' a man said. He was sitting on the pavement.

John stopped. Perhaps he was thinking about giving the man some money.

'Are you asking me for money?' he said.

'Yes,' the man said.

'Stand up then,' he said. 'I'm not going to give money to someone sitting on the ground.'

The man got to his feet quite suddenly. Suddenly he was tall.

'Hunchback,' he said.

'Yes,' John said, still quite relaxed. 'Yes, I'm hunch-backed.'

'And I'm asking you for money,' the man said. 'I'm asking some fucking hunchback faggot for money.'

For a moment he paused; like Louis, the man had got something right; but there was no need to show it. He began to walk on.

'I'm asking you for money,' the man said. 'Fucking hunchback faggot. Give me some money. Give me your money.'

The shift from some to your. The terror. The man loping beside you.

'Just do it. I can run. Can you run, cripple, can you run?'

There was terror showing. He had seen it. He did not know how to hide it now, too late, he could not run.

'I can't give you money,' he said, muttering, not showing anything. 'I can't, please.'

'You've got money,' the man said, and John wondered why he hadn't realized immediately that he was mad, and wondered now why no one came and no one who walked past thought that he was about to be punched quite severely and robbed. He knew, at once, how he could stop it.

'Look,' he said, stopping quite dead. He got out his wallet from his pocket. There was only thirty pounds in it and some cards. 'Here's my wallet. Take it. Just take it.'

The man stopped with him, and John realized quite abruptly that he was not asking for money in a serious way; not asking for money in the way people serious about money ask for it. He looked at the wallet, as if he had heard of wallets, once, but did not quite believe in them. Then at once a marvellous huge grin broke across his face in the wet black street in the west of London, and it was between his hands. It only took a moment for his great arm to swing back and, like a suspended side of ham, his fist to strike against John. The unfairness, John thought as his knees went, always the knees to go; the impossibility of return; the great swing and exhilaration of the movement of the bone and the flesh through air.

After a while there was no one there, and Giacomo's flat was near.

'I've no money,' John said, as soon as they were inside.

'It's all right,' he said. 'You can pay next time. It's coming to be. It's getting.'

His English magically failed. Grinning, he pointed at Henry's eye, then his own eye.

'My eye,' John said ruefully. He fingered it, waiting to wince. 'A shiner.'

'A shiner,' Giacomo said eventually, not grinning.

'A black eye,' he said.

'A shiner,' he said eventually, and reached out and touched his eye, the other's eye. Giacomo joyfully made the wince John had waited for. 'Pay me next time,' he said again.

'That wasn't what I came for. We have an expression,' John said. 'A tart with a heart of gold. Do you get it?'

'Yes,' Giacomo said. 'I'm not one, though. If I was, you could have it free. I'm still going to charge you. I'm sorry about yesterday.'

'That's all right.'

'I didn't give you away,' Giacomo said. 'Nice boy.'

'Fat.'

'Fat, but handsome. Very nice. What did you come here for?'

'I don't mind you charging me. That's all right,' John said. 'It is your job, I suppose. I came for help.'

'You came to me for help?' Giacomo said. It was as if John saw a surge of electric happiness through him, and his face was the face with which he had waved at John, with joy, in the street.

'You were near,' John said.

'Not just that,' Giacomo said.

'No,' John said. 'Let's not have sex. I don't think I want it.'

'That's okay,' Giacomo said. 'It's nice to have you here anyway.'

'Okay,' John said.

'I know what to do,' Giacomo said. 'For your eye.'

'I don't need anything,' John said. 'I just need to sit here quietly for a while.'

'No, you need to do something about it,' Giacomo said. 'Or it'll be worse tomorrow.'

'I don't know what to do,' John said. 'You're supposed to put raw steak on it, aren't you?'

'That's something for the movies,' Giacomo said. 'And I don't have raw steak. I don't eat meat.'

'Are you vegetarian?'

'Yes,' Giacomo said. 'Didn't you know?'

'No,' John said. 'It's unusual, an Italian who doesn't eat meat.'

'No, not unusual,' Giacomo said. 'I don't eat it because I don't like it. I never did. I only ever wanted pasta and cake when I was a boy. I used to cry when they put steak in front of me. My brothers used to laugh. And when

I was a bit older I said I wouldn't eat it and I never do now.'

'There's only one sort of meat you want in your mouth now,' John said, with an attempt at sex.

'No,' Giacomo said, puzzled. 'I don't eat meat at all.'

'No, I meant –' John said. He didn't press it.

'Oh, I see what you mean,' Giacomo said. 'Yes, that's true. But I don't have steak and I don't think it would work. My brother's a boxer, I told you, and he just has salt water on his eye when he makes a shiner. A shiner?'

'A shiner,' John said. 'We could try that.'

'Why were you in Earl's Court?' Giacomo said when he came back from the kitchen.

There was no reply. They sat for a moment with a bowl of salt water between them.

'Here,' Giacomo said. He took a sausage of cotton wool, and tore a strip from it. He dipped it professionally in the water, and wrung it. John thought of him, a boy with an adored hero of an older brother, dabbing at the victorious wounds. He hissed slightly through his teeth, but it did not sting; he hissed and winced through the pain of the happiness he ought to feel.

'You know I don't always answer the telephone,' Giacomo said.

'No one always answers the telephone,' John said, not understanding.

'Do you want my number?' Giacomo said.

'I've got it,' John said.

'No,' Giacomo said. 'I've got a phone I always answer. You can have that number if you want.'

Thank you, John thought. Thank you, with a deep and

terrible black dread in the pit of his stomach at what Giacomo was giving him.

They looked at each other for a long long time, before they began.

'I'll pay you next time,' John said.

'Don't bother,' Giacomo said. 'That was fun. I had a good time.'

'It was fun?' John said. 'You really are a tart with a heart.'

'No I'm not,' Giacomo said.

'You mean,' John said, testing a node of surprising pain, 'it's good for business?'

'Mmm,' said Giacomo. His face was down on the pillow, but he could be seen to smile.

'If you let me have one visit without paying,' John went on, 'I'll keep coming back? Is that what you mean? You'll never make a living.'

'I'm not interested in making a living out of you,' Giacomo said, sitting up leaning on one elbow.

John sat at the edge of the bed and felt the trickle, like happiness, of Giacomo's fingers down his poor snaking zip-like spine.

'Why not?' he said dully. He thought of nothing, and not of Giacomo. He looked at his fists, clenched against his naked thigh like the great hams of his mugger, and clenched in no rage or violence that he could understand.

'Because I'm going to give this up, and I'm going to come and live with you, if you want. I want to stop this and be with you. You don't have to have me. That's just what I want. That's all.'

'And if I don't want?'

'If you don't want that,' Giacomo said. He seemed to speak with too much care; his care frightened John. 'Then I'll just go on as before. You can come. I won't stop you. But you'll just be another one I won't talk to. It could be all right for us. Either way.'

John looked at the wall. He couldn't see Giacomo. For the first time, he noticed that above the television set and the line of pornographic videos there was a reproduction of a picture which was quite attractive. Densely brown, it appeared to be of rounded glowing balls, an abstract pattern. Out of the gloom of the room it, glowing, resolved itself like a sock turning inside out, into a tree, some sheep, a sun, two breast-like hills. It looked like nothing; then it looked like something; and he knew, for once in his life, where it had come from and what had made it happen. 'Samuel Palmer,' he said, half to himself, and the words began to pull him out of the stomach-clenching terror, as if before his own attacker, he found he had gone into. He remembered to breathe. The hand down his spine, redolent of puzzlement, of not having heard, stopped in its path. John considered the path of its goodness, its beauty, its love. Then he turned and he killed Giacomo.

KITCHEN VENOM

T HEN SHE DREW the silk vest over her head and, like silk, felt her soft flesh flush coldly against its tender softness, like flesh. A crack like tiny lightning clung it to her sides, where looseness and wrinkling only seemed to show how soft it was, her skin. She stood in her drawers, her vest (she called them these things, to herself only, a child again; her dresser and she had quite a different set of words; they used them quite normally). She stretched inside her skin, without moving.

These are the things the Prime Minister liked. She liked the look of unworn stockings, their white sheen laid out across a white bergère for wearing. She liked the crackle of silk when pulled over hair and the pricking of invisible hairs on flesh, with electricity. She liked the feel of a shirt in a box between tissue paper, as if it were new, even if it were new. She liked even things she would have worn three years ago, which were now beginning to seem a little strange; the enormous plank of shoulders in the jackets, the silk tied in a bow at the neck for neatness. She did not find them ugly yet, or absurd, as she did with the handbags and dresses she wore ten years ago; but she was accustomed to the processes of disillusionment, and, discerning the first stages, knew how things one had always relied upon could turn, could become not worthwhile, could become worth rejecting. People, too.

Most of all she liked detail in her clothes. She had suits she wore because she was fond of the buttons; she had other suits from which she had had the buttons removed and new, or old, favourite ones put on it in their place. Zips and hemlines she went on about; hemlines, she said, were things she understood. She turned jackets inside out, and examined the finish. She counted the pockets, as if she would ever use them. She tugged at piping and hooks. She tried on ballgowns, and stretched upwards and outwards like the Nike of Samothrace to examine the pull and stretch and fit. She said she wanted wear; she wanted perfection, and perfection forever, which she could not have.

It was two-thirty. She was dressing after lunch. She drew on the narrow skirt – perhaps too narrow, but flattering, a rich bouclé nubbling under the hand, a shade between mauve and blue, and with the clips and zips and hooks, did herself into it. It was something she loved, here. There were so many devices to hold the skirt together, and when it was done, and she was in, no ripple or lump or hard metal glint remained to show how it was achieved. It was, ungravitied, just there. And only she knew how it fastened, and the buttons which were covered, and the little flap of material covering the zip. A tightrope walker's art, to stay up without a sign of difficulty or a sign of cause.

When it was done, the shirt was not pulled but billowed beautifully, and her waist both emphasized and not specified. She looked in the mirror. Perfect. Perfect forever.

She went to the rack, and unzipped the clear plastic bag in which the coat, in a shade between mauve and blue (for the eyes, to emphasize the blue of the eyes) was kept. She drew it on, and stood for a moment. On a whim, she buttoned it, and stretched her arms out in both directions. It tugged a little, but the line held. She swivelled the top button of her suit and held it firm, liking it. Her left hand went to the hem of the coat, and quickly pulled. As she did, quite suddenly the top button of three she held came off in her hand. No warning. Five minutes to go. It must be mended immediately. No; tonight. She turned her back on the mirror, removed the suit, and from other zipped clear plastic bags in the wardrobe found another suit, another shade between mauve and blue (for the eyes). She was not annoyed, not even with herself, although the button might have been her fault. There was plenty of time. That was the secret; never rush.

That day no one dressed at half past two in the afternoon unless they had good cause to. People dressed in the mornings and, satisfied with what they wore, or not thinking about it, continued to wear the same clothes until they went to bed. Some changed their clothes when they returned home from work, not wishing to eat their dinner while wearing the suit they wore for work. Only a few people habitually dressed after lunch, or changed their clothes then; the idle; the powerful; those who had taken their clothes off before.

The sun was shining, inappropriately. The newspapers referred to what was occurring in the Palace as Shakespearean. But on their back pages the weather was reported, imperturbably, and the sun was shining, with the appearance but no feeling of heat; and in Shakespeare the Shakespearean events the newspapers thought of are accompanied by storms and thunder and lightning. After a while they wrote the word with no thought of its meaning or appropriateness.

Jane ate lunch in her pyjamas. It was not a meal her mother would have recognized as lunch, beginning with cornflakes and ending with cold fried bacon from the fridge. After she ate, in further defiance of her mother, she risked a heart attack by having a hot bath and reading in it. And then she dressed.

Jane's friends hardly thought about her clothes, because neither did she. There were a number of things she would not do, because she thought they diminished her. There were people she knew who acted from principle, who lived their lives as an argument. She was not one of those, but, because she thought of herself as important, there were things she would not do. She would not learn to type. She would not wear make-up habitually. She would not spend her days shopping for clothes. The pleasure she got from her clothes was a small but strong pleasure, and it was the pleasure of comfort. She did not care how she looked. She believed that if she was satisfied in her clothes, her satisfaction would change into appeal to others.

If many people believed this, they would be wrong; Jane did not quite believe it, and was only partly right in her partial belief. Today she dressed not for herself, and not for nothing. Today, at half past two, she dressed to wow the street.

She had one dress for this purpose. She wore it once a year; not to parties, although it was a dress made for parties, and not to walk in. She wore it to walk in. In the street she swung herself, not in sex, not to appeal, but to insult and to intimidate. On other women, the dress would not have struck; on her, it seemed like a grand dress, like a ballgown, and in it, with her mouth an angry gash and her face white as the dead with powder, she looked as feminine and terrifying as a drag queen.

Her knickers were white and clean and tiny, and she pulled on the dress. It was black, with some kind of rubber in the material which made it stretch when on and cling to her as if in fear. Sex in the clothes of the Prime Minister came from the air which floated between her garments; on Jane, the sex was in the lack of air, the fact that it stuck to her as if in vacuum, as if underwater. The skirt she was accustomed to pull up until it folded tightly over itself like black bandages. She combed her hair, but upwards into a great angry flourish. In the end, she put on her shoes, a pair of black stilettos shiny like the screen of an unplugged television, knowing how unfashionable she looked in the skirt and the shoes, and how wonderful. She telephoned for a cab, because anything else was out of the question, and looked forward to walking the street, and talking to no one; and while she waited, she took up a book she had never read, and she read from it.

'She loves situations and she wanted to see how I was facing this one.'

'Yes, to see if you were jealous of me, hoping perhaps, that life here from now on would be full of interesting little scenes between us, something to sustain and nourish her while she chops the parsley – which she does – doesn't she? – with not just *kitchen* venom?'

She thought about the sentences. She thought about her own venom; she thought about the ways in which it was kitchen, and the ways in which it was not. Venom could not be limited to its reason, and when she dressed, venom came into it. She thought that her own venom often seemed to be about something it was not. She wondered, and she thought she knew the answer, what was at the root of her own venom.

She had had two gin and tonics with her lunch, in her pyjamas, and her thoughts wandered. Kitchen venom; a place nourishment was produced, and a place from which poison could come. Like the heart; a place where love rose, and a place where killing sat, and dwelt. If she had his neck now, between her hands, she did not know, and never would, whether her hands would tighten and squeeze and kill, or whether they would hold the precious dark head and keep harm from it. She wanted both.

When she gashed her mouth with lipstick the colour of a Bloody Mary, she did it for those she did not know; but the way she did it was for Henry, or against him.

Jane rarely read books all the way through. Sentences were enough.

At the same time, Louis, off work supposedly sick, was swathed like a pasha in towels. Around his head was a tur-banning towel to protect the clay he had, an hour before, painted on to his hair. The earth under the towel, formerly hot, worked and polished his chestnut-shiny hair. Under his arms and over his ample bosom, extending down to his knees, a blanket-sized towel. Draped across his shoulder was a third, and to dry his legs and feet he used a fourth. As he worked at his toes he sang his flatmate's favourite song, pausing between lines to breathe, which, bending, he found difficult. Come on come on come on come on baby now, he sang, twist and shout, twist and shout. He became a singer as he sang, in his head, but also some backing singers, and a band, and, if he could, an orchestra.

The two things he could never do, twist and shout, except in pain. Except in pain.

These four towels were a purple he called mauve. As he advanced in the song, alone, he flagged about him the towel for his feet, then, waving like cheerleaders do, he took a towel in each hand, and, in his fashion, he twisted and, in the song, in his fashion, he shouted. His purple excesses; he quivered and the huge towel about him fell, heavy and flaccid, in a puddle to the floor. He regarded, with sorrow, his grey bulk.

Time passed, and no time passed at all. The Prime Minister was in her smooth perfection, and in one minute she would walk downstairs and into her car. Jane stood with her legs apart and waited for her car, which she would pay for, which she would direct. The Senior Vote Writer in the House of Commons, tired of the idea of doing any work, tired of manning the office for the Clerk of the Journals who had disappeared and the bottom boy who was off sick, had retired to the small bathroom on the same floor as the Journal Office and was taking a bath, while reading a book which was, to tell the truth, just the job. Another man, who had tried to telephone Giacomo and found his telephone unanswered, undressed before a muscular paid Brazilian, one street from the street in which Giacomo lay, and expected to be charged too much for too little, which he was.

Most people were already dressed, and did not think at that time of the clothes they wore. Francesca, whose clothes irritated most people around her with their calculated silly billow, walked across the common, thinking in a fug of lust for Henry. The Clerk of the House was dressed in his second-best suit; he only had two, since retirement was near; and he did not think of it. Henry was in a perfect suit, and noted the suits of those around him with degrees of scepticism. Members; their lack of hygiene; their badly cut suits; the halitotic stew of their breath.

In a room, somewhere, and somehow nowhere, one man was sitting where ten minutes before two men were sitting. John looked at Giacomo, and his gaze did not move. He could have felt him, and felt the warmth of his flesh, just for the moment. Would that have done? It would not. He could have told him what he felt for him, and that could have been good. Would it have been good enough? He did not answer. He did not understand, and now that Giacomo was dead, no regret came to him, but only the beginnings of worry at discovery. He, too, began to dress, and gave no thought whatever to the clothes he wore, which, like flesh, could be put on and taken off easily, at will, by others.

BEING FOUND OUT

FOR EVER AFTERWARDS, a small part of John's brain was in a room, too little, in Earl's Court, while his hands clasped each other around the neck of the most beautiful boy he had ever – the most beautiful boy he had ever seen. In his mind, in this little room in his mind, it was him who was struggling for air, like a man rising from the black depths of water into the black stuff of night. And in his struggle, which for him then and in his mind always afterwards was a struggle, not against the most beautiful boy, but a struggle against the strangling torsion of his back, like a killer behind him, he panicked into breath, knowing as he held it that he held it, while he acted. Always afterwards. And the shaking; the shaking as he went through with it, and the shaking of the hands after it was over; no, not the hands, the shaking was not in the hands, but in the stomach. A place fear was felt, and bravery. Two things that could not be told between. He did not know the difference between fear and bravery, and never would. A feeling he never felt, except at the prospect of his job defeating him, or, in his poor ugly bespectacled difference of a childhood, the dash of a schoolteacher over him, the run of adult rage towards him in vengeance and unmotivated hatred, and the yelling, the horror, the instant, unstoppable hot fear. A naked boy was under him – a naked boy, oddly yielding under the pressure which was not his, which could not be his – and for the moment, before there was suddenly nothing beneath him, there it was once more, in the inside of his stomach. The great lurch in the pit of the stomach, exactly synchronized with the way the boy's legs kicked, just once, against the air. Always afterwards. If he had ever written down what he had seen, he would have lied. He would not have denied killing; he would have lied about something quite different. He would have written that in the boy's eyes he saw a love which surprised him. It was not true. It would not have been true. And he would have written it down.

Dishonesty strikes us, when we kill, and at other times. It strikes us in ways which surprise us and others. And being found out takes different forms, many forms.

Being found out takes every form.

This is what is true. If he had looked at Giacomo's face while he was killing him, he would have seen not love, which would not have surprised him, but surprise, and terror, which would.

He finished. It could not be said how long it was before his breath slowed into a normal quietness, a rhythm which had nothing of spasm in it. *He did not look*. He did look; but that is what he would have said about himself, *he did not look*. He began to dress, quite calmly; his shirt and tie a success, his trousers and shoes quite normal. It was only when he reached the bottom button of his overcoat that it went wrong. It would not go through, and one hand was suddenly no use. He would not turn, he would not look, now that he knew that he should not, he knew that *he did not look*. He turned away with the bottom button of his overcoat undone. He reached the door and stopped. 'I've got to go now,' he said to the empty flat. He left. He was half-way down the shaking road before he thought of wiping the glass, the door handle, the body. There was no point. He couldn't return. He was found out.

The sky over the city; it did not arch overhead, but, like an egg, seemed to dip towards the city's earth, as if, somewhere, it would touch, or had touched the earth. And egg-like now was the way it broke in an easy shatter and dripped water in a great weight, with a great crash; and the air, and the earth, and the waters of the river, and the flesh of the city steamed with the rains as if hot. They ran, the people of the city, as if they could run from it; but they only ran under it. Only John did not run, having nothing to run to, having everything to run from only. And what do murderers do afterwards? They do what John did; they carry on. They go back to their wives and their daughters, and their jobs, and they might be noticed, or they might not. It depends. Because murderers are ordinary.

But murderers are always found out, by themselves and by others, and there was one more thing. Not something he left, as he feared. Something he took. It gave him away.

In the midst of death was death.

What Giacomo left with him was the thought of his face, which John knew, and the means of John's death, which he did not know he carried within him. What Giacomo had done that afternoon, with his penetration which proffered only pleasure, was send the little messengers on their way. The little messengers, of which John knew nothing and thought nothing, hurtling round his blood, with their unfeeling annunciations and unplanning revenge. When he looked at himself, he did not see death, and for ten years, he did not and would not know. Giacomo left nothing to the world, except the memory of pleasure, and the phantom of love. He did not know that what Giacomo had left with him, the only legacy Giacomo had left to the world, was his own imprisonment; his own guilt; his own death.

As he walked down the street, when people looked at him, they looked at him as people always did. They did not see what they should see, that they looked at a murderer. They did not see that they looked at a dead man, a man under sentence of death while the tiny lawyers in his blood argued for his reprieve or execution. They looked at him because he was a hunchback, a thing not often seen. They looked at him, hunched over his own walk, and with a black eye. No one knew as they were looking at him that what they looked at was a man who had found death in a little room, and a man who carried death with him in the street.

Then there was a blank in his mind.

It was like the asterisk authors use to separate the chapters of a book. It was tiny when he looked at it, but it could have contained within its infinite tininess days and weeks and months. He knew he was leaving the flat. He knew he walked down the road where the man who had assaulted him still sat on the pavement, unnoticing the man who had left him to assault other men, in other ways, worse. And that was that. He knew no more.

He knew no more. He knew nothing else. He knew nothing whatever. And there he was at the foot of some stairs, brown-carpeted, stretching upwards for ever. He was

Gollum at the foot of the stairs of Shelob. He recreated something in his mind which was not there to recreate. He recreated his journey. He knew what he must have done. He must blindly have stuck out his arm and got into a taxi. Bloodstained. He must have listened to the driver's twaddle, or he must have heard it. He must have pressed his small plastic pass – identifying him identifying him – to the window of the glass of the car as the man carried on his garbage and the state of the nation and the scandal it was. He must have got out and he must have paid – how? – and he must have walked. He must have. He must have. The obligation. Bloodstained though no blood was on him.

And here he was, at the foot of the enormous stairs with its hushed carpeted heat. John thought and he knew where he was.

He was at the very bottom of some stairs which he had never climbed. Above him there were a million stairs and a fast lift, which he had, every day for many years, taken. It took him from earth to the spires where he worked.

He began to climb. Somehow the lift was beyond him – the thought that other people might get into the lift. And as he climbed, there seemed behind him a tugging, increasing as if it would never let him go, and as if before he reached the top the tugging and his tugging of himself forward would equal each other, and he would stop, and breathless, begin to topple, helpless, backwards. Breathless he pulled himself up, and what struck him suddenly was an amazing silence which was nothing to do with him, and was not the usual silence of carpets and corridors and hush. It was the silence of a building as if everyone had gone from it, but it was not the absence of people his ear registered in the hum of machines and no other. It was the silence of people who were waiting, the silence of a huge building in which every man had withdrawn into a tiny chamber, too tiny to hold every one of them, and silenced, waited, as if for him. Only John's breath made a noise to him, as he pulled himself upwards, and upwards looking, saw that there was no end to the enormous padded staircase and no end to the climb upwards into the sky and the spires he had never made before and never – never – would again.

'I remind the House,' the Speaker said in his clear peremptory manner, reading from a crib sheet the Clerks had prepared, 'that a resignation statement is heard in silence and without interruption.'

The House was full. It could not be seen how so many Members and Strangers could be pushed into one Chamber. The Chamber was not big, when, in the morning, it was walked through – fifteen strides from beginning to end. But now there were six hundred and fifty Members in the Chamber, in their seats, behind the bar of the House, behind the Speaker's chair, in the galleries where Members sat and Clerks could sit, squatting in the gangways and hanging half out of the division lobbies. And the Strangers were made to sit, and when the seats they could sit in were taken, that was an end to it, and the other Strangers were asked to wait in the lobbies. And the press, two hundred of them, somehow, in the gallery they could use. And the doorkeepers, who, every single one, had found an excuse to be in the House, as if carrying messages. And the Clerks, who crowded into the galleries for Members, and in the little space behind the Speaker's chair, and the bigger space at the end of the Chamber, every single Clerk, except one, and his absence was not noticed.

The man who had once been Leader of the House and was not any longer began to speak. She had offered him everything she could. She had made him everything he was, and everything he could possibly become. She had not sacked him when he deserved it, and perhaps she should have done. He could become nothing more. He had had his time, and he had reached the limit of his ability. The time for him to go had come, and she was glad, he, too, had seen it. He had been Chancellor of the Exchequer, for a time; he had been Foreign Secretary, for a time. He had been good enough for that, mostly. He had had the opportunities for greatness which she had given him. It was not for her to say whether he had taken it. It was not for him to say whether he had taken it. In the last thing he could do, now that his time had come and almost gone, he would say it, anyway. The little Chamber was packed with flesh and was hot. Perhaps only the Speaker and the three Clerks before him found that they were not pressed against, and they did not find that they pressed against others. Sweating in their wigs, their space was history, and they found they could move in it.

The Prime Minister even was pressed against, and she did not think of what she was about to listen to. Her attendance in the House was pure courtesy. Naturally she would listen. There was no obligation on her to be here. Naturally she would be polite to the House. And afterwards, swiftly, she would go.

He began to speak, and there was silence. She listened to him, and in a way, he was saying to her what she knew he was capable of saying, but always thought he never would.

She wondered whether the rage she felt about his words; the violence she suppressed when she heard his words gave them any truth. She wondered whether the fact that she knew exactly what he would say meant that she saw the justice in what he had to say. She wondered whether her knowledge meant anything at all.

In the street, the policemen ran; not knowing, yet, what they ran to; knowing only that there was something to run to. Queer acts after nightfall, and violence in silence they found; they found an act, and they stopped it. And another act rose up, to be stopped, and another. And after a while the line of acts ran on for ever, unstoppably, unpreventably, and the line of policemen, one tired policeman taking the place of an exhausted one, could no longer even think about the consequences of the desires of the heart. They thought only of saving themselves, and of how much worse things might be. They thought of New York, of Palermo, of Rio de Janeiro, and they thought that the city was not as bad as all that. But in the desires it held, in the wickedness it held, the city was as bad; as bad as anything; and at the end of all the desires and the violence and the murder and the officers of prevention, one after another, there was a man killing what he most wanted and loved, because it was what he most wanted and loved.

Alone, perhaps, in London, Francesca took no interest in any of this. She had given up writing poetry. Instead, she was lying on a sofa reading the novel Henry had lent her. She was pleased she had it. It gave her an excuse to see him again, to hand it back to him. Otherwise it might have been hard for her to call him and manufacture a reason to see him, after the night on which he had given it to her.

She was not given to shame, not familiar with its hot ways across the skin, but whenever she thought about her voice saying to Jane on Henry's telephone, 'If Henry and I fall in love . . .' she could barely credit it. She knew as soon as the phone was down and the words still hung in the air that she had done it, and silently gave thanks that he had already handed the novel over. Worst of all was coming out of her room at two in the morning, roused by the noise downstairs rather than any sense of what was causing it, and the sight of Jane, dishevelled, her mouth ringed with black after red wine, yelling down the telephone at Henry, and all the time, the boy who had come to dinner that time sitting there apologetically drunk, looking up at her in no surprise, but only observing.

She had really done it, and no mistake. The only thing she could decently do was read the novel, and this is what she did. All the time she read she did not think of what she was reading. Instead she thought of Henry. She would not have been a bad reader of Henry's novel, though she was not a good reader of the one Henry had lent her. It disappointed her. It was his favourite novel, and yet there was nothing of him in it. She lay on the sofa and thought about Henry and about a poem she might write about him, although now she had given up writing poetry. Almost entirely; she might start again now that she had something to write about. Or perhaps – still better – she might write poems about his home, and the poems she would write about the rooms would reveal his personality through the beauty of their clutter. Like casual lovely snapshots. His clothes, she saw them, lying about romantically strewn on his furniture, the debris of his self. Sometimes Francesca shocked herself with the originality of her ideas.

She turned the pages, thinking. What she did not know is that he never strewed his clothes about, never did anything but place them in cupboards and wardrobes.

She would ask him. She had to go back to his flat to take back the novel, and, realizing this, she saw that her hands had passed pages, she did not know how many, between them without her looking at what was printed on them. It did not really matter. She read for his character. She knew she had that already. And it wasn't in *Two Worlds And Their Ways*.

At the other end of the long room there was Jane. She too was lying on a sofa, or rather on two. She had pulled two floral sofas together, facing each other, into a private hedged garden of patterned furnishings. She lay on the bed she made and did nothing. She only smoked, and her only sign in the room was, behind the hedged-about sofas, a blue line upwards of smoke and a sometimes quiet cough. She did not want to read. She did not even want to pretend to read. She had no shame, but, if she were shameless, she would have spoken to Francesca, and this she did not do.

Francesca feared her sister, and only now did she realize it. She had always known, from a very young age, when a tiny Jane intimidated those paid to teach her the piano with her fierce gaze, her disarray, and her confident unpractised inaccuracies, that Jane was feared. She had always known that Jane was worthy of fear. She knew that everyone who did not know her well, and some of those who did know her well, feared her. Francesca had never feared her, not knowingly. She had told those who said how frightening her sister was that that was simply her manner. She said she was fond and lovable. She said, even while devoting time to trying to appear as distant and unapproachable as Jane, that Jane was not distant and unapproachable at all. But though Jane did not work at her terror, at her grand imposing manner and untouchability, it was there, all the same. It was not diminished by her small-hours ranting. It was not touched by her approximate lipstick and staring wildness and stained clothes and her irrational, house-rousing telephone fury. And for the first time, she felt, Francesca felt the full force of not being spoken to by Jane, and for the first time, she knew what she had always felt and never named, fear of Jane.

Even when Francesca went out, in her habitual wrappings and layers of clothes for no good reason, Jane did not respond to her half-goodbye as she shut the door. But this was because she had not heard her. For seven hours she had done nothing except smoke. She had said nothing to anyone. But she was not thinking about Francesca, or even consciously ignoring her. She was thinking about nothing, and smoking. She felt, like Francesca, that she had been found out. And when Francesca had left the house, she decided to telephone Henry's sister Nancy.

Nancy was someone Jane told her secrets to, but only if she wanted them broadcast, as she usually did. Similarly, she telephoned Nancy when she wanted to know the secrets of other people. Nancy was shockingly indiscreet, and a good listener. She felt as if she would not understand the night she had spent drinking with Louis until she had told Nancy the story; she would not see its point; she would not know if it were a funny story or not; and she would not know if she had behaved well or badly.

Nancy would tell her what Henry had said, and Nancy would listen.

In this case she had a feeling she had behaved badly.

'Hullo darling,' she said. 'How are you?'

'Awful,' Nancy said. 'I've got the most awful cold. I met this man and he took me for a walk in the country and it rained the whole time and I didn't enjoy it one bit.'

'But why did you go in the first place?'

'No idea,' Nancy said, with her evident lie.

'Do you want me to come round and make you hot drinks?' Jane said with a fit of kindness.

'No, not really,' Nancy said. 'It's just rather nice of you to telephone. The annoying thing is that I was supposed to go out tonight, with the same man who gave me the cold, and I can't really, I feel so grim. It's supposed to be called something, this cold. Hong Kong or Singapore or something.'

'What do you mean?'

'Hong Kong Flu 2, or something,' Nancy said.

'I think my granny's got it. Where were you going to go?'

'Oh, just round the corner. But I'd bought a new dress and I thought I'd wear it tonight, and now I've got no reason to wear it at all.'

'You could put it on in front of the television. Or ask him round to look after you.'

'I don't really know him that well.'

'Well,' Jane said with an inspiration of guile, 'you could ask Henry round. He always likes new dresses. That is, if he's not too busy fucking my sister.'

'Is he fucking your sister?' Nancy said, equal to this. 'I'm sure he's not.'

'Oh, why?'

'I think he would have mentioned it,' she said. 'And he doesn't much like her.'

'He likes her enough,' Jane said. 'What's the dress like?'

While she let herself be told, she thought about clothes; she thought about the reasons people bought and wore clothes; and she realized there was only one reason people wore clothes. For display, and to hide.

'And it has a sort of white collar,' Nancy finished, 'which isn't very nice, to be honest, but it comes off.'

'Good,' Jane said. They went on for a while, and then they agreed to meet the next week for a drink, said their goodbyes, and Jane put the telephone down. They had not discussed Jane's behaviour. There was no point in saying anything, in fact. Jane knew how she had behaved.

It was a week before it occurred to John that he might be discovered by the police, and arrested for a murder which he had committed. By then, the ordinary fictions of existence had taken over, so that he had to stop himself from saying to himself 'arrested for a murder which he had not committed'. In quite the same way, he denied to those who solicitously asked, that his black eye was due to what it was due to. He said a door had slammed in his face. In a way it had.

He was suffering from influenza. It was the sort of influenza which the people who telephoned him referred to as one which was more enjoyable than anything. But for John there was no pleasure, none at all.

'I think you must have the same cold granny's got,' Jane said. 'And Nancy. Nancy said it was called Hong Kong 2. Like a bad film.'

But colds are not the same, and suffering is not the same, and disease is not the same, and he lay back and put his face in his pillow, when she had gone out of the room, knowing that suffering has to be endured alone.

It taught him what his daughters presumably knew, the length of a day. In his ordinary day, there were things to do which filled it. There was work; there were people to talk to, and advice to be given; and papers to write. Even on a Saturday and a Sunday there were these things; even in recesses there were these things, and he wondered, now they were taken away from him, whether he created these things for himself. He wondered, now they were no longer there, why he put these things in his life, and what they were there to replace. He could not remember the last time he was ill, and he could not remember the last time his days were empty like this. There was nothing in his life except sleep, and, when he felt like it, food, and a kind of suffering which was not pain, but just suffering.

Even when Helena had died he had carried on, for a while. And her death had been such a social event – had required organization and civility and letter writing – that it had only filled his days further. It had taken illness to make him mourn, and a death he had brought about, the death of a boy he, in the end, barely knew, and could hardly say he loved. And who would he say it to. And for what he was mourning, except his own suffering, he did not know.

The influenza went on for four days. By that time, John had whiffled his way through three boxes of tissues. And then it left him, or began to leave him. The red abrasions of the nose and mouth would take some time to soften back to skin; his throat would smooth, and the pitch of his voice was already beginning to rise. Sometimes he stretched his joints and there was a delicious, not a sore ache, which, by stretching, he relieved. The mark for him that he was getting better was not a day when he got dressed. This is the measure many people use. John always got dressed, even at his most weeping and liquid and hot. The mark for John was the day he felt like a shave. The day the flu left him was like a day, the marked end of summer, when over a hot brown cracked earth-skin of a volcano just once, a sky cracks. And rain, falling on the hot earth, calls up a softness from the new moistness of the earth, and a green life from nothing.

His skin, which, before, was wet, but cracked with drying, was bearded. He smiled at himself in the mirror, so unaccustomed; a disguised criminal on the run. As he put shaving foam on his face, he thought, with a blade in his hand, of his own mortality and terror. His terror, which, for the first time, like the great horse plunging down on him the metaphor evoked, he let have full rein. The first time. He let his terror loose on him, as he began to shave, in the hope his hand would not falter, and if he did not cut himself or tremble with it, he believed he would be safe.

His guilt and terror now for him were like the Journal he spent his life working on. The Journal did not record what was said or felt by men in the House. The Journal wrote what was essential. The Journal wrote the beginnings and the ends of things. It wrote the decisions, and the truths. It was as if until now he had been living by ephemera, and distracted by unessential things; what men said, and their laughter; and their bodies' movements. It was as if, until now, he had been living by Hansard. He had been writing down, in his head, what only was felt by him, in his head. And now did he see that, as if in an office no one had ever heard of, the essentials and the truths had always been there, being written down. And the end of the session had been reached, and presented to him, in a big blue book, were the decisions that had been reached. And, in his flu and his temperature, these are what they were.

He had telephoned a boy. He had offered him money to have sex with him. He had had sex with him, repeatedly. He had murdered him. The boy's body was now lying in a flat in Earl's Court. There was only one ambiguity, one unacknowledged truth yet to come. It was whether anyone else would know, and if anyone else had found the body of the boy.

As he shaved himself, he began to see a way in which no one else would discover the body, and in which he would not be caught. He wanted anyone else to be caught, and what he feared was not being punished, but, once caught, having to explain. And that he could not do even to himself, even in silence, inside his head. But, as if in parentheses, an irrelevant but comforting plot came to him. If the plot worked out, the police could never, and would never, discover who he was.

This is what happened, inside John's head, and what would happen. He had been assaulted for no reason in the street by a tramp. He visited his boy, had allowed himself to be buggered by the boy, with pleasure, and afterwards had killed him, for no reason. He had no reason to come up with reasons for killing him, because the reasons would never be called upon. Reasons could be come up with, if needed, but they never would be needed, because of what would follow.

It had been a surprise visit, and there was no reason why any sign of his traceable presence should have been recorded, in advance, by Giacomo, in the flat. Nor did anyone have any knowledge of his visits there; not his daughters, not his colleagues, not his wife, because she was dead. Not the friends of the boy, because he had none. Not the boy, not Giacomo, because he had never known John's name, and was dead. Only Louis. He would not think of that.

So the many signs of the past life of his body about Giacomo's body could and would be discounted. The many millions of men, the many hundreds of thousands of murderers, the many thousands of murderers who acted on their desire and murdered; they would not be tested, their fingers would not be blacked and printed. And if they were, it was of no account, because John would not be.

John even found a guilty man; a man who would be found guilty. There was a man before him, presumably; a man who had left some minutes, presumably, before John had arrived. The boy had not known him; he would not have known him, as he did not know John. The boy, when the man had telephoned, would have taken the man's telephone number, which now would be lying on a telephone pad by the bed; a number from which the man could be traced. That man, too, would have left his traces about the body, about the flat. He would have no argument when asked by the police where he had been on the morning of the murder. This ghost of a murderer, this man who, perhaps, had never been, took on flesh and reality. He was everywhere, and he was a murderer. And John was nowhere, and, although he killed, he was innocent.

There was one more thing. One more reason why the doctors of the dead would be unable to see the difference between the hands of a man who left at twelve, and the hands of a man who left at one. The body of the boy had not been found yet. He knew this with absolute certainty. He knew the boy had no friends. He knew he had no lover. He knew now what he never knew when the boy was alive. He knew the boy lived in his flat with a ringing telephone for strangers, and a silent telephone for both his beloved brothers, and his beloved mother, and his beloved father, and he lived alone, with this unringing telephone, in silence. The body of the boy would not be found by those who knew him, because there was no one who knew him. There was no reason why the body should ever be found, he thought, as he realized that the shaving foam had dried on his beard and prepared to apply some more.

He kept his mind from the body. He kept his mind from the body's quick loss of heat and its stiffening. He did not think of the tanning of the skin, like leather, in the clock-like on-and-off of the central heating, set months before. The telephone would carry on, like the central heating, and no one who overheard it would think from its continuing ringing banter with the silence that a death had taken place, and no one would think anything different, or worry when, from a failure to pay the bill, the central heating ceased, and the telephone stopped ringing. He did not think of the insects which, somehow, would find their way into the curtained flat, and they would settle, and they would feed. The liquids from the body would seep from it into the carpet, looking for an earth to rot into; what could evaporate would evaporate, and stink. The soft living beauty of the skin would go, and the fond warm glow of the eyes would freeze over, and the quick firm tenderness of the muscles would, as if panicked, cling on to each other, and pull. And in the end, someone, somewhere, who did not know Giacomo, would object to the smell – one could not hope that anyone would miss him, or notice his absence – and into the flat the policemen would force their way, and a cloud of tiny flies like a cloud would rise from the fucked body and the grinning rictus of what had once been a beautiful ungrinning beautiful man, and the hunchback who killed him had left his traces all about, and could not be traced.

He closed his eyes before the mirror in which he shaved. He did not think about these things.

'I think you're getting better,' Jane said.

'I hope so,' John said. It was a Thursday afternoon. Francesca had gone out, perhaps for a walk, or for some purpose of her own. John had dressed in the morning, as he normally did, and had sat in an armchair and read a novel, or appeared to read a novel. He had not felt much like eating at lunchtime, but Jane produced some electric-orange tomato soup from a tin, and a little toast with some anchovy paste, if he wanted. After all, he did feel like eating these comforting things. Then he had a little nap on the sofa, and woke to the comforting click of Jane's cigarette lighter, opposite him. She made him a cup of tea; she made him some more toasty things. He accepted them without making a show of his pleasure. When he was fluey, he often felt like weeping, for no cause, from his heat; now it was over, he felt like weeping from his fondness for her. He loved her so much, and he felt as if he feared she, too, were about to die.

'Do you think it was flu?' Jane said.

'No, just a sniff,' John said.

'Oh, it was worse than that. It was definitely a cold at least. I worried it might be a proper flu,' Jane said. They both had an austere regard for the degrees of illness, and with scorn they considered the reports of people who claimed on Tuesday to be in the depths of influenza, only on Wednesday to reappear with the faintest drip and wipe. A sniff was brief but unpleasant; a cold lasted a week; the flu was not far short of pneumonia in severity, and could kill, and did. They kept awfulness at bay by not invoking it without severity.

'Granny's really quite ill, you know,' Jane said. She had gone into hospital the week before.

'I know,' John said. 'When I'm better I'll go and see her.'

'Go tomorrow,' Jane said. 'I honestly am rather worried about her. She was terribly ill two days ago.'

'All right,' John said. 'I'm sure she'll be fine.'

'She's eighty-five,' Jane said. 'All right, but do go tomorrow.'

'Is she desperate for visitors?'

'Oh, no,' Jane said. 'I didn't know they'd done away with visitor's hour, and the result is that there's never a spare moment for her. You know what they're all like –'

'All those old beaux,' John said.

'Yes, but all the same, you ought to go.'

'Lovely muffins,' John said. 'I can't remember the last time I had muffins. I'm surprised you can still get them, actually.'

'I like them. You can always get them in supermarkets, in fact. They're just not very exciting, I suppose. Nice, though.'

'Maybe you can get them at work. I don't know,' John said.

'You've got butter on your chin.'

'*I know*. They're the sort of thing one always says one ate as a child, but I don't think I did. I know you never did, when you were little.'

'Grandmother likes them.'

'Does she? You know, I don't think I've seen her since the funeral.'

'Oh, you are bad. I'm really very cross with you.'

'Of course, one doesn't feel one has to keep up social obligations. It's a bit of an excuse, of course, but I really haven't felt up to it,' John said.

'Well, it can't be nice for her, either.'

'All right, I'll go tomorrow.'

'Good. Now tell me what I liked to eat best when I was tiny.'

'Oh, I can't remember.'

'Yes you can.'

'Well, you liked liver, I remember. At least when you were very tiny you did. It was always your favourite, and your mother and I were always amazed, because, of course, it's a great trial to get most small children, and I have to say, most small girls, to eat anything. When you were a bit older there were these gruesome birthday parties for ten seven-year-old girls, and your mother went to immense lengths to make cakes and sandwiches, and none of these little girls would eat anything but crisps and gassy drinks. But when you were tiny you did like liver – it was awfully convenient, because, you know, the cost of it – and, really, it was only when Frances came along –'

'Francesca,' Jane said.

'Francesca,' John said, not quite managing to suppress a smile, 'and she was terrible, a classically picky eater, and certainly wouldn't eat anything like liver that had been inside an animal. Eggs were all right for a bit, until one day somebody told her what eggs were and then that was hopeless too. So then you wouldn't eat anything either. It was a great bore, because then we had to find things that she would eat, and that you would eat as well, because you certainly wouldn't eat anything that Francesca turned up her nose at. Quite often you'd refuse to eat things which she wanted to eat as well, just because she wanted to eat them, and, heaven knows, there was little enough food she would eat. I think in the end you both lived for about five years on toast and peanut butter and jam. Didn't do you any harm. But muffins, no.'

'The odd thing is, I seem to remember them,' Jane said.

'Projection,' John said. 'They seem like a nostalgic sort of thing, and the sort of thing you would have eaten in your childhood, and so you do remember them, in a way. A bit like being abused as a child and then suppressing the memory, as people are supposed to, only in reverse. Are there any more?'

'A few.'

'Will you do me a favour?'

'Of course I will,' Jane said. To anyone else on earth, she would have said, That depends on the favour. But at that moment, she would have done anything for her poor father, from whom she had exacted one favour. But she knew, before he asked, what he was going to ask.

'Ask Henry round for dinner and be nice to him.'

She looked at him with the momentary pretence of aghastness. She was not aghast, of course. It was what she wanted.

'When Francesca's gone out for the evening, of course,' he added quickly.

'Done,' she said. They did not need to talk; they heard each other, and, that afternoon, they sat with their muffins and, before they licked, they let the butter run down the outside of their wrists. He allowed himself pleasure, for now, and when he sweated, it was with his illness, and nothing more serious.

When Henry's telephone rang, it was Francesca. And whenever he got home, his telephone answering machine was flashing to indicate that there were messages on it, and they were messages from Francesca.

He was grateful and pleased that he was telephoned. Of course he was. He knew now that, before he knew Francesca, hardly anybody telephoned him; he had so few friends, compared to the sort of people who had friends. That is what he thought. When he imagined what his life had been like before he met her, before he had anything to do with his life except go to his colleagues' houses for dinner and go to work during the day, he imagined that he had been unhappy, that he had felt a lack of things for him to do and people to see.

But was this true? Had he been unhappy? Or was it simply that, now that his life was more full, he was aware, retrospectively, that his before-life was not up to much? What Henry thought, he could not say to Francesca. He thought that perhaps he could not have been unhappy and not known it. Because unhappiness depends on one knowing it. And if he, then, had been unhappy without knowing it, there was no reason that he might not be unhappy now, without knowing it. He would not speculate.

Francesca was pursuing him – that was as far as he would

go. And now he enjoyed the ordinary parts of his life. His job, for instance. He had always quite liked it. Now that Francesca was there to telephone him, and to talk to him about her life, to share as much of his life as she possibly could, he enjoyed going to work even more. She did not call him there. He said to himself that he liked the change she had brought to his life; the new fullness, so that he now never had an afternoon with a novel, or in front of the television with a bottle of wine he would soon finish. Instead, there was work, which he enjoyed, or a dinner with her, which he enjoyed, or work on his novel, which she asked him to do, and which, nevertheless, he now knew he would never finish and never publish, because it was rubbish. He was so busy, and his life was so changed that he frankly admitted to happiness, and did not inquire into himself before he said it. His happiness belonged, too, to points in his life where Francesca had no hold, where she was not, and never was. Points of solitude. Perhaps even more so. His happiness was not apparent to others, until they were told. He did not mind; he knew he did not mind.

They were coming out of a cinema.

'What did you think?' she said, once they were half-way down the street and had allowed time for them to walk in silence for whatever reason for a while.

He had been bored by the film. 'I liked it,' he said.

'I thought it was terribly beautiful,' she said. 'I particularly liked the part with the horses.'

'The horses?' he said.

'Yes, the horses on the statues.'

He had no idea what she was talking about.

'I haven't seen any of his films before,' he said.

'No, nor have I,' she said. 'At least I don't think so. Did you find it moving?'

'I think so,' he said. 'Well, I wasn't moved by it particularly, but I could see that it was moving.'

'I was terribly moved by it,' she said. 'You know the other night.'

'Yes,' Henry said. It was the first time she had raised it.

'About what I said.'

'Don't worry about it,' Henry said. 'Jane just has this knack of driving people mad and then making them say things they regret afterwards.'

'It's not so much regret,' Francesca said. 'It's more embarrassment. After all, if you and I fell in love, it would be none of Jane's business.'

'No,' Henry said cautiously. He was only vaguely aware that this was what Francesca had said. 'It isn't any of her business.'

Only then did he notice what he had said. If he had said, 'It wouldn't be any of her business,' it would have been quite different. Nothing would have happened.

'I'm glad you feel like that,' Francesca said, taking his arm.

'Oh, shall we go in here?' Henry said. They were going past a bar.

'I thought we might walk for a while,' she said.

'All right,' he said.

'You know,' she said. 'You always want to be inside. I've noticed this about you. Whenever we go out together, we walk for five minutes and then you want to go into a restaurant or a café or a bar. Why don't you like to walk?'

'I imagine I have weak ankles,' Henry said. 'No, I didn't realize that. It is true.'

'Do you dislike the outside?' she said.

'I don't know,' he said, not knowing. Perhaps he did; after all, he didn't much care for the garden, he never went to the country, and he never, if he could avoid it, walked anywhere in town.

'Do you ever exercise?'

'No,' Henry said, shuddering, 'what an *idea*. I haven't exercised since I was at school, and I don't intend to exercise ever again.'

'Nor do I,' said Francesca, and a strange chill came over Henry. He wondered to himself, while they walked, what he had intended Francesca to think when he had expressed his horror at exercising. He wondered what had happened to the two of them in the last five minutes; he wondered what had made it happen, and the conclusion he came to, quite quickly, was that it was the will of Francesca. For the first time, he recognized something of her sister in her.

'I walk, sometimes,' Francesca said. 'And I like the countryside, really. I do.'

'I don't think I do,' Henry said. 'Though, actually, the only time I ever go to the country is when I visit my parents. I might be disliking that and just thinking I dislike the country.'

'Do you dislike visiting your parents?' Francesca said.

'Yes,' Henry said. 'That's what I just said.'

'What are they like?' Francesca said.

'Oh, ordinary,' Henry said. 'Like everybody's parents. Haven't I ever told you about them?'

'Not much,' Francesca said. 'Look, there's that boy who came to dinner.'

And, as they were walking past the café they happened to be walking past, there was Louis sitting in the open floor-length window with, if they had known it, Joey. And Joey was saying, 'I told her, I don't care, I simply don't care, and she said to me –' and Louis was laughing, and Joey's cigarette was throwing arms of smoke around the diners next to them on every side.

'Shall we stop?' Francesca said.

'No, let's not,' Henry said. He was respecting the pleasure of Louis's evening, and only afterwards, when he turned to look at the way she was beaming at the street, did he see the way she, inevitably, had taken it. He saw in that moment how their evenings would be; how, from now, they would always be.

There were many houses, actually, quite near the Palace, in which discussion took place at that time. Around a church, very near the Palace, there was a square, and off the square there were six eighteenth-century streets. These streets were full of houses which were full of beautiful plain innocent eighteenth-century paintings. But the people who lived in these houses, who were politicians and lobbyists, and sometimes publishers, lived in their houses and looked from time to time at their minor but interesting Zoffanys, or Devises, or, in the case of the richer inhabitants of the tiny quarter, Gainsboroughs, and hardly thought about them.

In these little houses, that evening, there were a good many conversations about the question of the Prime Minister. And in the rest of the square mile or two around the Palace, too, they talked; somewhere near, two Members talked to each other.

'She's finished,' one said.

'I know,' the other said. 'But that's only what everybody

is saying. If she pulled herself together, we'd all vote for her. I'd vote for her. I will vote for her.'

'So will I,' murmured the other. 'She's really our only chance.'

'That's so true,' said the second. 'But no one seems to see that.'

'We see it, don't we?' the first said. The two of them had, long before, at university, slept together; they had expressed their love for each other, in full seriousness; they had committed fellatio, willingly, on each other. They did so no longer, and talked about that time very seldom.

'Yes, we see it,' the second said. 'I'm sure everybody does, in fact. It's simply that we all believe that nobody else would vote for her.'

'And yet she's finished,' the first said, getting up. He went to the sideboard and picked up a photograph, of a woman. 'She is finished, even if it's only that everyone thinks she is.'

'No,' the second said. 'I can't believe it.'

'Where is she?' the first said, referring to the other's wife, in the photograph.

'Upstairs,' the second said, untruthfully. 'It's her evening for the telephone.'

'I see.'

Elsewhere, in Lord North street, a dinner was taking place, a dinner for thirty. Members were there, and three Cabinet Ministers, and yet, because there were business-men, and the wives of businessmen, and Americans, and the wives of Americans in the room, they did not talk about what was going on. They all merely said, when asked, that the Prime Minister would stay for many years yet, and that her rival would find that his day was past, and her day was still at its zenith. The foreigners and the businessmen nodded, finding the idea of the casual deposition of the Prime Minister an unimaginable idea.

Elsewhere in that small town, there were blocks of flats; blocks which somewhere else would house forty, and here held two hundred. Blocks split up into depressing two-room flats, where men slept alone from Monday to Wednesday, if that, and telephoned their wives from, and went back to, drunk, three nights a week, and left thankfully on Thursday afternoon. Men of every party lived in these flats, and, although they had never spoken to or seen the Prime Minister very closely, they found at this time they were questioned with a nagging closeness as to her fate. And some of them gave their opinion, seriously, as if they knew what they were talking about, and as if their opinion was worth anything at all.

As for me, as for me . . .

Listen. I was dreaming all this time. I dreamt about my future as a woman who was not Prime Minister. I dreamt that I would take my red boxes with me, and my power, and the men who surrounded me always. In this last I was right. The men who surrounded me are still with me, with their bouffant hair and their immaculacy, and their intense gaze at me, as if I were other than, better than human.

But I dreamt all that time that I would always be as powerful as I was. Power came to be thought of as the same as the power I held. The power I held was not the power of the Prime Minister. It was my power. That is what I thought. And that is what it was. I had power over everything. I had power over the Cabinet, and the Government, and the Party, and the House, and the House of Lords, and Westminster, and London, and England, and

Great Britain, and its islands and its dominions and the fragments of its history and the glorious trailing light of its past, every privatized tiny glory of the kingdom added its unknowing lucent fragment to my power.

Therefore, I do not know, at this time, why I was in France. But that was the case.

I ran down the steps, and I elbowed a man aside, and I cried to the world, I fight on. I fight to win. I remember going to a ballet; and I was late. I remember the presidents of the many countries were kind to me, and I remember thanking them. I was good at their names, and I had always been good at recalling the names of their wives; I imagine it is one of the things I am famous for. I remember nothing of the ballet. Men passed notes to me throughout the evening, and through the dinner which followed, of which I ate nothing, or almost nothing.

'Nothing to be concerned about, Prime Minister,' one of the notes said. And that was it. I was concerned about nothing. I was concerned at this nothing, this fact that nobody around me saw anything to be concerned about. I could not say that. They were all doing their best, and I had never done anything but my best. But it concerned me. And somehow, for the first time, I knew that the nothing I saw, the unofficed nothing which stretched out before me like a future, which is what it was, this nothing; I knew it was waiting for me. I would not wait for it. But it could wait for me, and it did.

'I came here with Louis,' Jane said. 'It was rather good.'

'Who is Louis?' Nancy said.

It was a date they had arranged the week before. Jane

and Nancy spent a good deal of time having cups of tea together, and drinking in each other's houses. From time to time – perhaps every six months – one or other of them felt dissatisfied with this, and made the effort to suggest going out for dinner, or once for a drink. They had agreed to go out for dinner, and Jane had suggested the fashionable, small restaurant she had gone to with Louis and eaten dried salted pig's liver.

'It's rather early to eat,' Jane said to the waiter, who was hovering. 'Can we order a couple of drinks and order food in half an hour?'

'The trouble is,' the waiter said, 'that we have to have the table back at nine-thirty, I'm afraid.'

'Oh,' Jane said. 'I didn't realize that. Well, can we have a bottle of the St Veran?'

'I'm not drinking,' Nancy said. 'Antibiotics.'

'A bottle,' Jane confirmed. 'And some water. I'll just think about food.'

'It isn't all that early,' Nancy said when the waiter had gone. 'Seven-thirty is quite respectable.'

'We'll be finished by nine,' Jane said. 'And if you're not drinking you'll be bored by then.'

'No, I won't,' Nancy said. 'Who is Louis?'

'Louis?'

'You said you came here with him.'

'Oh yes. He works with my father and Henry. I met him in a pub once by chance and again when he came to dinner at my father's. Are you sure you don't know him?'

'Quite sure.'

'Well, he brought me here and we had a very good time. The food is good.'

'What would you recommend?'

'Oh, I don't know. The menu's changed since the last time.'

'I don't know what I want. What are you going to have?'

'I don't know,' Jane said, with a slight sinking feeling. 'Something to go with the wine.'

'Will you want all that wine?'

'Yes, I think so,' Jane said.

'And then – and then – and then –' the man at the next table said. He was explosive with laughter and his friend's face was paralysed in suppressed expectant merriment.

'Have you seen Henry recently?' Nancy said.

'No,' Jane said.

'I saw him a couple of days ago.'

'I'd rather not talk about him.'

There was no one else in the restaurant but them and the laughing people at the next table. Out of the window a pneumatic drill was going. It seemed quite close. The wine arrived.

'Thanks, that's fine. Are you sure you don't want any?'

'No, these antibiotics.'

'Would you like to order now?' the waiter said.

'Yes,' Jane said. She ordered.

'Oh, but I was going to have that,' Nancy said.

'Well, we can both have the same thing,' Jane said.

'No, we ought to have different things.'

'All right, you have that, and I'll have the pork.'

'But you wanted the pheasant.'

'I don't mind.'

'No, I'd rather have the fish anyway,' Nancy said.

'So what do you want?' the waiter said.

Jane sorted it out.

'Was that right?' Nancy said. 'I don't think I wanted that.'

'You said you wanted the fish.'

'I thought you said I could have the pheasant.'

'Do you want me to call him back?'

'No,' Nancy said, 'it's all right. No, please don't call him back, it'll be fine.'

Silence fell.

'How is your job?' Jane said.

'Oh, it's fine,' Nancy said. 'We're quite busy.'

'I'd like to be busy,' Jane said. 'I don't have enough to do, really.'

'I've got plenty to do,' Nancy said. 'Too much, almost. How is your father coping?'

'All right, I think,' Jane said.

'I thought I saw him in Putney High Street a week or two ago. He had the most enormous black eye.'

'Yes, he fell over at work.'

'Does he often fall over?'

'No,' Jane said. 'Why?'

'He could sue the House of Commons for work-related injuries, or something.'

'Don't be absurd. He's had that awful cold you had and my old granny. He was off work for almost a week with it. I've been lucky so far.'

'Is Francesca going out with Henry?'

'No,' Jane said. 'Not as far as I know. Whatever made you think that?'

'You told me he was.'

'I don't think so,' Jane said.

'They might be quite well suited,' Nancy said.

Jane poured herself another glass of wine. She was pleased

to have discovered this wine. It was not especially well known; at least not to her, who knew little about wine. But she liked it. The food arrived and they stopped talking.

'That's a horrid dress you're wearing,' Jane said after a while.

'It's new,' Nancy said.

'It's horrid.'

'What's so horrid about it? I like it.'

'I don't like that collar at all. It makes you look like a sacrificial victim with your head on a plate, and a lace doily all round it.'

'I like it. Really, Jane, you are unpleasant.'

'I'm just telling you what I think.'

'I'm not interested.'

'Doesn't the collar come off? It might be all right without it.'

'It does, but I tried it and it looked too plain. And anyway I like it with the collar.'

'It doesn't suit you.'

Nancy pushed her plate away, still loaded with fish and potatoes. It was difficult to make a point while plucking fish bones from your teeth.

'I honestly don't come out with you to be insulted,' Nancy said. 'You know what your trouble is.'

'No,' Jane said. She enjoyed this conversation.

'You got into the habit of being clever and rude when you were young, and now you can't get out of it. Nobody minds someone who's twenty and beautiful and clever being clever and rude, but look at you now. You haven't combed your hair, your clothes aren't very clean, you look terribly unhealthy, and you're still being rude. And you're thirty. Just ask yourself what there is to recommend you.'

'Nothing,' Jane said.

'Yes, nothing, that's exactly it,' Nancy said. 'Just ask yourself why anyone would ever want to spend time with you, or go out with you. So don't waste your time telling me that my collar doesn't suit me, or whatever. Think about yourself.'

'I will,' Jane said. 'Thank you. Can I have another bottle of wine please?'

It was nine o'clock when they left the restaurant. It was the middle of the week and the streets were surprisingly empty; those who were still in London were dining, or in pubs. Jane had drunk two bottles of wine. Nancy had drunk a litre of mineral water.

'Do you want a cup of coffee?' Jane said.

'I'm still quite tired after the flu,' Nancy said.

'I don't think it was flu,' Jane said. 'It was just a very bad cold.'

'No, it was definitely flu,' Nancy said. 'Anyway, you haven't had it.'

'I saw what my father had,' Jane said.

'But I think I'd better get home,' Nancy said. 'Are you walking to the tube?'

'No, I'm going to get this cab,' Jane said, sticking her arm out.

'Well, thanks for a lovely evening,' Nancy said. The cab was already driving away. Nancy stood for a moment on the kerb; then, turning towards the tube, she decided that when she got in she would telephone Henry, to whom she hadn't spoken for some time, and chat about Jane and Francesca. She, too, wanted to know what he planned to do.

*   *   *

The next day, a problem arose.

This is what happened. A Member was made into a junior Whip, to his surprise and to those who knew him. He was, until then, a member of a committee which supposedly existed to supervise the expenditure of a Government department, and, in fact, did nothing but bore its Clerk to rigidity. He could, daily, be seen in the Tea Room, day after day, in his slightly holed cardigan and horrid beard, reading every single newspaper which there was kept. The only pleasure in his life, and one of the biggest in the lives of the members of the committee, was the skill the committee showed in extracting money from another committee to go to the warmer parts of the world at the colder times of the year.

The Member was obliged to leave the committee of which he was a member as soon as he was made a Whip. After a time, the Whips, of whom he was now one, negotiated with one another, in lobbies and corridors and over cups of tea and glasses of whisky, and fielded bribes from some evidently hopeless Members and bullied recalcitrant other Members, and promised some that they would be put on the committee if they were good, and promised other Members that they would be put on the committee if they were bad. And in the end, they all decided on another Member, thought to be unobjectionable, harmless, loyal, and dull, about whom absolutely nothing was known, who should be put on this completely unheard-of committee.

Another committee met, whose job it was to meet, and agreed to nominate the Member whom the Whips had nominated, and placed a motion on the order paper – drafted and subsequently corrected, with a good deal of tutting and groaning and exclamation by Henry – which proposed the discharge of the first Member, who was now a Whip, from the committee, and the adding of the second Member to that committee.

This was all quite normal, down to the tutting and the groaning and the exclamations, of which nobody took any notice whatever, quite rightly. Now problems began to arise.

The second Member was not, in fact, as unobjectionable as it seemed. In fact, he was widely known, to everybody but the Whips, to be regularly receiving rewards – quite indirectly, quite correctly – for small investments. Such rewards were of a small but agreeable nature. His investment in areas which would be affected by the committee's deliberations in the warmer parts of the world at the colder times of the year came to the notice of parts of the House. Parts of the House was the polite phrase the Clerks used: by which they meant a lunatic Member. The day occurred when the motion removing one Member and replacing him with another arose. The Government had no idea that the motion or the Member was more than usually obnoxious to any part of the House, and anticipated that no objection would be received.

When the Whip moving the motion sat down, another Member stood up, as if to make a speech.

'On a point of order, Mr Speaker,' he said. 'I do not know the correct procedure for objecting to this motion.'

'Objection taken,' the Speaker said. The Clerks before the Speaker looked aghast.

The problem now arose.

'There's nothing to write, of course,' the Clerk of Public Bills said, later, in the Journal Office, looking at the big green-sheeted minute books in which he had written what had happened. 'No point in minuting unopposed business that's objected to after the moment of interruption.'

'But something has to be written,' Henry said, who that night happened to be writing the Vote. 'Because at that point, Standing Order Number Fourteen bites.'

'Oh, stuff Standing Order Number Fourteen,' the Clerk of Public Bills said, and there was, of course, nothing more Henry could say.

So Henry and Louis, who were both on duty that night, decided to issue the Vote with no mention of anything that had happened relating to select committee membership.

Louis did not worry about these things overnight, because he did not understand them well enough. But once Henry left the House and went home, at twenty-to-three in the morning, he started to think about the consequences of not having minuted something from which consequences could flow. It was his job to take account of consequences which had not yet happened, and to take responsibility for them, and he realized that he had not yet done so. It was his job to write history as it happened, and he had not noticed actions which could precipitate consequences.

As he ate breakfast the next morning he discovered before the end that pieces of food had lodged themselves in a gap between his teeth he had never noticed. He knew from television advertising that this caused tooth decay and gum disease. So he searched for something with which to extract the bits of food. A needle suggested itself, but so did a narrative in which Henry swallowed the needle, which perforated his stomach and led to his hideous and painful death from peritonitis.

Finally, what he found was a paperclip. Extended, it

plunged into the soft matter which might have been gum, but, unfeeling, was probably old food.

'What are you doing?' said Francesca.

'Finishing my breakfast,' Henry said. He lied quite readily to her, he found, and it did not alter what he thought of her. 'Thanks for telephoning. I'm in a bit of a rush. See you soon, I hope.'

'Yes, I hope so,' Francesca said. He put the telephone down and did not think of her. Rather, he thought of the telephone conversation – a strange telephone conversation – he had had with Nancy the night before.

'Jane's completely unbearable,' she kept saying. 'You just have to make it completely plain to her what the situation is.'

'What is the situation?'

'The situation is that you don't love her and you're not going to go back to her,' Nancy said.

'But I've made that plain to her.'

'She doesn't believe it, and she won't till you marry someone else.'

He pushed it out of his mind, and thought again about work. All the way to work he heard, with the faintest of his bat's ears, a noise which might have been the distant noise of his confidence and knowledge and control, a great rock of control, being worn down, as if by wind and rain, by the passing of time and the occasional careless foolish slip. What he saw, or heard, or, distantly, like a tremor, felt, was the weight and thinning and threat of a mistake. He feared mistake as other men feared death, and in it he saw the passing of time and the erosion of his ability. He did not wish to go to work, and he did not see how he could not.

He stood on the escalator of the underground in his not much worn suit and prepared to take his luxurious two-stop journey. A pigeon had ventured underground somehow and applauded its way desperately from one end of the escalator's diagonal vault to another. Its panicked speed made one see how small the space cut out of the earth was. Henry was heading downwards, and, as he did this every day, this inevitable journey, he did not look back at the pigeon, as if he did not care. He did not, except by the continuing castanetting slaps of its wings, trying for air, and finding only new roofs, new walls, see that it would never get out. Unless it met with the kindness of those who had nothing to lose. Which it would not meet with, because something to lose is what everyone has.

When he arrived at work at ten past ten o'clock, he found John, whose first morning back at work this was, and the Senior Vote Writer in the middle of an argument. He deduced that the Clerk of the House had visited the office some moments before, and withdrew behind a bookcase to read the Standing Order.

'(e) proceedings on a motion such as is referred to in paragraph (2) of Standing Order No. 104 (Nomination of select committees) for the nomination or discharge of members of select committees appointed under Standing Order No. 130 (Select committees related to government departments) which has been opposed at or after the interruption of business on a preceding day: Provided that any such questions necessary to dispose of the proceedings on such a motion shall be put at eleven o'clock or one hour after the commencement of these proceedings, whichever is the later,' he read. Or something like that.

'Fuck all to do with the Journal,' the Senior Vote Writer said, tottering with rage.

'But,' John said.

'You're going to say, but what about the Standing Order. I know about it. I don't care. The fact is we don't minute business if it's opposed and isn't proceeded with, and I don't see a case for starting now.'

'The point is surely that we have a consequence now following from something which hasn't been recorded in the Journal and nobody would ever see the necessary reason why this motion now has to be given an hour on the floor of the House unless we now minute the objection in retrospect,' John said.

Henry listened for a while longer, looking at the words on the page, which were as if no human being had ever written them, and hearing the words in the air. For a moment he understood them, and then he almost understood them, and then he knew he did not. He kept silent about his failure to understand, as about his mistake, if it had, indeed, been a mistake, which he did not quite understand. When Henry left the House to walk home, or if he ever left his job, when he mastered the facts he needed, he knew what would happen. The facts would quickly slide away from him like smooth laughing girls on ice in pompoms, away from a learning fat top-heavy boy skater. Their significance, like the ice melting into the warming seas beneath, would go from him into nothing. Once more the lessons of facts about the world he had once learnt, when young; lessons of figures and numbers and rocks and metals. It was an effort which he would come to mount, as he had mounted most efforts until now, successfully. He had gained his knowledge with effort, and knowing it would cost him no effort, at some unimagineable imagined future, to lose.

'The Clerk of the Journals,' the Senior Vote Writer pronounced, departing grandly from the office, 'has gone quite mad. I thought I was the maddest in this office, but I find not.'

The Clerk of the Journals had left the office, and became oblivious of the Senior Vote Writer's venom, directed at his back. Louis, sitting ignored, felt himself becoming the whole of boredom. The silence between him and Henry was soporific as heat or afternoons are.

'What's the time?' Louis said, that afternoon.

'Guess,' Henry said.

'Half-past three.'

'Better than that.'

'Four o'clock.'

'Not so good.'

'You're quoting something.'

'Yes, I am,' Henry said, and laughed. Louis looked at him as if it were not common, Henry laughing. Perhaps it was not.

'What do you think will happen this afternoon?' Louis said.

'The same as usual, I imagine,' Henry said.

'I meant, with the ballot.'

'Oh, *that*,' Henry said. 'No idea. Hundreds of lunatics casting their vote with no one to tell them who to cast it for, hundreds quite possibly drunk, and all we can say is that they will be voting for someone who next month will be Prime Minister. And, anyway, who cares?'

'I do,' Louis said. 'Probably everyone cares, except you.'

'Probably,' Henry said. Silence fell. Louis went to have

a cup of tea, and came back. The sun moved in the sky.
The Senior Vote Writer, who had, that day, spent almost
four hours in the office, one of them reading a novel, and
another one and a half of them asleep, went home.

'Are you busy?' Louis said. It was Thursday. Both of
them had been sitting in the office with nothing to do
but make occasional notes on pieces of paper, and wait
for Members to come in. No Member had come into the
office for thirteen days, and that had been by mistake.

'Not in the *slightest*,' Henry said, smiling brightly.
'So long as you don't want to talk about the doings
of the Conservative Party. I don't want to start that
again. It's too utterly sick-making and tedious. I can't
remember the last time it was so completely dull and
boring.'

'Don't be so affected, Henry,' Louis said, and Henry
noticed something he had never observed before, that Louis
got pleasure out of saying his name. 'They're just about
to sack the Prime Minister out of not much more than
naughtiness and boredom. That's fairly interesting.'

'When you've been here as long as I have, though we're
not going to talk about it,' Henry said, 'you won't find
any of this in the slightest bit interesting. You'll be madly
excited by clauses outside the scope of a bill, and questions
of hybridity instead.'

'What's hybridity?' Louis said, picking up the newspaper.

'Look it up. Do you think, by the way, there are any
intelligent Members?'

'I can't think of any,' Louis said, a little sycophantically.

'I think you're being a little harsh,' Henry said. 'I can think of five.'

'Who are they?' Louis said. Henry named them. They were all quite unknown to Louis. 'Yes, I think you're probably right about them.'

'They are a dim bunch,' Henry said. 'God knows who sends them here, or why we have to put up with them now they're here.' They carried on working for a moment or two. Henry reflectively sucked on his pen. The door to the office opened, and they looked round, but it was only John. He took down a copy of the Journal for 1988–89, and began to look something up. They ignored him.

'What are the five greatest operas?' Henry said, as if talking to himself.

'What, ever?' Louis said.

'Yes,' Henry said. 'Not just your favourite ones, of course. And not just the immortal masterpieces, but genuinely the most important ones.'

'I don't think there's a difference,' Louis said. 'I think the ones universally recognized as great probably are the most important ones. After all, what other standards would one have other than consensus between informed judges, or a purely subjective opinion?'

'Truth, of course,' Henry said. 'Most people have no independent judgement at all, as Pope said.'

'He didn't say that at all,' Louis said. 'He said, Most women have no characters at all. Good god, there really is nothing whatever in the newspaper.'

He turned the page. There, half-way down the page, was a photograph. Louis looked at it, and then he read the story. He read it again, and looked at the photograph of the beautiful laughing boy.

There he was.

John was at the other end of the office. He could not speak.

He could only stop himself from speaking.

What he had been about to say was to call to John, and say, That boy, that boy; but then he saw almost immediately that he should not. He looked again at the picture, and he knew what had happened. It was utterly clear to him; as clear as the events in the Journal, once he had learnt to read it. He understood the meaning of his black eye, two weeks before. He understood what acts had passed between them. And he understood that John had already read the newspaper that day, and had a good reason for not bringing the piece to Louis's attention.

He saw that there, in the hundred and fifty words and the photograph, three inches by two, was everything he needed, to do what he was going to do. He knew what he was going to do. He knew every awful thing he had to do, and the single act of betrayal, and he knew that, once he had done it, it would follow him, in his mind, for ever. He read once more, about the dead boy, and looked at the photograph of Giacomo, who was dead.

'Yes,' Henry said. 'That's what I was thinking of, though it's not frightfully relevant. What I meant was that independent judgement isn't the same as subjectivity. I was being complimentary, of course, in supposing you do have an independent judgement. One only has to look downstairs to see how quickly a judgement – even a judgement which isn't rooted in any kind of truth at all – how quickly a judgement spreads. The Tory party thinks the Prime Minister's time is up, so it is. The belief that her time is up, that she's going to lose them the next election has spread so quickly it doesn't matter a bit whether it's true or not. If they had any independent judgement, they might be able to see whether it were true or not, and act in a sensible way. As it is, they only know what most people think, or what some people think, and they're going to act on a cumulative opinion. Watch them. It might be right, or wrong. There's no way of knowing what the electorate would do, of course, or whether they really are going to throw her and them out at a general election. It's just a matter of what they believe.'

'But,' John said. 'If everyone acted in accordance with their wishes, we would have anarchy and moral chaos and everyone would be raping and murdering. Excuse me.' He left the office, not looking at Louis reading the newspaper.

He had read the newspaper that morning; he had spent two hours staring at the same page; and now that he had seen Louis reading the newspaper, and not looking at him, he knew exactly what was going to happen to him, and all he could do was leave the office, and not look at Louis reading the newspaper.

'Quite,' Henry said. 'That would never do, although it wasn't really what I was talking about.'

'But the five greatest operas,' Louis said.

'Yes,' Henry said. 'Now, quite a lot of people would say *Boris Godunov*, which is frankly inferior, obviously inferior to *Prince Igor* or *The Queen of Spades* or quite a lot of things. Not that those are in the five greatest operas either. It's just a matter of exercising personal judgement in favour of truth.'

'Well,' Louis said.

'*Tristan*? I think so,' Henry said. 'But a Mozart? Which one?'

'*Marriage of Figaro*,' Louis said.

'No, I don't think so,' Henry said. 'I think more highly of *Così fan tutte*. Musically, I think it's more ingenious and more tightly bound together, if you see what I mean. And more serious, in a way.'

'Yes,' Louis said.

'I wish,' John said. He had come back into the office without either of them noticing. He stood by the bookcase, holding the huge plank-like object of the 1988–89 Journal. 'I wish sometimes I would come into the office and find one or other or even both of you doing some work. Instead, I just come in and you're both just nattering pointlessly about opera or novels. You know, the taxpayer pays you both large sums of money just to sit there and talk about Mozart. And there's work to be done. I'm working. You must have work to do.'

'No,' Henry said. 'We've nothing to do, actually.'

'Well, just get on and do something,' John said. 'Just do something. It drives me up the fucking wall to see you doing nothing. There are so many fucking things you could be doing and you're doing fucking nothing, and there are people outside starving and dying on the streets and for all you know there are people murdering each other for no reason at all. I look at my payslip every month, at the end of the month, and I know I fucking well deserve it, I would deserve any sum of money they felt like paying me, but do you have that feeling? Do you feel you should? I don't think you do and I don't think you should. And here you are talking about whether one fucking novel is better than another, and it's not good enough, and if you can't find anything to do in your fucking job description then you should be going out and finding things to do and listening to what's going on in the Chamber if you think that'll do any good either. I don't know, but for Christ's sake just fucking stop doing fucking nothing.'

'Actually,' Louis said. 'We weren't talking about novels. We were talking about operas.'

It was brave of him to say it, although it was true. It was something that Louis could have said, knowing what he knew, and knowing now what he could do, or what he could refrain from doing. John didn't seem to see or hear him, but he stood, red-faced and strangely broken for a second with his enormous book in his hands and his suddenly enormous hump on him before he strode to the window and, with a grunt, threw the volume out of the window. It could not have been more than half a second, and that is all it seemed, before there was a crash from a car, which must have been parked underneath. They could not see the damage it had done. The telephone was ringing. John turned and walked out of the office. Henry picked up his telephone.

'Yes,' Henry said to the telephone. 'That seems all right.' He looked at John, as he spoke, with his coat and without his briefcase, leaving his office, although it was only late in the afternoon. He could see he was shaking, and that he did not wish to meet anybody's gaze, and not Henry's, whom his daughters wished to marry. It was as if, not as if he were ashamed of his rage, but as if he did not understand where it had come from or why. Or as if he had understood where it had come from but not why, not then.

'Tomorrow then,' Jane said to the telephone. 'About eight.' She picked a time when she knew Francesca would be out. When Henry agreed, Jane put the telephone down and smiled at the man in the black coat and white tie. Henry had understood her to be telephoning from her house. But she was in the Palace, waiting for Louis. It was a long-agreed thing; it was to balance out the dreadful immense evening they had had in the Dome and the French House and a restaurant neither of them could agree they had ever been to. Jane was to come to the office, and Louis would take her to a bar, and perhaps to dinner. Henry, they had both independently decided, should not know about this occurrence.

She was very early for their appointment, and sat down on the green benches. She knew she could not smoke, and so had brought a book to read.

After a time she looked up. The lobby was full, in its usual way, of people of only one sort. Today, she realized that she was almost the only person in the lobby without a child in her arms. Everybody else was holding an infant. At the back, a chorus of bawling was just starting up, and spreading quickly, like a pox. She regarded them dispassionately. She did not mind children, but did not think of them as serious human beings. She would never talk to one, and had never thought of having one. It was always left to Francesca to bill and coo when a visitor came with a small child. Francesca too clearly wanted a child. This was apparent from the way she always said she would never have a child, with emphasis. And when she had a child, she would come to the House of Commons to protest about it. It was possible that that was why she wanted to marry. A Cabinet Minister passed; not the one who had come to her mother's funeral. Jane took no notice. Like her father, she did not regard them as serious human beings either.

As she waited, her father left the building, to go home, to go to bed. He left by another door, one of many many guarded doors.

'I might go a bit early,' Louis said, upstairs. 'I've got someone coming in for a drink.'

'Oh,' Henry said, 'pleased to see you have as much interest in the ballot as I have.'

'What time is it announced?' Louis said.

'Oh, half past six, I think,' Henry said.

'Not that you're interested,' Louis said, leaving the office. His telephone was ringing. Henry picked it up, as he said 'No,' to the closing door.

'Is that Mr Cobb,' the Central Lobby attendant in his white tie and tails said. Jane stood by him, bored of waiting among all the harassed and harassing women.

'No,' Henry said. 'He's out of the office just at the moment.'

It was Henry's policy never to admit that anyone had ever left the office.

'Could you tell him when he returns,' the attendant said, 'that he has a visitor in the Central Lobby.'

'I think he's on his way down, actually,' Henry said. He put down the telephone, lit a cigarette and carried on reading his novel, just for the moment.

'Darling,' Louis said, coming through the guarded passage-way where Members sat and gave their indiscretions to the press. 'Have you been waiting long?'

'Not long,' Jane said. 'I don't mind.'

'Where do you want to go?' Louis said.

'I don't think I really want a drink,' Jane said. 'I've been sitting down all day. I think I'd like a bit of a walk.'

'A walk?' Louis said. 'What sort of a walk? Along the Thames or something?'

'No,' Jane said. 'An indoors sort of a walk. I had the most awful boring evening with Nancy.'

'Who's Nancy?'

'Henry's sister, but a friend of mine anyway. So I hope you're going to make up for it. My father's often saying there are surprising bits of the building not many people know about. Why don't you show them to me?'

'I don't think I can,' Louis said. 'I don't really know the building at all. I've only been here six months. I can find my way from my office to the Tea Room and the bar and the Chamber and that's more or less it. I'd get lost in two minutes if I went anywhere else.'

'Let's get lost,' Jane said. She grinned suddenly; her mouth was huge in her pointy face with its clipped short boy's hair. 'What's through that door?'

'No idea.'

'Less than two minutes, then,' Jane said, but a policeman was through the door immediately behind them.

'Can I see your pass, sir?' the policeman said.

Louis got his pass out. The policeman looked at it. 'And yours, madam?'

'I don't work here,' Jane said with disdain.

'I'm afraid strangers aren't allowed in this part of the building, even if they're accompanied,' the policeman said.

'Oh dear,' Jane said. 'We were only trying to get to the bar.'

'Which bar?' the policeman said.

'Is there more than one?' Louis said, a little hopelessly.

'Oh, yes, sir,' the policeman said. He smirked in an un-policemanly way.

Louis and Jane went back into the central lobby, and turned right. This time they were not stopped. They went into another lobby, where a policeman was standing. On the benches in this lobby, two Members were sitting, each deep in discussion with a journalist. To the right a huge stone staircase rose up, lined with pursed-mouth busts of unknown Prime Ministers. To the left a carpeted staircase sank into the basement. Louis and Jane took this down, decisively, and found themselves in an underground, dimly lit, hot carpeted corridor.

'Try and look as if you know where you're going,' Jane said. 'Or we'll be stopped again.'

'I dare say we'll be stopped anyway,' Louis said. 'You know, Henry never knows where he's going, I think; he's always taking the wrong turning and ending up in the House of Lords.'

'There's an allegory in that,' Jane said.

'Oh, I hope not,' Louis said. 'This way.'

They were before two lifts, labelled Members only, and got into one. At the top floor they got out, and found themselves in another dim, hot, carpeted corridor. This one was deserted.

'Are we lost yet?' Jane said.

'Oh, yes,' Louis said.

'I'm sure not,' Jane said. 'Those are the booths Hansard work in.'

'How do you know that?' Louis said.

'It says on the doors,' Jane said. 'It doesn't make us any less lost, of course.'

They went past the Hansard booths and quickly found themselves at another staircase.

'Which way?' Jane said.

'Up, of course,' Louis said. It was as well to have principles. They bounded up the stairs; their breath was in gasps, like dogs for hunting, and at the top of the carpeted stairs, they became stone steps; and at the top of the stone steps, there was a ladder; and at the top of the ladder there was a shut door.

'It's shut,' Louis said.

'What's on the other side?' Jane said.

'I don't know,' Louis said. He was so out of breath.

'It's not locked,' Jane said, looking up at it. She just knew. Louis went first, and at the top of the ladder he pushed. For a moment it stuck, and then it quickly fell from him. And they were on the roof of the Palace.

Such acres of flagstones; and such air above them. The blue like the blue eyes are, and all around them, and beneath them, the air of London. The fields of stone spread out, in the sky, around them, and their hedges of tiny spires, their gothic encrusted fences keeping roofs apart. And the tower, the clock tower, so truncated from these high roofs, and so perfect, its gilt and its unfeeling movement like the toytown clock it so resembled; they had to lie down.

'Exhausted,' Jane said.

'Wonderful,' Louis said.

'Wonderful,' Jane said. 'Do you know where you are?'

'Somewhere up in the sky,' Louis said. 'Do you know where you are?'

'Above politics,' Jane said. 'Like the Queen.'

It was the funniest joke, just for the moment, and, head to head, they lay on the blank clean flagstones, like the least trod-upon pavements in the world, and laughed at the sky which seemed, no closer, but less interfered with. They lay there for so long; laughing; undrunk.

'I've got something I've got to do,' Jane said. 'Watch me do it.'

She scrambled up with her bag, and out of it she got one perfect egg.

'How did you get it through security?' Louis said.

'I put it in my pocket,' Jane said. 'The metal detector wouldn't have picked it up. Do you think they would have objected to it?'

'Of course,' Louis said. 'You might have thrown it in the Chamber.'

'Do people do that?' Jane said.

'All the time,' Louis said. 'What are you going to do with that?'

'I'm going to throw it,' Jane said. 'But I'm not going to throw it at anything. It's a good-luck thing. It's going to show what our luck is going to be. You have to go to the highest place you know, and then you throw it as far in the air, upwards, as you can. And when you throw it in the air, you watch it going up as long as you can. But when it looks as if it's going to start to drop back to earth, you have to shut your eyes and not watch it dropping. It doesn't work if you watch it dropping. The place where it lands shows what kind of luck you're going to have.'

'And if it lands on you, then that's bad luck or good luck?'

'Neither, because it never does. You never see where it lands. It lands where it's going to, and you never know anything about it. It's just like luck, you see.'

'So it shows what your luck is, but it doesn't show it to you, because you don't know anything about it?'

'That's right.'

'So what's the point?'

'The point is throwing an egg in the air,' Jane said.

'Is it hard-boiled?' Louis said, for some reason.

'Of course not,' Jane said, and then, like the lucky girl she was, she hurled the egg in its column of air up into the blue. She flung herself back down on the roof, and together, they found themselves chanting Watch it watch it; and together they cried Shut your eyes when it was time to shut them. But for ever afterwards Louis knew that he had not seen the egg begin to drop, and knew that it never did drop; and knew that this egg, of all the eggs in the world, carried on climbing into its empyrean, thrown wonderfully by Jane, and taking the luck of Jane with it. The luck of Jane went with it into the blue, the blue which for now was above them, and would not be there much longer.

A long time passed, and the silence they felt around them was like the absence of wind.

'Tell me about Henry.'

'Nothing to tell.'

'Everything to tell. Do you still love him?'

'Of course.'

'Have you always loved him?'

'I felt when I first met him I loved him before I knew him.'

'What was he like?'

'I don't know.'

'Try.'

'Okay,' she said. She swallowed, lying there. He waited for her to begin. 'Everyone always says the man they love is like nobody else on earth. But it's not like that. Maybe it's like that if you're not really in love. If you're not really in love the man you love is like an alien, or completely strange, or weird, or impossible to understand, but he wasn't like that at all. When I met him he was like everyone I'd ever met in my life and when we began to talk it was as if we were just starting a conversation again which we'd abandoned the day before or a week before or a lifetime before. We just knew each other. I knew what he looked like. I knew what his skin would be like when I put my hand on it. When he held my hand for the first time I just knew that his hand would be my least favourite bit of him, I knew it would be that slightly damp feel people always say they hate. But even that was familiar. I didn't mind it. I knew it.

'It was the same for him too. It was just the way he looked at me. We just relaxed the first time we saw each other. You know that grim week at university at the beginning when you don't know anyone, and five people who live on your staircase have just decided to cling on to you, and you go out for pizzas in huge gangs and argue about who had the garlic bread and who had more wine and who didn't have a pudding, and all the way through dinner you know they don't really understand what you're talking about, and they look at you as if you're really really weird? Perhaps you don't. But that's what it was like for me. I was meeting people all the time who were incredibly neat and hard-working and stupid. But after a while I met Henry and I knew it was going to be all right.

'I went to his house once, and that was that weird feeling all over again. His parents didn't like me one bit. They thought I was seriously mad and probably alcoholic, and they had that way of looking at me when I said something, as if I'd dropped into Chinese without noticing or my nose was dribbling. I said that to Henry afterwards and he didn't believe me, he said I was imagining it. But I wasn't. Henry never noticed that sort of thing.

Even the mad girls with their tidy rooms and their pen sets and their pink eiderdowns from home, the way they looked at me he never really believed. You see, he just understood me so well he couldn't see that not everyone did.'

She stopped for the moment. She had to. There was something in her voice she wanted to keep out of it, and she wanted a wind to carry the noise of her words away from her, away from Louis, away from the roof and into the sky. There was no wind.

'Is that why you never slept together?'

'Yes,' Jane said. 'We didn't need reassurance. We didn't need that kind of intimacy. You know that thing about friendship, that friendship's a stuff in need of constant repair. It wasn't like that. It didn't need repair at all. There were no holes in it. That's what I always thought all the way through, and that's really what I think now. I think if we went away together and talked to each other for a week with no one else there and not even a romantic landscape, then we'd never ever leave each other ever again. It was always perfectly all right. There was never anything at all wrong with it.'

'Until the end.'

'Yes,' Jane said. She was lying down, and the tears from her closed hot eyes ran down the side of her face and wet the lobes of her ears. She could not stop them, and she could not help the noise she made. They were there together until silence came, and the faint noise of the wind could again be heard.

'That's it,' Jane said. He saw how brave she was. 'We can open our eyes now.'

The egg was nowhere to be seen.

'Look,' Jane said. 'That door. That different door. Through there.'

They got up, and walked together towards the other door. The door slammed shut behind them, and they found themselves at the very top of an immense wooden staircase. There was a faint echo of the noises they made, echoing downwards into the space delineated by the stairs. When they trod on the steps, their feet left their marks in the dust.

'No one can ever come here,' Jane said.

'I don't know where we are,' Louis said.

'You could get lost for ever here, and no one would ever find you,' Jane said. 'Except in a hundred years, they'd come across two skeletons. Look, here's another door.'

She tried it, but it seemed to be locked.

'It's locked,' she said.

'There's the key,' Louis said. It was hanging on a hook by the side of the door. Jane took it, and wiggled it in the lock for a while before it seemed to bite.

'Are you sure?' she said. 'It's not like wandering aimlessly, opening locked doors.'

'Might as well,' Louis said, though he was unsure.

'All right,' she said, and opened the door. There they were. Like wandering through a theatre, and suddenly finding themselves on a bright-lit stage, it was, and facing a huge, unseeable audience. They were in an immense room, a shock of a space after the enclosed and snailing staircase. But like the staircase, it could be seen that no one ever went there. They could be there for ever, and they would never be found there. And it was full, this enormous room; it was full of great piles of papers, and broken chair legs, and cardboard boxes, and a sofa with torn green leather upholstery. The roof of the room was high, and through a high window the last of the sun lit the dust they had raised by entering. A cathedral of ruin, this hall they were in, and every bit of detritus which could not be thrown away and every tiny fragment of thought the House had ever generated, and everything the House had broken and destroyed in its unchanging progress through history was here. The House maintained its perfection, unaffected by death or change or pity, by sending all evidence that time passed for it, that destruction fell on it as well as the men which passed through its offices and its chambers, by sending all this detritus and ruin and forgotten thought to a great hall which was never visited and from which nothing was ever retrieved. Somewhere in this great pile of papers and the dust which, having risen, was almost immediately beginning to fall and to settle, there were the names of the Prime Minister and her Ministers; and the names and the handwriting of the Clerks; and the names of Louis and John and Henry. And there was recorded, in this pile, their acts and their small triumphs, which would soon be forgotten and would never be looked at or thought of again.

John lay on his bed.

He was clothed. His boots were off.

His face was held down into his pillow.

This is the way he would stay. He would never act again. He would never see them again. He knew this was what he had to do.

Both Louis and he knew that it would be a month before Louis gave his name to the police. All he had to do was wait.

There was no choice. He asked himself in silence, ceaselessly, if there ever had been.

'I know where I am now,' Louis said. They were walking down a long plushly carpeted corridor.

'What's that noise?' Jane said.

Since they had stepped out of the lift, they had not seen anyone. They had been walking through deserted corridors and unpeopled rooms; they had walked on empty roofs. The noise they heard struck them as strange, but it was only the noise of people yelling. Somewhere near, three hundred people were shouting at each other.

'It's the ballot,' Louis said.

'Let's go and see,' Jane said.

'She hasn't made it,' a man said, running past them. 'She's two short.'

'Did you hear that?' Louis said.

'Was he talking to us?'

'There's no question,' a man in a pinstriped suit was saying into a microphone another, shabbier man was holding, 'that this appears like a serious problem. But the party is not divided. There is no question of any serious division here.'

'Where is it?' Jane said. 'I've never seen anything like it.'

They pushed into the crowd of men yelling the same four or five facts at each other.

Another woman would have cried, in Paris.

But I did not. And a woman who would have cried at

that; a woman who would have sat in her beautiful gilt and pastel embassy bedroom with her officials around her and sat on the bed and cried; such a woman would never have reached Paris. And I did not cry.

'She's finished,' a man said.

'She's finished,' the man he was talking to said. They were pushed against each other and could not look at each other, and they shouted.

'Jane,' Louis said, but behind him she had gone. She was somewhere in the crowd, but lost. He carried on.

'She's got to carry on,' someone said.

'You're out of your mind,' someone else said. 'It'll be a complete rout.'

'They'll come back to her,' a Member said. 'They will.'

'She's got to go now,' Louis said. He did not know who he was speaking to, or how he knew what he was saying, and yet he still spoke. 'She's got to give the Chancellor a free hand.'

He was in the middle of the great crowd in the corridor now, like a mob at an execution, a mob howling for its victim, and deprived of one; and next to him a small woman Member was shouting Stop pushing, stop pushing, over and over again.

'He won't support her.'

'He's got to.'

'She's got to release him.'

'Why should she?'

'It's her best hope now. She can't stay now.'

'She will.'

It would be a month before Louis did what he knew he

had to, and picked up the telephone and telephoned the police to tell them the name of the murderer of Giacomo. He knew he was the only connection; he knew it was his responsibility; his role. He knew it was the only important thing he would ever do in his life, and when he considered what he would do, it did not trouble him. He knew that his obligation lay with Giacomo, whom he did not know; he knew he had no obligation towards John, whom he worked with.

Downstairs, the secretary to the Chief Whip picked up his telephone and dialled the thirteen figure number which by now he knew by heart. When it was answered, he spoke briefly, then pressed a button which allowed the Chief Whip to talk directly. He allowed himself the luxury of listening to the first few words before he put the telephone down and prepared to get on with his job.

The next day, Jane got on the bus to go to the hospital to visit her grandmother. She wanted a long journey to begin to think about preparing her dinner for Henry. She had picked the first day when she knew, from Francesca's diary, that she would be out, and an evening when her father would be working. She did not want to seduce him; she only wanted him not to go to bed with Francesca, or to have anything more to do with her. The thought that she was jealous occurred to her, and she accepted it, not wanting to think any better of herself. In fact she was not jealous. Not any more. She did not want him for herself; she wanted nobody to have him. If she had been living among people who did such things, she might have considered killing him.

Jane did not cook more often than was necessary. But on this occasion she had no alternative; she had supplied herself with none. On her way to the bus stop, she bought a cookbook from a bookshop. She did not feel she could use her mother's books. She chose a book by an author whom she had heard her father's more affected friends speak highly of; her literary style, her revolutionary simplicity, her personal charm. She did not see how any of these things could make for a reliable cookbook, but she bought it in any case. On the bus, she began to read, with a pencil in her hand. Next to recipes which sounded delicious, which she would order in restaurants, she put a tick. Next to recipes which sounded easy, she put a cross. Next to recipes which sounded both easy and delicious, she put a tick, a cross, and circled it. When she had reached the end of the book, she went through it quickly, and found that she had identified five recipes as both easy and delicious. She eliminated two immediately by trying to imagine Henry eating them, and found that she had a meal which, she hoped, she could cook.

(All the time she wrote, on the bus, John was at home, upstairs, in bed, silently. She assumed he had gone to work, and he did not feel now that he would ever get up, ever again, but just stay in bed and weep the tears he had to.)

Jane looked up. She had forgotten where she was, and found that, mildly sick, she was reading a cookbook on a bus. Around her there were ten old people, who seemed to know each other. They all talked constantly; they did not seem to want to stop to listen, and perhaps they were all too deaf to hear anything. They were perhaps her grandmother's age, but her grandmother would never class herself with these people. Their voices were strange, partly in their vulgarity and partly through their lack of teeth and jaw; their skins were spotted; they, palsied, shook. Their conversation was about food and illness; they travelled, like her, to hospitals for somewhere to go.

Sole véronique, Jane read, *is an impressive dish for dinner parties, and is not too difficult to prepare and serve with panache.* They were almost there. London thinned out at these edges. A strange notion of healthy air had placed these great palaces of recuperation and death near the small fragments of country between the cities. When her mother had died, she had had a view of trees.

The bus stopped and the driver, accustomed to groups of the elderly, called out the name of the hospital to alert them. The ten old people got to their feet and helped each other up. Jane observed them. They were visiting their wives and brothers, but their turn would come soon. She followed them out of the bus, and quickly found herself directed to her grandmother's ward. She went along with it.

Her grandmother was asleep, and pale. Jane sat by the bed and quietly took her hand, so as not to wake her. She muttered in her sleep and, once, smacked her lips as if they were dry; once, a little saliva formed a bubble and burst. Jane stayed there and looked at her frailty, white with a favourite white angora bed-jacket on the chair by her. Even here, her grandmother thought of her clothes, had planned her wardrobe to die in.

'Lou your nana?' a passing nurse said.

'What?' Jane said.

'Is she your nana, then, Lou?'

'She's my grandmother,' Jane said coldly. 'Lower your voice.'

The nurse went off into peals of laughter. 'Won't wake that one,' she said over her shoulder. 'Deaf as a post, Lou is.'

'How is she?'

'Oh, much better,' the nurse said. 'We're thinking of turfing her out before much longer. Nothing wrong with her, really. You've just got to keep an eye on them when they get flu like that. Oh, she's waking up.' She wheeled her trolley off.

Jane found that her grandmother was surfacing from her sleep.

'It's Jane,' she said immediately. Her great fear was being mistaken for her mother.

'I can see who it is,' she said. 'Do pass me my bed-jacket, dear. You are kind to come all this way.'

'I was worried about you,' Jane said.

'No need for that,' her grandmother said. 'I'm much better now. They thought I'd cashed my chips, but I knew I'd be all right once I stopped coughing. Naturally, I'm not letting on that I'm better. I'm hoping for another couple of days in the lap of luxury.'

'I would want to be out of here straight away.'

'Oh no,' her grandmother said. 'What a shocking idea. It's jolly comfy, the food is lovely, and the nurses are really very nice.'

'They call you Lou,' Jane said.

'Yes, they do. But that's not so important. It makes me feel like a little girl again, all this being looked after and having a nickname.'

'Don't you want to move to a better hospital?'

'There's not much point,' she said. 'All that money one would have to pay. I thought, well, I've jolly well paid my taxes all these years, I don't see why I shouldn't take advantage of it. Oh, look, it's nearly lunchtime.'

A trolley was rattling past them.

'Is it hot outside?'

'No, just sunny.'

'How nice, sunny and cold. It does get hot in here, they will turn up the heating all the time. Did you get a taxi here?'

'No, I came on a bus.'

'It must have taken simply ages. It is kind of you.'

'Well, I've nothing much else to do, and I haven't been to see you for a while.'

'How is your father?'

'Oh, he had a very bad cold, last week – the same one you had, I suppose.'

'Well, poor him, it was ghastly.'

'Everyone's been getting it a bit. My friend Nancy said it was called Hong Kong 2.'

'Really? No one here told me it had a name, though I don't think I would have been any fonder of it if I'd known that. Is he better?'

'Getting better. He's quite subdued, if you see what I mean.'

'I do. Subdued is what I feel, or possibly a bit faded.'

'Are you tired?'

'No, stay. Do stay and help me eat my lunch,' she said. 'The ghastly old trout in the next bed always offers to eat whatever I leave, but I don't see why she should have my leavings every single day.'

'What is it for lunch?' Jane said.

'Well, that's rather the nice thing,' she said. 'You see, they come round at six-thirty in the morning, and you have to choose what you want for lunch and for supper. Lunch is at twelve noon, and supper is at five-thirty. And of course by then you've quite forgotten what you ordered, partly because it's so long, and partly because I'm completely gaga, and it's far too late to change what you thought might be nice at the crack of dawn.'

Jane laughed.

'The thing is,' her grandmother went on, 'I was thinking about this – really, one has far too much time for thinking here – and I was thinking how like life it is. You get asked what you're going to want when you're almost bound to make the wrong decision, and then you're stuck with it. When the trolley lady comes round in the end, you might fancy the sole, but you're stuck with the sausage sandwich. Or perhaps you could only really manage a small salad, but you have to get through an enormous beef stew. Am I rambling?'

'A bit,' Jane said. 'Francesca sends her love.'

'Frances,' her grandmother said. 'Tell her it would be nice to see her. I get so bored with all my young men sniffing round for a legacy. It would be nice to have her for a change. And your father, of course, when he's better.'

'You are tired,' Jane said. 'Why don't you have a little sleep?'

'Stay here until I've gone off,' her grandmother said. 'It's so nice of you to come. I'll be home tomorrow. I don't think I'll be able to wangle much more than that.'

Jane stayed by her grandmother, stroking her hand, until her eyes were closed and her breath had resumed its regular whiffling. She left a fond note for her to find when she woke up, and found her own way out.

*　　*　　*

Much later in the evening, the House divided. And upstairs, at ten, the Senior Vote Writer sat at the Vote Writer's desk and wrote what he thought was happening, downstairs, fifty feet below him, in the Chamber. He had written what he thought was to happen, some hours before, but now he sat and wrote what was really happening. It annoyed him that the House did not fulfil his prediction precisely, and he took off his coat and loosened his tie in annoyance, as he crossed out what he had written, and replaced it with what he wrote.

> Adjournment. A Motion was made, and the Question being proposed, That this House do now adjourn; a Member rose in his place and claimed to move, That the Question be now put. And the Question being put, That the Question be now put: – It was agreed to. And the Question being accordingly put; The House divided.

He wondered what had happened to the Clerk of the Journals. John had left the office, most unusually, rather early in the afternoon the day before. He had not returned that day. Nobody would tell him precisely what had happened, but clearly something had. He wondered, with pleasure, whether the Clerk of the Journals had actually gone mad or on the rampage. A pleasant picture filled his head of the Clerk of the Journals, wig in hand, hanging like an orang-utan from the chandelier in the central lobby and howling, ignored by everyone beneath.

He turned his attention back to his work. He had written all he could without knowing anything more, and until anything more happened, he could not know it. This was unusual. He finished writing, and relished the smooth unfeeling poetry of the Journal, its hard beautiful repetition of the word Question as if the pronoun had been abolished. He loved its casual abolition of Members; he loved the lessons of vanity it taught. It taught that the names of Members were of no account, that controversy and policy and the arts of the politic were of no interest, but only the motions that the figures went through, and the decisions that the House made. In the perspective of the Journal, men and women vanished, like the uproar of the Chamber disappearing when the adjournment was called; and they went to other lives; to disappointment; to death. No one had ever heard of them, and yet they thought they were famous.

The House divided with its shrill easy clamour. Louis was drinking a cup of tea when the division bell rang, and he got up and out of the Tea Room. He walked round the Chamber, the long way, and past a policeman who tried to stop him.

'Division, sir,' the policeman said.

'Officer of the House,' Louis said. The policeman stood aside sharply. Around them Members milled pointlessly, trying to discover which lobby they were supposed to go into. There was no reason, they all knew, in trying to find out what they were supposed to be voting for. They spoke to their Whips, who directed them. Louis knew what they were voting for. Nobody asked him.

He reached the division lobby within the statutory two minutes, but only just. On the other side of the locked glass doors, Members were crowding round the division desks. At the front, he could see a member of the Labour party of the old school who represented a south coast constituency, who was ridiculed by every Clerk because of his complete lack of friends and allies, his failure ever to brush his hair and his poor personal hygiene. Because of this, and his constituency, the Clerks used an insulting nickname for him.

'There's Halitosis Hastings, I see, first in line,' the other division Clerk said as he arrived.

'What took so long?'

'Oh, I was having a bath,' the other Clerk said. 'Can you open the door?'

The doorkeeper did so, just as, in the Chamber, the Speaker could be heard to put the Question to the House again. They scrambled into their tall chairs like infants. The division began. Members whose names began with the letters from L to Z filed past Louis on his left; some gave their names; some, who considered themselves famous enough to be recognized or known by a Clerk, simply nodded, and Louis either recognized them, or stopped them with a tug on their coats or an arm out, and said 'Name'. Some who considered themselves famous were not so, and some who did give their names were famous. Perhaps they rightly saw that their fame was temporary, trivial, and that humility suited them.

They milled and crowded, the unheard of, the marginally great, the famous for doing nothing and the famous for talking to newspapers. Louis marked their names, and the names of most of them he did not know. Some were impatient with him; they were drunk and incoherent. Some made a small joke, of the sort they made indifferently with every Clerk, with every constituent, with everybody they ever met. Most thought nothing of Louis; some considered him young; some considered him fat; one member of the Cabinet, passing, noticed his sexual availability, and allowed himself for a moment to imagine an idyll of sodomy, with pleasure. Lulls came in the crowd, and billows of men, and laughter burst like a balloon of water among them.

And then there was a silence, and if Louis had worked there longer, he would have known what was coming. The men before him turned, affecting to continue their conversation with each other, unaffected by what came before and behind them. But love is complicated, and to each other they burbled their nonsense, and did not listen, and did not notice the nonsense that they spoke. And the bellow outside the lobby, the great heavy echo of the men in their wigs, like great black trees at night under white blossom, shouting into space their sentences. 'Lock the doors,' one shouted, and, distant, the locks and clank of the doors shutting behind the Members seeking to vote, to register their thoughts and their opinions, which their managers had told them. And before him, before Louis at his desk, if he had looked up to see what came before him, came the tiny crowd of favoured men, and inside them, inside the crowd, there she was, there she was, there she was.

(Fifty feet above, there the Senior Vote Writer was, writing on a proof of what the printer had sent back to him, and he was changing things he might have written; he changed '". . . on its success in achieving low inflation by its economic policies" instead thereof [The Prime Minster]' to '". . . on its success in achieving low inflation by its economic policies," instead thereof [The Prime Minister];' and he was pleased at what he had seen, the two changes he had made, and yet he thought nothing of it, and nothing of what was happening fifty feet below him.)

She said her name. And she pointed to her name on the big yellow sheet. He looked at her, the division Clerk. He saw her. Did she see him? Just the sudden flash of blue in a gaze, and what stayed with him – what he thought at that second would stay with him for ever – was the soft radiance, like the glow of chemicals in a tube, of her skin. It was as if her skin was so lightly furred that the hair could not be seen, but, wonderfully, light had seen it, and it fell on her, and her face, wonderfully, held it. 'There it is,' she said, her baritone husk like the voice of sex itself, and he brought his pencil down to mark her name, knowing he would never see or speak to her, never again. How well she passed on, and how well she left the lobby, and the office of Prime Minister, and her power, and her decade, and, in the end, how little she mattered, how little he mattered in their roles and their purposes, their histories which were not only their own. For now she was brave, but it would not have mattered if she had not been, not for one second. Not in the end.

The House finished dividing, and it was as if they all breathed once more, and it was as if something had come to an end. But history does not come to an end. History continues. The life of offices does not know death, or departure, or change; only, like a baton, the name of the office passing from one temporary holder to another, whose names are quickly forgotten. And the office lives on, for ever, and does not change. And in the end; but there is no in the end for offices; and for offices men do not matter, and speech does not matter, and breath does not matter. But for men the stifling air, the cold black night outside the Palace, was everywhere, and nowhere, the unbreathable. And for men something had come to an end.

Dear Father, Henry wrote, *I have decided to get married. I have met a wonderful girl whom I am very fond of and who loves me. I have always wanted to settle down and marry and have children, and I feel that I am lucky now that I have met someone. I hope you will meet her very soon, perhaps if we come and stay with you in the country, and that you will like her as much as I do. We have many interests in common, and I am sure we will be very happy together. We hope to marry in June.*

Henry went on; his letter came to a lengthy conclusion. He had never written so fluently, and when he had finished writing, he had three pages which he could send. He printed them out, and he sent them. He had given up on truth. Lies were easier.

Something went wrong with the food. Jane opened her recipe book, and followed a recipe for ice cream. It seemed very complex. She opened a bag of sugar, and began to weigh eight ounces. She poured it into the weighing scales, but it moved terribly slowly; she had poured almost the entire bag into the bowl before it registered eight ounces. She continued anyway; she boiled the pile of sugar with fruit; she boiled more sugar with water, and whisked it into egg yolks; she whipped cream; she combined everything, and put it into an ice-cream maker. It was only then that she realized that a piece of cardboard was lodged in the weighing scales, and making it impossible to weigh properly. She removed the cardboard, and as she did so, it came to her that her mother had bought the scales earlier that year; that her mother had never used them, and that no one else had used them since her mother's death.

She left the jam-like confection circling uselessly round the freezing bowl, and went to have a bath to brood over it.

Jane was in the bath when Francesca came back, and she dressed quickly in what she had been wearing. She did not want to dress for Henry. She wanted to be as she had been, and as she would be again.

'A strange coincidence,' Francesca was saying, rather loudly, as Jane was coming down the stairs.

'What?' Jane said.

'Oh, Jane,' Francesca said. 'I didn't know you were in.'

'Who were you talking to?'

'Henry,' Francesca said. 'He's in the lav.'

'Did you let him in? I didn't hear the doorbell.'

'No,' Francesca said. 'He came back with me, actually.'

'Hello, Jane,' Henry said.

She fixed Henry with what she hoped was a look of utter venom as he came back from the lavatory, but his head-down walk avoided her look. A bad sign; a bad sign of something. Francesca smiled in his general direction as if she would have liked to ask about his bowel movements.

'A strange coincidence. Or rather a series of coincidences,' she went on, stretching her arm out along the back of the sofa, as if waiting for Henry to rest his head against her. 'My class was cancelled, you know. At very short notice. And having nothing to do, I bumped into Henry at the tube station. And he had nothing to do, so we've been having tea all afternoon in the Savoy.'

'How smart,' Jane drawled back. She was not going to

be outdone. 'I thought you had a job to go to, Henry.'

'Well, I do,' Henry said. 'I just took the afternoon off. I thought I owed it to myself.'

You owe yourself nothing, Jane thought, but kept quiet.

'I went to see granny this morning,' Francesca said.

'How is she?' Jane said.

'Much better.'

'I went to see her too,' Jane said. 'Her memory must be going; she said you hadn't been for weeks.'

'I had no idea,' Francesca said. 'Till Henry said, I had no idea he was coming round this evening. You should have mentioned it. I would have liked to see him. Not that I can't see him any time I like, of course.'

'Well, now you are seeing him,' Jane said. 'Aren't you going out?'

'Well, yes,' Francesca said. 'I think so.'

'Just a second,' Jane said, and went to the kitchen. She could see there was no getting rid of Francesca, and started cutting the bread, with a viciousness it did not altogether deserve.

'Fucking, fucking, cow,' Jane said inadequately. Strangely, she worried whether there was going to be enough food for three. It was a stew; it was divisible into three. And no one would eat the ice-cream, which had proved impossible to freeze, and was now merely jam. She said this to herself, even though she knew things are never divisible into three. Things are planned for two, or for multiples of two. Nothing which began life as something for two – a stew, a sofa, a bottle of wine – is ever divided into three with much success, and when people said it was enough, it was good, they lied in their politeness.

'No, not particularly,' Henry was saying on the other side of the open door.

'Oh, really, Henry,' Francesca said. 'That's too absurd. Do you mean to say that you're seriously claiming that you have no interest in who's going to be the next Prime Minister?'

Jane carried on, intently. She saw that everything she had made could be divided into three parts; the vegetables could be chopped into slices; potatoes could be mashed, although she frankly didn't know how. It could be done. She did not know why she should do it, but she felt that there was nothing else she could do.

'How many children would you want?' Francesca said.

It was all a matter of coping. If Francesca wanted to behave like this, she could be coped with. There was something horrible on the other side of the door, and however horrible it was, whatever it was, she could always put on her best dress and her shiniest heels and get out there. She went back into the drawing room, where they sat without talking.

'What a delicious smell,' Francesca said. 'Are you cooking something special for father?'

'No,' Jane said. 'He's not in. I was cooking for Henry.'

Henry shuffled in his chair and affected surprise.

'For Henry?' Francesca said.

'And for you, if you want some,' Jane said. 'There'll be enough for you as well. I thought you were going out.'

'We are,' Francesca said. 'I think we ought to celebrate. I've booked a table, I'm afraid. If it'll keep, you and I can have it for lunch tomorrow, surely.'

'What are you celebrating?' Jane said.

Francesca performed a one-sided pantomime of exchanging loving glances with Henry. It wasn't good enough; it wasn't convincing; and Jane knew what it meant.

'I asked Francesca if she would marry me,' Henry said.
'And she said yes she would. And we're getting married
next month, very quietly. From my parents' house. It
happens.'

'Poor you,' Jane said.

'What do you mean?' Henry said.

'These awful things are always happening to you, aren't
they?' Jane said. Her irony hurt her, and there was no other
way she could respond.

'Do be serious,' Francesca said.

'I'll be serious when you are,' Jane said. 'You're getting
married?'

'We're getting married,' Francesca said. 'These things
happen.'

'We decided,' Henry said. 'Together.'

'I always thought you said she had a face as fat as a
farmer's bum,' Jane said.

'Please try and take this seriously,' Henry said. 'I'm
willing to be polite to you, but not if you say things
like that.'

'Well, that is what you used to say about her,' Jane said.
'Why?'

'It happens,' Francesca said. 'And we love each other.'

'It happens,' Henry said.

'I'll fucking kill you,' Jane said, very quietly. Holding a
bread knife, she meant it.

'Oh Jane,' Francesca said, laughing. 'You don't mean it.
I know you don't.'

'She does mean it,' Henry said.

'You must be pleased for us,' said Francesca, earnestly.

'I must be pleased,' Jane said. 'Yes, I must be. Yes, it must
be compulsory, just to make everything so much easier for

you. Only I'm not and I just can't see, just for the moment, any possible reason why I should be pleased.'

'I really think we ought to go,' Henry said. 'Francesca, we really must go.'

'Are you going to go on calling her Francesca?' Jane said. 'You could take to calling her Frances. A sort of pet name. You don't have to go. Why should you go? No need to go, no need at all.'

'You'll get used to it,' Francesca said. 'People get used to anything. I wish you would be pleased. Think of it from our point of view. I was unhappy and lonely, and now I'm not. Henry was unhappy and lonely, and now he's not. You have to be patient, and you'll be happy with someone. They just come along, unexpectedly. What about that beastly drunk boy you were necking with on the sofa the other night? What's his name? Louis? Or someone else? You should just be patient, and you should be happy for us. Do you think, in the whole of London, there's anyone who, when they hear their sister is about to get married to an old family friend, would threaten to kill them? Do you think that a reasonable attitude for someone to take?'

'I'll fucking kill you if you don't tell me right now that this is some not very funny, but still your feeble attempt at a joke. I'll fucking kill you.'

She waved the bread knife in their general direction. She could not see well what she was doing. She could not steady her hand or her voice or her face, as if they were the hand and voice and face of someone else. Only the noise in her head seemed her own.

'You don't mean it,' Francesca said. 'I think we'd better go. The table is booked for eight o'clock.'

'She does mean it,' Henry said, not getting up.

'You see?' Jane said. 'You know when I say something true. You know when I mean something. Do you know that about her? I don't know when she's just saying something, I don't know when she's lying, I don't know when she's telling the truth. She's going to claim to, you know, she had no idea you were coming round, and you're going to claim to her that I must have misunderstood, that I'd just asked you round for a drink or something. You've already said that. Haven't you? Haven't you? And that's what your life's going to be like. Remember, I know her. You'll be married, and all the time, you'll be lying to each other, and not telling each other the truth, and all the time there'll be Jane, somewhere around, getting drunk and spilling things on herself and not being introduced to the children in case she spills things on them, like the truth about what their parents are like. And there will be children, you know, lots of them, and they'll all look exactly like her. Is that an appealing idea? And every minute of every day, you'll think to yourself, I've married this woman who drives me completely and utterly mad, and who hasn't the faintest idea about anything except how to irritate me, and this woman's just awful beyond belief, and every minute of every day, you'll think, what would my life be like if I married her sister? What would my life be like if I was with Jane and Jane was with me?'

'No,' he said. She had stopped. His face was pale. 'I don't think I will.'

'I think you will,' she said. She placed her emphasis on every word, as if it were the last thing she would ever say to him.

There was an awful silence. Henry looked down at his wrists, and he saw, with a sudden shock, that he had put on a double-cuffed shirt, with cufflinks; and he was wearing a single-breasted jacket. He thought, with a fit of terrified irrelevance, what had led him to this pass; he wondered whether ever again he would care enough about what he wore. He wondered whether he would be permitted to, and the pointlessness of his worries shocked him. He looked up, at Francesca. He had no one else to look at.

'You've forgotten that I love him,' Francesca said, with the appearance of anger.

'You've forgotten that *I* love him,' Jane said. 'I never knew that you loved him. I still don't know that you love him. And I know that he doesn't love you. He's marrying you for reasons which have nothing to do with you. He would marry you if you looked like the back end of a bus and had the IQ of three cockroaches. He would marry you if you were a Sicilian dwarf with sideburns. He would marry you if you were a man, practically. He's got to marry you because his father said he ought to marry someone, and it couldn't be me, and he doesn't know anyone else. And he's marrying you because he used to want to marry me, years ago, B.C. – Before Cowardice – and now he doesn't want to marry me any more. And you're as good as me, he thinks, but you're not me. You're reliable and not mad and not plate-smashing and not drunk, but otherwise you might as well be me. You're practically the girl next door, and he's too lazy to go any further to look for anyone. He just wants someone who will be no trouble, who won't mean he's got to move, who's nearest. It's all so logical. You're the only person it could be. But it has nothing to do with anything he feels for you, and it's nothing to do with you being a nice person, even if you were, or loving him back, even if you did. All his life has just collapsed on to this, and he doesn't know what he's doing any more, except that you'll do. If you really loved him, you wouldn't marry him. You'd save him from himself. And don't ask me if he's any good in bed. I've no idea.'

'I don't need to ask you,' Francesca said.

'You always wanted to say that,' Jane said.

'No,' Francesca said. 'Not always.'

Jane stood there for a moment, and it could suddenly be seen that Jane and Francesca were almost the same height. Francesca stood there and would not move. With a yell, a silent inward yell, Jane found the knife in her hands, and she turned with it, and threw it into the kitchen. What it hit fell heavily and broke. She followed it. Francesca did not flinch, but stood there in her sense.

'You see,' she said to Henry. 'I knew she didn't mean it.'

They stood there for a long time, before Henry followed Jane into the kitchen. On the kitchen table there were three plates, and on to them, Jane had poured the stew. Still hot, it steamed. Like a fearless Goldilocks, he stuck his finger into the first, and tasted.

'It tastes jolly good,' he said to Jane, sitting on the floor. Her wet tears scalded her face; she did not reply.

'Jane,' he said.

She did not reply.

'Jane,' he said. 'Please.'

'Let's go,' Francesca said, standing in the doorway. Henry went to Jane and helped her up. They stood like that for a long time, before Henry, scared, moved to Francesca, and they went. Unwilling, Jane followed them to the front door, watched them put their coats on. The coats were like the suitcases of a new life. Francesca opened the door, and stepped out. Jane looked at Henry although she had said to herself she would not. She had never deceived herself before, and she did not deceive herself now. She had no hope that this was anything but an ending. She had no hope that anything would happen after this, since she knew it would not, and it did not. He did not look back, although he had said to himself he had not feared to, and he saw her without looking. Her sister was outside the door, and did not see what they saw, which was the eyes of the other.

She did not see Jane's speaking goodness and Henry's fear, his doglike spanieled terror at what lay before him; his fear at what lies for every one of us outside the door. It was as if his eyes spoke, not to her, because they were not focused on her, and did not look on her, but on some point of promise and protection and safety behind her, somewhere. Like the audience at a pantomime, his eyes cried out silently, Behind you, behind you; and what was behind her was not danger; was not murder; was her father's house. And no one knew what was in her father's house, and what, like some rough beast, slouched towards it, and what awfulness was in it already. Waiting. As he left with her sister, doing up her collar and thinking of what on earth they could talk about, he shut the door on the house, and on everything, and on her. He shut the door on the good brave girl he might once have married, and for now still might, and it was as if it were a sound, the door shutting, he would never forget, which was the case.

She turned back to her father's house. Upstairs, she did not know that her father, like her, wept. He lay and waited for the police to arrive.

They would not be long.

They would not be for him.

She walked to the kitchen quite calmly, when it was over and all the doors were shut. She had never given way to self-pity, and perhaps this was the moment to give way. There were plates on the table, still full of food, cooling as corpses do. She walked past them. In the kitchen there were saucepans, and, open, there was the newly stained good cookbook, with the mark of the tick and the cross against the recipe on the page it was open at.

She began to scrub a saucepan with the chemical green washing-up liquid they seemed to use. It came off, all that food. Next, she took a plate, which had not come from the dinner she had just cooked, but from the lunch she had made for herself, while cooking. It was encrusted with food, and dried, and she did not trouble too much to get the stains off. It did not matter. It was hard to see who would care if the stains were not removed.

On the floor was a bread knife, and it needed washing. She had, impatiently, taken it and stuck it in the butter and spread, unable for a second to find a butter knife and unwilling to wait. And then it had been thrown.

She looked at it.

It was a solid knife. It was a knife she had never seen consciously before, and was suddenly aware that someone, somewhere, had considered and debated the mock-wood texture of its handle and the effective serrations of its blade. She sat on the floor, for some reason, examining the knife for a long time. She felt as if she had never examined any object with such exactitude, such care, and as if she never would again. Perhaps she would not. Her knife was in her hands. It was hers. She took the knife in her unshaking hands; in her one hand. She found it was good enough. It was there.

THE CITY OVERHEAD

I WAS BEING driven down a street today. It is more usual than people perhaps think. I was on the way to a function – an official function, I should say, except that now, for me, no functions are official any more. I am a private individual. And, as if to remind me, on the corner of a street on the Fulham road, there was a shop, an antique shop. Susan Foster, the name read above the window; it was a strangely familiar name. I thought for a moment; perhaps I had bought a chair there, long long before; perhaps it was the name of a girl in the garden room, or the maiden name of a Member's wife. And then it came to me. It was the name of a girl my age, in my form, at school; a girl never quite clean, a bright girl with pink glasses and a stutter, whom I was almost friends with for a time, because of our cleverness. A name and a face from long long before any of this started, when I was no one, and I was myself. For decades I have lived in a world where none of this mattered, where jobs and roles counted, and names not at all; and, in a second of pensiveness, I was back in a world where individuals counted, where names without jobs mattered. Perhaps I am back there for good, now.

The car stopped at a set of traffic lights, and a cyclist, pausing, breathless by us, happened to glance in. I caught his eye just as we drove on, leaving him, amazed, agape, behind at the lights. The moment, I think, had passed.

And now the happy ending. Where are they now? What are they doing? Is it not true that every glorious perfection, every imagined eternity lies, waiting to be taken up, every possibility before them? What deaths, what promotions, what new blisses have carried them off? What sweetness of perfected life have these temporary inhabitants of space and time seen before them, or behind them? And what possibilities?

What possibilities are there, and what possibilities are gone, quite gone? I knew everything once, but now I only know what they did not do. Giacomo, for instance, did not retire to run a café in Taormina with the enormous amounts of money he had made from the sad. Jane's grandmother recovered, and lived for a while longer, but she died, in the end. Francesca did not marry Henry, in the end, for obvious reasons. Nor did Jane, for a still more obvious one. Louis never lost weight, nor did he ever perfect his hair; once he had carried out his act of betrayal in a single telephone call and a series of interviews with police, and lawyers, and judges, he never spoke to John again, and never saw him again. He did not become happy, and, despite his intentions and his wishes, he did not live for ever, nor will he.

Is it my job at all to answer the question, *What happened next?* Is it something I ever knew?

Some possibilities are no longer there to take up; and no one ever remembers that, until it is too late. Only the Members and the Ministers carried on being Members and Ministers; the Prime Minister is immortal, although from time to time the pronouns pertaining to the Prime Minister may slightly change. The Clerk of the House changed his name and went on for ever, a wig and a black flap of garments denoting his presence in the Tea Room. Only Louis still believes in every possibility, who every minute of every day thinks to himself of the boy he might have followed in Trafalgar square and somehow saved; and believes in his own goodness and his betrayal; and every now and then thinks of the moment when he picked up a telephone and began to dial, and changed his life, and the life of everyone he knew; and only Louis thinks every minute of the idyll he might have found in Trafalgar Square, in the November world and every minute of every day recites to himself a mantra:

> Every wearied body must
> Late or soon return to dust
> Set the frantic spirit free
> In this earthly city we
> Shall not meet again love yet
> Never think that I forget.

And Francesca lived happily ever after.

Years later, when the announcement of the death of the former Prime Minister had come over the news, Francesca had a dream about the dead, her dead. She dreamt that she was alone under her blanket asleep, when through the door came her dead mother and her dead father and her dead grandmother and her dead sister. They all got into bed with her, and they were laughing. But, just as when she was a child, she did not laugh, and she knew they were laughing at her, and at something she did not understand. The bed was too small, and they were quickly lying on top of her, crushing her, and it was with a great panic and inrush of air that she woke. She stretched her arm out into the half of her double bed which had always been empty. She had not seen Henry for many years. She never dreamt about him.

And John?

'Can you help the homeless help themselves?' the boy sitting on the ground said. It was that strangely mild time in November between funerals. Everything was over, and no more awfulness could possibly ever happen to John. He paused. He was struck by the boy's unquestion-like question.

'What do you mean?' he said.

The boy looked up at him hopelessly, a face above him on Victoria street, not knowing if he was serious or not.

'I mean, can you help the homeless help themselves?' he said.

He looked down at the boy, in return. He reminded John of everybody, and yet he reminded John of nobody. That is the trouble with people; they are always different, and always refuse to fill the roles we supply for them; and yet they have their roles. And the boy's way of squinting reminded him of one man; and the way he sat on the street and asked hopelessly for money reminded him of another; and yet he was a boy with his own history, and his own life, and, no doubt, his own name. He had a beginning which was only his own, and would come to an end which was only his own; but John, looking down at him, thought only of the men who had preceded him and the men who would follow him.

'Are you asking me for money?' John said.

The boy considered for a while. He was surprisingly not dirty.

'Yes,' he said. 'I am really.'

'So, why don't you say, Can you give me some money?'

'I don't know,' the boy said. 'I never thought about it.'

'Try it,' John said. He noticed a truculence in the way the boy spoke, and he realized that those who beg do not feel that they need to please those whom they ask.

'Why?' the boy said.

'Are you successful now?' John said.

'What does it look like?' the boy said.

'Well, try it,' John said.

'No one would give me any money if I just asked for it like that,' the boy said. 'The thing is, you need to look as if you're doing something to help yourself. You need to make a bit of an effort. Even if it's just saying something crappy like Can you help the homeless to help themselves.'

'What happens if you don't,' John said.

'You die,' the boy said.

'You die anyway,' John said.

'You die anyway,' the boy said, agreeing. He paused, still looking up at John. He appeared to be thinking; he seemed to have decided in favour of John.

'Like,' he said in the end.

'Why don't you do something to get people to give you money?' John said.

'Like what,' the boy said.

'Can you sing or something?' John said. 'Have you got a guitar you could play?'

'No,' the boy said.

'Well, can you dance?'

'No,' the boy said.

'Oh, come on,' John said. 'Everyone can dance.'

'I can't,' the boy said.

'It's not difficult,' John said. 'You just smile, and then just imagine the music in your head and begin to move to it.'

'You know,' the boy said, 'when you put it like that, it seems really hard.'

'No, no,' John said. 'Watch me, then you do it.'

He moved a little forward, and put his case on the ground. He flashed a brilliant smile at the boy, who just looked back. He began to clap. A quick twist, and you saw how very much his suit was not made for dancing in. He bent, and his feet tapped at the pavement in a quick tattoo.

'What's your name?' he said.

'You didn't make any money either,' the boy said. 'Can you give me some money?'

'No,' John said. 'You're not worth it.'

He picked up his case, and walked off into the crowd. Some of the people looked at the hunchback, who a moment before they had seen dancing; and some just looked at him as he began, out of tune with the music in his head, unrhythmically, to walk with his own worries. A hunchback is used to being looked at. But they did not look at him for the real reasons. They looked at his deformity. To the boy on the ground, and to the people who walked the streets of the bereaved city that November day, his deformity counted. To him his deformity was trivial; from now on he would live inside his worries like a show house, furnished by others, and as long as he lived, which was not long, he would not escape from the visions and knowledge in his mind, which he had let other people place there.

I could no longer watch him, since my omniscience and

my office had gone in those few terrible days; but I can pass on the power to watch. I pass on my power in a command and a request. Look, reader.

Look, reader, at this man; this good man, filled with his bad acts. Look at his dancing in the street; look at his twisting, his shouting, as if in pain. Look at the way his spine puppets him down the street, like a marionette dance which only to the dull seems like the steps of a man walking. Look at his goodness moving, like a body through air. Look at his evident love for those whose ashes are thrown to the winds of the air. Wait, and breathe, and look, if you can see it, at what is coming to get him; look at the police running towards someone who will never kill again; look at the death in his step; his crippled jingle before it; the noise he makes, his own noise. Look at him. Look. Look.